RONA

Twenty Eight Days

To Mum

With love always

Rae Jamson x x

HFCA Publishing

ISBN 978-1986002806

Twenty Eight Days

Sentenced to death...
All hope gone...
Until he receives a visit from victim #6

Condemned for a crime he didn't commit, Quinten Peterson sat on death row praying for a miracle. He just never expected his angel of mercy to be the girl he fell in love with so long ago.

The press called her a victim, but Saige Lockwood was a survivor. And she had twenty-eight days to discover the truth about what really happened to her that fateful night, eight years ago.

With time running out, Saige desperately needed to unlock her memories ... before it was too late.

Novels by Rona Jameson

Come Back to Me

When Esmé Rogers meets Luke Carlisle in 1987, she never expected to end up on board the Titanic for its maiden voyage from Southampton to New York in 1912. What started with confusion and questions turns into the greatest love of her life.

Summer at Rose Cottage

McKenzie (Mack) Harper needs to get away and the small cottage just outside of Cape Elizabeth is the perfect location to unwind and bond with her six-year-old nephew, Lucas. It's here at this quaint summer rental that Mack discovers a diary dated March 4th, 1947, which pulls her into a world of love and heartache.

Twenty Eight Days

Condemned for a crime he didn't commit, Quinten Peterson sat on death row praying for a miracle. He just never expected his angel of mercy to be the girl he fell in love with so long ago.

To my family

Authors Note

Port Jude is a fictional town and is located approximately two hours west of fictional, Harlington Prison, for the purpose of this story.

This is a work of fiction. Names, characters, businesses, places, events, and incidents are products of the author's imagination and used in a fictitious manner. Any resemblance to actual persons, living or dead, or actual events is purely coincidental.

8 years ago

Saige thought her head would explode as she gained consciousness, fighting through nausea, pain, and dizziness. A groan burst from between her dry cracked lips. She shivered. Cold clammy sweat coated her skin, as she lay naked on a hard surface. She tried to move her arms, but they wouldn't budge. Restrained at the wrists. Panic like she'd never known welled in her throat.

Frantic, she tugged on the restraints. No give. She cried out in fear and frustration. Her legs weren't restrained. *Why?*

Her eyes snapped open. Dark. A blindfold? The dizziness cleared and she knew that she had to think. She had to remember.

Where was she?

What was she doing?

Who was she with?

An icy fear twisted around her heart—she remembered nothing.

A noise slowed her breathing while she listened—the thump of boots. The scrape of the door over the floorboards as it opened. A gust of cold air hit her flesh and goose bumps followed. The draft disappeared as she heard the creak of the door being forced closed, and then the shuffle of feet.

She wasn't alone anymore.

"You're awake," he said, his voice distorted, emotionless and cold.

Dark fear crept down her spine.

Saige, God dammit! Pull yourself together, and think!

A calloused hand caressed her ankle, making her skin crawl. *Survival.* Saige quickly bent her knees, and with as much force as she could manage, she kicked out. Her right foot connected with hard flesh, followed by a groan and then a long, brittle silence.

"Fucking bitch," he roared.

He roughly grabbed her ankles. She struggled to get them free, but he had strength and freedom on his side. His torso fell across her legs while his fingers fumbled to restrain her ankles.

He grunted and used her body to push himself up and away. His hands had felt large and rough. His feet shuffled on the wooden floor and then the clank of instruments against a metal tray made her heart race.

A sharp prick in her thigh and her strength swiftly disappeared. Her body felt heavy.

"I'm going to make you pay for breaking my nose," he growled. "You will pray for death."

She began to shake, the fearful images his words created built in her mind.

"That's right, *Saige*"—he fastened something around her neck—"you can't cause any more trouble now." He laughed, a frightening, manic sound that was almost worse than everything else he was doing to her.

"Nothing to say?" His voice was inflamed and hostile.

Panic welled in her throat when he trailed his fingers down her torso to her feet.

His eerie laugh terrified her more than anything.

Tears seeped into the fabric of her blindfold. As she drifted into sleep, her last conscious thought was of the man she loved. He'd find her.

4 days later

A trail of white mist filled the air in front of Quinten the cold unusual for Florida.

He rubbed his gritty eyes as tiredness overwhelmed him. His feet were heavy as he moved through yet another section of forest, ducking and just missing being hit in the face by a stray branch, only to walk straight through a spiderweb. He reached up and wiped the sticky web from his face.

He felt desperate, which kept him searching. He'd been that way since his brother, Alex, and he had discovered Saige's abandoned car. It had sat at the side of the highway with all four tires flat. Shredded. She'd been so close to home.

Days later, he was exhausted and knew he'd have to rest soon or he'd pass out from lack of sleep or lack of nourishment. Energy snacks only lasted so long.

Sweat trailed down his back. His thighs quivered as he pushed himself harder. Light wasn't his friend with the thick, tall trees rising out of the earth to brush the sky. He tripped and went down with a hard thud thanks to a rotten fallen log. His attention hadn't been on where he would take his next step. His eyes had been busy searching, and his heart full of the need to find Saige. The girl he loved.

He brushed dead leaves and pine needles from his clothing and continued pushing forward. Listened for noise that didn't belong in the forest that would indicate he wasn't alone.

Fatigue settled over him like a thick black cloud, which is why when he took his next step he fell to the hard ground. He scrambled for a foothold. Earth disappeared under him and he started to slide down through the muddy underbrush. His hands reached out for purchase and got scarped and pierced from prickly thorns.

He continued to race downwards and when he burst between two thick and bright berry bushes a wooden structure appeared in front of him. Before his brain registered what his eyes saw, he came to an abrupt bone-jarring stop.

Stunned, Quinten moved into a more comfortable position, his body aching from head to foot. The shack was hidden so deeply in the foliage that it would have been missed but for his undignified fall. He caught his breath and glanced around unable to pick up any other sound. Not even that of an animal.

The shack was a small structure made of mud-chinked logs. He slowly moved around the perimeter until he found a half-rotten step leading to a warped doorframe. The wooden door had a shiny new padlock. *Keep strangers out? Someone inside? Both?*

Moving forward, he tested the two steps before he allowed them to take his weight. His breath became heavy as he took another look around and noticed the drooping roof covered with dead leaves and twigs. He prayed the shack would stay together until he'd had a chance to check inside.

He dropped his knapsack to the ground, and took out his pocketknife. He'd never been good at locks, so he stabbed and chipped at the rotten wood surrounding the padlock. As splinters of wood started to fly off, he finally exhaled. He was getting somewhere.

He turned his head to make sure no one was creeping up on him.

Big mistake.

He missed the door and stabbed himself. Pain shot up his arm to his shoulder, radiating throughout his body as he caught his breath on a hissed curse. Blood ran in rivulets down to his hand, dripping on the ground.

The good news: he'd managed to pry the new padlock from the rotten frame. The bad news: he needed to stop the bleeding before he did anything else, or he'd be of no use to anyone.

The door in front of him didn't open as he thought it would so he stood back and kicked with all his strength. The door broke from the frame and thumped to the ground.

He paused on the threshold and let his eyes adjusted to the dim light. An overwhelming smell hit his senses. His nostrils flared and his stomach rolled as he tried not to gag.

A quick glance noted three kerosene lanterns hanging from rusty hooks. A workbench filled the left side with a lonesome shiny silver tray sitting in the middle of it. Instruments a surgeon would use laid out neatly in a row.

His legs trembled as he took another step inside, and that's when the true horror hit him. *"Saige?"* He staggered to the wooden table, which was bolted to the floor in the middle of the room.

"Saige?" His voice sounded broken. She lay motionless. He hesitated and pressed two fingers to her ice-cold skin to check for a pulse. Relief rushed through him. She had one, albeit faint.

He became lightheaded which drew his attention to his arm. He'd forgotten about his injury. He took a quick glance around the shack, and moved to the workbench. On the shelf below he found a torn pale blue shirt. He wound it around his wrist and tied off a tourniquet before he moved back to Saige's still body.

So much blood.

The leather straps around her ankles and wrists felt new and were stiff and unyielding as his fingers fumbled with the buckles.

He grabbed a surgical knife from the tray and cut through the bindings before he moved to her neck. He gulped and swiped at the tears and sweat that blurred his vision. He couldn't afford tears.

They'd have to wait until Saige was safe.

The leather strap around her neck was wide and thick with no give. He was surprised she hadn't choked to death. But he thanked God when the buckle was easy to work because he sure as hell didn't want to risk using a knife near her neck.

The leather gave and he hesitated, he had no idea where to touch her because of all the lacerations covering her body. The majority closed with congealed blood.

He removed the blindfold slowly and placed a kiss to each closed eyelid, relieved that she would now be safe.

From his knapsack he retrieved a blanket that would keep Saige warm, and wrapped it around her. His eyes scanned her broken body and he held his breath, praying he didn't hurt her further as he lifted her into his arms.

Without wasting any more time, Quinten quickly dashed out of the shack and through the forest. He hadn't gone far when he needed to catch his breath. He leaned against a tree and scanned the area, analyzing where he needed to go from there. He needed to put distance between them and the shack.

There was hardly any weight to Saige as he carried her against his chest. His body shook with relief that he'd gotten to her in time, and in fear that the sick fuck would come back before he could get her away.

Quinten looked down when Saige gave a slight gasp. Still unconscious, but he didn't want to risk her waking and struggling in his arms. He spotted a small patch of grass that was free of brambles and underbrush and hurried forward. He dropped to his knees and carefully placed her down, hoping he wouldn't cause her more pain.

She murmured slightly and curled into the warmth of the blanket.

He'd never felt as helpless as he did in that moment, hovering over her unconscious body. A searing rage filled him, knowing she'd been tortured and left for dead. He wanted to scream out in anger. Wanted to hunt the bastard down. He couldn't do either. Saige needed him. He dropped his forehead to hers and gave in to his fear and anguish and let his tears fall before they choked him.

"Don't." Her whispered word was so quiet he wasn't sure he heard her. Quinten lifted his head and scanned her face for any sign of her waking. Her eyelids fluttered open for mere seconds before they closed again. He wanted and needed more from her.

But nothing.

"Saige," his tears choked him as he spoke. "You're safe now. I won't let anyone hurt you. I promise." He caressed her face with frozen fingers, hardly noticing his own condition. "Saige, it's me." He softly kissed her lips and noticed they'd started to turn blue with cold. At the same time he noticed her pulse started to fade.

Panic coursed through him and chased away his rage. Not knowing what else to do, he lay down beside her, and pulled her into his arms. "Please open your eyes. Don't give up," he begged. "I won't let you. Dammit, Saige. I love you." He wrapped himself around her, willing his warmth and his life into her. She was so cold.

She would make it. She had to. He tried to give her what strength he had left as he slipped off to sleep. He was thankful he'd found her before she met the same fate as the other five victims.

Day 1

"Saige, this is yours. Table three," he yelled.

One … two … three …

Saige plastered a fake smile on her face and took the plates of greasy food from Barney the fry cook. The man was an asshole, and irritated her more than usual.

She hurried over to table three, placed the food in front of the two hungry tourists, topped off their coffee, and turned straight into her roommate, Tamsyn.

"We need to stop meeting like this," Tamsyn said, as they bumped hips.

The diner was crowded with the lunchtime

rush and lacked space between the stools at the long counter and the booths nestled against the windows with views of the ocean.

Lou, the owner had just arrived with several cakes and fruit meringue pies, which she placed under the glass dome on the counter.

A couple of tourists slipped past Saige to the old till, which was loud—even in the noisy diner— as Janet thumped down on the keys.

Saige laughed and moved behind the counter to wipe the sticky spots of spilled syrup from the white Formica counter.

"Hey, honey. Turn that up."

She glanced at the man who'd made the request and raised a brow at his rudeness.

"Please," he added, and grinned.

She mumbled under her breath, and twisted the volume knob on the television. Her hand froze and slowly dropped to her side while her gaze stayed fixated on the images flashing across the screen. A cold knot formed in her stomach.

A younger version of herself stared back at her—a picture taken from her prom. Her blonde hair was clipped at the nape of her neck, the ruby red dress showing off her youthfulness. Her heart sped up, slamming into her chest as her throat tightened around her breath. She wanted to run ... to hide from the prying eyes that would be staring at her now, but then she remembered she wasn't that Saige any longer. She'd changed. Her hair was no longer blond, but auburn. Her body wasn't adorned with a perfectly cut prom dress, but was hidden under the frumpy, grease stained waitress uniform.

She glanced around at the customers who were watching the screen—and not her—and sighed in relief. Then her gaze returned to the television.

Why was she up there?

The blood that had rushed through her ears finally quieted enough so that she could hear what the reporter was saying...

Earlier today, Governor Stafford signed an execution warrant for thirty-five year old Quinten James Peterson, who, at the age of twenty-seven, was found guilty of the premeditated murders of five college girls, and the abduction and torture of Saige Lockwood, who became known as victim number six.

In twenty-eight days, Quinten Peterson will

have the lethal injection administered at the death row facility in Harlington, where he's been incarcerated for close to eight years.

Harlington's warden, Jonathan Roscoe, has confirmed that later today Quinten Peterson will be transferred to a death watch cell, pending the execution of the warrant.

At this time, we've been unable to contact Quinten Peterson's ex-wife, Jocelyn, or Alexander Peterson, his brother, for a statement.

The governor will be giving a formal statement at three o'clock this afternoon.

And there he was, Quinten Peterson in his prison uniform, large as life on the screen. Her eyes stayed focused on him, traveling over his narrow shoulders, dark brown hair, and hard chiseled face half covered with a trim beard. His eyes held her gaze. They were so dark that it was like looking into pools of *despair*.

Saige's heart raced as fast as the blood rushed through her ears. She reached up to her forehead and pressed at the pain that threatened to bring her to her knees. There was something familiar about the man. But what? A memory teased her.

Gone just as suddenly.

"What's wrong?" Tamsyn grabbed her arms and pulled her into the hallway that led to the restrooms. "Saige," she whispered. "I know we're not best friends, but I'm here for you."

Tears flooded Saige's eyes and slowly slid down her face as she watched Tamsyn worry at her lip.

"I ... I don't know." Saige wiped at her eyes, but the tears continued.

Saige didn't want to be seen in tears, so she dashed into the restroom and grabbed a handful of paper towels from the dispenser. "I have to work."

Tamsyn stopped her mid-swipe when she grabbed her arm and slowly turned her. "Look at me, Saige."

Saige gulped. "I have everything under control, and then something happens and I feel like I'm about to lose it again."

"I can't begin to understand what it's like to suddenly have that slapped in your face. Your memories." Tamsyn stepped forward and wrapped her arms around Saige. "I'm here for you if you ever need to talk, cry on a shoulder, or eat a full tub of ice cream."

Saige tried to smile but it came out more of a wince. "I don't have memories."

Tamsyn stepped away. "What do you mean?" She frowned.

"I don't remember anything."

"That's probably for the best." Tamsyn wet some paper towels. "Here, you need to sort your face out, and clock out."

"I'm not leaving mid-shift."

She could have said more, but she didn't. She didn't want to get into it with anyone. She hadn't for years. Her family tried to get her to talk about her memories—her lack of memories. They'd filled in details, trying to lodge something loose in her memory. She was so sick of talking about it that she got used to changing the subject, and her family eventually got the hint. At that point she'd felt a sense of relief coming from them.

"Are you sure you're okay to go back to work? You still look pretty shaken."

She felt shaken and her nerves made her nauseated. Her hands trembled as she raised them to her face. Maybe Tamsyn was right. Maybe she needed to clock out early. "I'm going home."

"Let me see if Lou will let us both leave."

"She won't. I'll be fine, Tamsyn. I just need away from here for now."

Tamsyn didn't look convinced.

"Please don't take this the wrong way, but I just need my own space."

"Okay." Her roommate watched her closely for a few minutes and then nodded slightly before finally leaving the room.

Saige sighed in relief when Tamsyn left her alone to collect her thoughts.

The image on the television of the man would forever be engrained on her brain. As far as she was aware, she'd gone eight years without knowing what he looked like. She'd been afraid that once she saw him the horror of her time with him would suddenly hit her, so she'd never gone looking. Her memory was just as blank as it had been for the past eight years, and that scared her.

She couldn't stay at work. She had to get back to her apartment. She needed to be surrounded by her things. Feel the comfort they gave her.

Saige closed the white door and pressed her back against the solid wood as she tried to draw energy into her body. She had none. She was exhausted and had only worked a half-shift. Moving slowly toward the table by the door, she placed her purse down and sighed with relief. She was home.

She took a few steps farther into her living room and dropped into the oversized chair—her comfy chair that everyone else hated. The battered brown leather didn't match anything in the elegant apartment, but for some reason, she had insisted that it went with her when she moved. The chair had always been in the boathouse, so she guessed it held happy memories that she wished she could remember.

And that was the biggest problem. She didn't remember *anything*. Not the attack. Not the rescue. Not the time prior to the attack. Memories erased from her life as easily as her attacker had tried to erase her.

Sometimes she would try to remember, but all it did was leave her with a terrible headache. The doctors had told her not to push it. Months would go by before it started again—wondering what she wanted to remember—so she'd try to regain her memories, only to be left with the usual headache. It was an unhappy cycle.

Her father thought it was a godsend that she couldn't remember what had happened to her, but what they couldn't understand was that she had nearly two and a half years stolen from her mind. Those years were just gone.

The summer before she was taken—gone.

The days of being tortured—gone.

Two years afterwards—gone.

Her father had once said that for the two years after, it had been like she hadn't existed. She'd been in a private hospital. Withdrawn. Mute. Completely pulled inward with no contact from anyone other than her immediate family and the medical staff.

It sounded like a lonely existence and sometimes she was glad she couldn't remember any of it. Other times, she felt like she'd go insane because she couldn't remember.

One question she constantly asked herself was, what happened to her afterward? Why couldn't she remember anything after she'd been found? It didn't make any sense. Why couldn't she remember the hospital when she'd been there for such a long time? Even now the smell of antiseptic made her physically sick.

Saige kept so much locked away inside her where no one could see. She was tired of being her. Tired of being afraid. Tired of not remembering.

Seeing Quinten Peterson on the television today had really thrown her for a loop. There was something about him that teased at a memory. He'd been familiar, but not in a frightening way. She'd always expected him to be terrifying to her when, or if, she ever saw him, but that reaction hadn't come.

Instead she felt a hint of affection. Perhaps after all these years she could finally admit to herself that she was crazy, because why the hell else would she had felt affection for someone who'd tortured her for days and then left her for dead?

Her father had kept her locked away from the awful truths. He'd kept her away from the trial and from seeing *him*. She hadn't testified at the trial. She'd been in the hospital recovering from all the injuries she'd suffered. Later, she remained in a private hospital for close to two years.

Saige shuddered and hoped like hell she'd never have to step foot inside the walls of that hospital again. Every time she thought about that place, chills of fear raced down her spine. She often asked herself what had happened to her while she'd been a patient—she would probably never know. She struggled to get herself up from the chair and slowly dragged her feet to her bedroom where she stripped out of her work uniform and climbed under the covers—wanting to hide from the unknown that haunted her. Just for a little while.

For eight years he'd waited for the execution warrant to be signed by the governor, and now that it had been, Quinten felt nothing but fear and anger.

He'd constantly asked himself, why him? He'd never gotten an answer. All those years ago, he went after the woman he loved. He didn't regret finding her. Even knowing how he ended up, he would do it again as long as it meant that Saige lived. Despite the odds against him, he'd managed to save her.

Even now, as they led him in shackles to one of the death watch cells, he could still see the blood covering her—his beautiful girl. Just her smile had been enough to bring him to his knees.

"Steady now," one of the guards said.

He blinked a few times and realized his body had tensed, and that his fists clenched together in front of him.

Four heavily armed guards flanked him while the warden led the way. The death squad. He didn't know any of these guards, but he'd certainly get to know them now that he was under twenty-four seven observation. That was, until they transferred him to the execution chamber, adjacent to his new home.

Quinten briefly closed his eyes and tried not to think about the end. He'd prayed since his incarceration that he'd be freed. He hadn't done anything wrong, and wondered if he was being punished for that last night when he'd seen Saige before she'd returned to college.

"Nearly there," another guard grunted.

The shackles around his ankles and wrists rattled when he slowly shuffled forward, and then he froze. His legs wouldn't carry him further.

He couldn't do this.

How the hell was he supposed to willingly walk inside that cell? He felt sick to his stomach with fear while he told himself he had to be strong, not just for himself, but also for his brother. Quinten just wasn't sure he knew how to anymore.

His legs weakened as he stared into the small space in front of him. The metal-framed bed with a thin mattress sat to one side, while the shower, stainless steel toilet, and sink had been placed to the back of the cell with a small window above.

He really couldn't do this.

"C'mon, Quinten. You know you have to step forward." The guard looked younger than him. He also looked sorry that he had to force him inside.

Inhaling, Quinten forced his legs to move him forward. The minute he stepped inside, the door closed and locked behind him.

"Turn around."

On automatic pilot, he turned and let them remove the chains while he kept his eyes closed.

"They're off. Move away from the door."

He followed their orders.

He always did.

He was a model prisoner.

His eyes finally opened as he moved closer to the bed and dropped to the mattress, his legs no longer willing to hold him up.

Quinten rested his elbows on his knees and dropped his head into his hands.

He stayed like that for a long time.

Saige gasped as she came awake, her heart jumped in her chest. She struggled free from the quilt and nearly knocked the bedside light over in her haste to switch it on.

A soft glow filled the room as she huddled against the headboard. Her skin clammy and her hands trembled when she wrapped her arms around her bent knees.

She felt warm, wrapped in a cocoon against a hard pulsing body. Something felt familiar about him, which told her not to fight. Not that she had the strength anyway. Or was she hallucinating again?

Her body was filled with pain and even in her fuzzy mind, she knew that she was dying. She wanted to die. No more pain.

Heavy eyelids fluttered open and she saw the shape of a man leaning over her. Trees were behind him and she heard birds chirping. The brightness made her head hurt worse to she closed her eyes. So tired.

The man. She knew him. He knew her. How though? Who was he?

"You're safe now. I won't let anyone hurt you. I promise." He caressed her face with fingers that felt like icicles. "Saige, it's me." He softly kissed her lips.

The dream had felt real—too real. She knew it to be a memory, which had been triggered by the news report. The man she'd seen who had promised to protect her, had been Quinten Peterson.

"Saige, it's me."

Quinten knew her. Why couldn't she remember him? He'd expected her to know him. Recognize him and his voice.

Unable to hold her tears, she let them fall unchecked down her pale face, overwhelmed with grief.

She should be happy because for the first time in eight years, she'd dreamt something that had felt real—something that she remembered the details of after waking.

If anything the dream and how familiar Quinten Peterson felt to her, made her want to find out everything from the trial. For eight years she hadn't wanted to know. Now though, time was quickly running out for Quinten and she needed to know why she didn't fear him. Shouldn't she if he'd been the one to hold her captive?

"Ugh!" Frustrated, she snapped the room into darkness.

Alexander Peterson, known for the past six years as Alex Peters, danced around the old leather bag in front of him, wishing like hell it were Richard Lockwood.

For eight years, his hate for the Lockwood family had grown and fueled his anger at the lies they'd told. And just like when his brother had been arrested and subsequently charged with the murder of those college girls, and the attempted murder of *her*, he felt helpless.

He loved his brother and knew he was innocent. Alex had never given up hope that one day Quinten would be acquitted because he was innocent.

Alex had hoped that *she'd* come forward and tell the world that it was all lies, except she hadn't.

She'd been hidden away by her family and he'd had no idea where to even start looking.

Quinten had needed her. Hell, even Alex had needed her. In the end he'd given up searching because their mother had lost all hope. Just before she'd died, their mother had begged Alex to get his life together instead of festering on the hate and betrayal he'd felt at his brother's incarceration. He'd kept his promise, becoming a firefighter, but he'd still let the hate and betrayal fester. He'd just learned to control it.

His brother's defense attorney had filed so many appeals and motions to try and get another trial, but he'd hit a brick wall with all of them.

Time now slipped through his fingers.

Twenty-eight days.

Just hearing those words made him want to hurl.

In eight years, they hadn't been able to get a retrial.

In eight years, they hadn't found new evidence to implicate someone else or tampering with evidence in his brother's case.

So what the fuck could he do in twenty-eight days?

Alex wanted to go and beg Lockwood to help free his brother, but he knew the man wouldn't. No matter what Richard Lockwood had said to his face eight years ago, he'd had no intention of helping Quinten.

He'd first met Richard Lockwood when he'd employed him and Quinten to create one of their masterpiece carvings for the wooden banister in the foyer of his home. And that was where they'd met Saige Lockwood. It had been the day before she'd turned twenty-one.

Alex realized his brother had stopped mid-instruction so he lifted his head, and that's when all thought fled.

The shy beautiful girl had frozen at the top of the stairs, a blush covering her cheeks as Quinten and he stared at her.

She cleared her throat and made her way toward them. His tongue stuck to the roof of his mouth as she stopped in front of Quinten.

Alex nudged his brother, amused because his brother had gone tongue-tied. "I'm Alex Peterson and this is my brother, Quinten."

"I heard my father had hired the Peterson

brothers. I'm Saige."

"You've certainly brightened up our day," Alex grinned, and rolled his eyes at his brother. "Ignore him."

Saige laughed.

Quinten frowned. "We have work to do." He turned back to the carving of a small bird he worked on.

Saige passed and Alex offered a knowing grin when he watched his brother, watching Saige from the corner of his eye.

"Hope you have a Happy Birthday tomorrow," Alex shouted.

Her head full of sun-kissed blond hair nearly touched her bottom, but she turned her blue eyes on him and Quinten. "I hope you'll both be here tomorrow night." She disappeared into the kitchen.

Alex knew better than to nudge into Quinten while he worked, but he loved to tease his brother. "Her eyes are like looking into the ocean on a sunny day." He sighed. "Don't you agree?"

Quinten ignored him.

Alex continued. "She's beautiful and I bet her hair is silky smooth to the touch."

"Don't you have anything better to do than bug

the shit out of me?" Quinten asked, a dark frown on his face.

"Lighten up. I'm just trying to get you to admit that she got to you." Alex turned back to the leaf he'd been working on. He loved working with his brother, and he was damn proud of the projects they'd finished. He wasn't an idiot and knew the only reason they had a business was because of his brother.

Quinten grunted, and leaned against the wall, his eyes found Alex. "Yes, she got to me. More than I care to admit, considering the baggage I have."

Alex groaned. "Your marriage from hell will be over soon. Why can't you get on with your life? You deserve someone good." Sometimes Alex felt like telling his brother 'I told you so'. Jocelyn had been unfaith to Quinten from day one. The sooner she left his brother the better.

"Saige invited us to her party. We're going." Alex grinned. "And don't worry about me, my eyes are constantly drawn elsewhere."

"I know exactly where your eyes are drawn, and if you're not careful, you'll get us fired."

"Relax," Alex said, feeling uncomfortable at his secret not being much of a secret. He should have *known Quinten wouldn't miss anything. He never did.*

Alex wanted to forget all about *her.* She betrayed his brother and him in the end by lying about the man who took her. What he'd never been able to understand was why? Why would she lie and let the real man walk free? For years, he'd wanted answers, and still did.

His gut burned. He wanted justice, just like she should.

He wanted his brother to be set free, and allowed to live his life.

It killed him knowing that in twenty-eight days his little brother would no longer be on this earth. He would never see him again. Even though he was behind bars, he at least lived and breathed. But in less than a month, his brother would be put to death for something he didn't do.

"*Fuck*," he roared, and punched the bag blindly. He just missed knocking his lieutenant down.

Alex stood gasping for breath while he tried to hold himself together. He ripped the gloves from his hands and bent at the waist. He gripped his thighs, dropping his head as he fought back tears.

At thirty-seven, he was man enough to apologize to his superior, but he was afraid if he opened his mouth he'd break down and cry like a baby.

His heart was breaking and there wasn't a damn thing he could do about it. Everything was out of his control and he wanted to scream at the whole world.

"Let's go to my office."

He nodded.

Two of the guys on his shift stood behind him. They held his gaze and patted him on the back as he moved past.

His lieutenant closed the door and indicated for him to sit in the chair opposite his desk.

Alex needed to pace, to run even, but instead he dropped his weary ass into the seat offered.

"I'm not going to ask." His lieutenant wasted no time in starting the conversation. "I know … Alexander Peterson."

Alex's mouth fell open in shock as he stared at his boss.

"There isn't much I don't know about everyone under my command." His lieutenant held up his hand when Alex went to speak. "I've known since the minute you stepped foot inside this station. I never judge anyone by his family. Mine weren't the best. I know from experience and we'll leave it at that. I should have told you, but I figured if you ever felt the need, then you'd come to me."

Alex glanced at the door. "Do they know?"

"I take it that you didn't see the governor's conference?"

"No," Alex said.

"The news station displayed your photograph. They're your friends, Alex. Don't lock them out, especially not now when you need their support."

Alex didn't know what to think or say as he sat and listened. They may still accept him as one of their own, but they presumed his brother was guilty. He needed to be away from the station house—he couldn't be here and listen to them all talking.

Alex finally found his voice. "I'm going to need some time off. Until after—"

His lieutenant nodded. "After the display I just saw, I have to agree with you. Your leave can start after tonight's shift, and you call when you're ready to come back." He paused giving him a searching look. "I mean that, Alex."

Alex nodded and looked around his boss's office. "Thank you."

"Don't thank me. No matter what he's been convicted of, he's still your brother."

He shook his Lieutenants outstretched hand.

Moving down to the shower room, Alex didn't see anyone else, which was just fine because he wasn't sure he wanted to know what they truly believed about him and his brother. He rubbed his chest where his heart felt heavy with sorrow.

After his shift, he'd sleep and then make a plan of action. He now had time on his hands and he wasn't going to just sit back and let them execute his brother.

He needed to make one last effort, even if it meant finally coming face-to-face with his past.

Day 2

Renting an apartment in the building next door to the one where Saige lives is a brilliant idea on my part. I hadn't planned on being back in Tampa for a long time, but here I am.

The minute I heard on the radio about the signing of the warrant of execution, I packed a bag and high-tailed it home. I wasn't about to miss the execution or the fallout from it.

My sources tell me that Saige Lockwood still hasn't regained her memory. I'm surprised. It's been a long time since her abduction, which makes me wonder what drugs she was given for the two years she'd been locked away. Perhaps I hadn't been told everything. I was well aware of what was being done to her, or so I thought. Why didn't I stop it? I'm still not sure of the answer. Saige suffered and I hope she eventually discovers who was responsible for that. The bastard isn't who she thinks he is.

Perhaps my plan should include him. I could get payback for the very beautiful, Saige Lockwood. We'll see what happens.

It's been a long time since I've spilled blood and just the thought excites me. The plan I've formed will be executed flawlessly while I follow a particular pattern. Can't have anyone looking too closely at me now, can I?

Sunset was a beautiful sight as Saige raced along the sidewalk toward where her father waited. She'd wanted to cancel the dinner and give in to the overwhelming tiredness.

She'd drifted back to sleep the night before with the memory repeating itself and the image of the man in his prison garb flashing in her mind. She needed to know more about him. She was terrified of what she'd remember, but that didn't outweigh the need burning through her to know.

Most of the day had been spent curled up in the brown chair with her laptop. She'd found quotes from newspaper archives and couldn't believe what Jocelyn Peterson, the man's ex-wife, had said.

He's a violent man...

He loved to use his fists on me...

He was cruel and unrelenting...

I'm glad he's finally somewhere he can't get to me.

It had certainly contradicted the comment from his brother, Alexander Peterson.

He is an amazing and loyal brother. He is innocent of all charges.

Alexander Peterson had obviously been close to his brother. He certainly believed in Quinten's innocence—unlike the ex-wife.

Saige felt more confused than ever as she stepped into the foyer of the Renaissance Hotel, her thoughts distracted with how to gather more information and from where. She'd start with her father. Because her reaction to the man she saw on the television bothered her—it bothered her a lot.

So with those thoughts heavily on her mind, she entered the restaurant, and found her father pacing five feet in front of her.

When he lifted his head, his eyes softened with relief and he tugged her against him. "Princess," he whispered against the top of her head. "I was worried."

"I'm sorry." She returned his embrace and pulled away when a server appeared in her peripheral vision. "I got lost in some research."

She winced when her father raised a brow in question. "Research?"

"We'll talk about it over dinner."

Her father watched her and nodded.

They followed a server through the quiet restaurant, the smell of fresh pasta and Italian sauce hitting her senses. Her stomach growled. She hadn't been hungry but her mouth watered at the delicious food she could see being delivered to other guests.

Fresh yeast rolls had been placed to the side of their table. A soft romantic glow from the tea lights on tables and fairy lights around the side of the building.

"So," he said, as they were seated. "I'm not sure I can wait until dinner to discover what research you've been doing."

Saige squirmed under her father's scrutiny. Sometimes she thought he'd have done well as a lawyer with the way he'd look at her. It was the, *I love you, but you better start talking*, look.

"I don't want to ruin dinner. We only get a chance to see each other a few times a month."

He raised a brow and waited for her to answer his original question. He wouldn't be ignored.

Saige bit into a fresh roll, and washed it down with a sip of water from the crystal wine glass. She needed a few minutes to ponder how to approach the topic without giving her father a heart attack.

"If I ask you something, will you be honest with me?"

He motioned to the waiter to continue filling his glass.

Saige tried not to fidget under his gaze and succeeded.

"Ask me your questions, Saige?" Although he sat back looking relaxed, she could tell by the twitching of his fingers that he wasn't.

Saige frowned at her father. "Why didn't you tell me about Quinten Peterson?"

Her father's eyes darkened, and with a silent breath he closed them while she watched him get his anger under control. "I saw the governor's press conference last night and planned on telling you today."

He took a long drink of his wine. "I'm sorry, Princess. I should have called. I just know that you don't watch television, so I figured I had time. Guess I was wrong."

"It's okay, Dad." She reassured him. "Really it is. It was a shock. But that's what I want to talk to you about."

He frowned into his wine before nodding his head, and patiently waited for her to get her thoughts together.

"I need to know what happened." Saige took a quick drink of water. "I'm not sure whether I want to remember what happened to me or not, but I need to know about the trial. I need to know what evidence was taken from me, and if I gave a statement. I also need to know what the convicted man said."

She reached out and took her father's hand into hers. "I need to know why, after all this time, even with his death close, he's never admitted to killing those girls, or what was done to me. Everything I could find online said he's never once admitted his guilt."

Silence descended following her rambling, and her father looked to have aged before her eyes.

"Daddy, please." She gripped his hand. "Please help me ... I've put it off for years. I need to know."

Her father took a few more gulps of his wine until his second glass was empty. "Think very carefully, Saige, because once you start reading about the past, your memory may start to return and I'm not sure how wise that is."

"Oh, Dad!" Saige moved to sit beside him. "I don't want *those* memories back but there has always been a chance they'd return, and it might not have been when I wanted them to. Regardless of how or when—if they do return, I'll have to deal with them. Since I saw the man on TV yesterday, I can't get him out of my head."

"That can't be healthy after what he did to you"—his voice broke—"or those other girls."

She exhaled and said what was on her mind. "What if he really is innocent?"

She let her words sink in, and when her father snapped his head back as though he'd been hit, she continued, "When I saw him on television, I didn't fear him. Shouldn't I have felt something like that?

Fear? Hate? Anger? The truth is I didn't feel anything like that. I had a sense of security. Why did I feel like that if he's the one? I have questions and I've finally woken up and want answers."

Saige leaned back in her chair and stared at her father. Anger flared in her chest and she couldn't help feel irritated with her father and his laid back attitude. While she'd been talking, all he'd done was shake his head as though he didn't want to hear what she had to say.

"You can't remember what happened, Saige. Perhaps you saw his photograph and felt sorry for him. If you can't remember what happened, why would you have felt fear?"

"I don't remember anything, but deep inside me the memories are there and my subconscious obviously feels safe with him. I need to know why."

Their usual meal was placed before them, and Saige picked up her fork and started stabbing at the pasta. "Did I know the man before I disappeared?"

It was barely noticeable, but her father paused before he carried on eating. She knew he wasn't hungry and only ate to distract her. It wasn't going to work on this occasion. She'd let her family control her knowledge but not for any longer.

"Define know."

In her confusion, she'd given up on the pretense of eating and glared at her father, wondering where the evasive man beside her had come from. He'd been on the defensive since the moment she'd started asking questions.

"Why are you doing this? I asked a simple question. Did I know Quinten Peterson before I disappeared? It's a question that requires either a yes or a no answer. It's not difficult," she snapped, realizing she'd raised her voice in anger. "I don't understand why you're reluctant to talk to me about it."

"Dammit, Saige. Why can't you leave it alone?"

She sighed. "Because there is a man who has twenty-seven days left on this earth, who has not once admitted his guilt, who I should get a sense of dread from when I see his face. All my questions begin with why and I need them answered. This man is going to die because of me, and I want to make damn sure they have the right person."

Sitting back, her father sighed warily. "Princess, he went through a trial. His DNA was all over you and the scene of the crime. He was found with one of the other victim's shirts wrapped around his arm. He was tried, and convicted. Sixteen out of twenty-five jurors agreed that he was guilty. He's guilty."

Saige paled hearing about the evidence, but she pushed forward, "What happened to the other nine jurors? Don't they all have to agree, at least in a death penalty case?"

"Not in Florida. If there had been less than ten jurors who voted the accused guilty, then he would have been sentenced to life in prison instead. But it was a supermajority vote, over half of the jurors, so he received the death penalty."

"There must be reasons why the other jurors didn't believe he was guilty." Saige wanted to know what they were.

"Please, Saige." Her father begged, almost fearful. "Don't start delving into his case. Can't you leave the past alone?"

She was afraid of her memories coming back from when she'd been taken and of what *he'd* done to her, but she didn't think she could give up on finding out everything she needed to know about the trial. She also had an idea on who would gladly help her with documents and transcripts, and if she guessed right, he'd probably answer all her questions if she could convince him that she thought Quinten might be innocent.

"Maybe I should."

Her father visibly relaxed before her eyes. "Thank God, Princess. I sure as hell don't want you remembering what he put you through. Just leave it in the past."

She hated lying to her father, but she couldn't see any other way. Saige folded up her napkin and placed it on the table. "I'll be right back. The restroom is calling." She turned to head inside the restaurant, and proceeded to trip over a laptop bag. Catching herself on the table, she glanced at the guy sitting there. "I'm sorry."

"No"—the stranger with dark piercing eyes quickly lifted the bag to the chair beside him—"I shouldn't have left it in the way. My apologies."

It had been quick thinking when Alex had placed his laptop bag in her way and she tripped over it. Why hadn't she recognized him? He'd kept his back to her father, but Saige had looked him straight in the face, and there had been nothing.

No spark. No smile. Nothing to hint of recognition on her part.

Why the hell had she asked her father about Quinten? She shouldn't have forgotten his brother as though he was inconsequential, not after the time Alex knew they had spent together.

He thought finding Saige Lockwood would be difficult. In the end it had been easy, thanks to her father's assistant. She'd told him where Richard Lockwood would be, so all Alex had done was wait, and then followed. He'd been led right to Saige Lockwood.

He wanted to go up and confront both of them but something held him back.

Saige not knowing who his brother was shocked him. He couldn't work out what was really going on with her.

Alex wondered whether or not her father really believed her easy acceptance to leave the past alone? Even to his ears she had sounded insincere.

He'd had it all planned in his head, what he'd say to her, or even how to go about approaching her. Her not recognizing him presented a new challenge or maybe an opportunity.

Originally he hadn't planned on introducing himself. He was going to just stand in her way until she recognized him. From what he'd overheard and saw, that wouldn't work now. He couldn't help feel a twinge of disappointment. He'd wanted her to be shocked and maybe even scared when he stood in front of her. He'd wanted to see fear in her eyes as she realized he was there for the truth instead of all the lies she'd told about his brother.

He now had even more questions.

Alex knew he had to talk to her, but tomorrow would do. He'd go straight to Saige for answers.

He wondered how she would be with him once he admitted who he was and what he wanted. He was a lot different now, and so was she.

Gone was the long, blond hair. It was now a rich, glowing auburn that fell softly around her strong chin and high cheekbones. She still had a delicacy about her that had been present before, it seemed fragile now, or maybe slightly hardened, as though she kept it hidden. He was glad she hadn't lost the softness. It was one of the things that had attracted his brother. Nothing could change the azure blue of her eyes. He'd know her from those alone.

Day 3

Settled in his truck outside of Saige's apartment, Alex wondered what had happened to Little Miss-Not-So-Perfect. One minute she was in the hospital and the next she had disappeared. He'd sweet-talked one of her nurses for information to pass on to his brother, who'd been going crazy wanting to know how his girl was. The nurse hadn't been much use, but at least he was able to tell Quinten that Saige would live.

He hated her for the lies, but he didn't think his brother could hate her even if she was the one giving him the lethal injection. For all intents and purposes, she would be.

She'd accused him.

It had been Saige who had selected Quinten's picture from a stack the DA and Detective Harris had given her. That one decision had been the start of the witch-hunt against his brother.

Catching a flash of movement to his right, he sat straight in his truck when he realized Saige was about to disappear behind the door to her apartment building.

Alex quickly opened his door and jumped down. "Saige," he shouted, trying to grab her attention.

She paused and when her eyes landed on him, she frowned as though she tried to remember where she'd seen him before. "You're the guy from the restaurant?"

He nodded as he walked closer, which seemed to set her on alert as her eyes darted between him, the entrance to the building behind her, and the coffee shop across the street.

"Have coffee with me?" He wanted her to feel safe so that she'd talk to him, although she'd probably run when she realized who he was.

Or would she?

"I don't have coffee with strangers." She edged

toward the building where the doorman had appeared, wary of their exchange.

He wasn't a stranger.

He figured that he didn't have much left to lose. "Saige, please. My name is Alex. Alexander Peterson. My brother is Quinten Peterson."

She froze at his words, all color drained from her face as her hand reached up and covered her mouth, muffling the gasp. "You look different than your photograph," she stated, tilting her head slightly.

He nodded in agreement, and continued. "I'm not going to hurt you, but I really need to talk to you."

He edged closer. "Please, Saige. My brother didn't hurt you, or those girls. Please just talk to me." He glanced toward the coffee shop. "Let me buy you coffee. It's busy so you won't be alone with me, if that's what you're worried about."

Saige stood frozen in place as the minutes slid by and Alex began to wonder if she was in shock, then she slowly nodded. "Will you answer my questions?"

He wondered what was going through her head and what questions she could possibly have.

His gut reaction was to tell her no, because of what she'd done to his family, to his brother, to his own life. He would have to compromise because he had questions of his own. "I'll answer them if I can," he alluded.

She waved to the doorman to let him know she was fine before she slowly moved toward the coffee shop. Alex watched her walk past him and turned to follow. Once inside, the waitress led them to a table by the window.

He didn't like the fact that the shop was so busy, but he was desperate and would take anything he could get at this point.

A young waitress strolled up to their table, took their orders and she was gone as fast as she appeared.

Saige rubbed her brow and frowned, her eyes searched his face. Tilting her head to the side, she asked, "Have we met before last night?"

He stared at her wondering what to say because she genuinely seemed confused.

"You really don't remember me, do you?" He searched her face, looking for the truth in her expression.

"No." Tears sat thickly on her lashes, but they

didn't fall as she blinked them away. "I think I should. My head has started to ache." She kept rubbing at her forehead. "When did we meet?"

He wouldn't mention her time with Quinten, but he could give her something. "We first met the summer before you were taken."

The waitress returned with two steaming cups of coffee and set them down before leaving them alone.

"I don't remember." Saige gritted her teeth and wrapped her hands around the cup. "I don't remember the summer before at all." She swiped at a lone tear as it trickled down her pale face. "I wish I did. My memory has a large black hole in it, and it drives me crazy. Surely, if anything, I should have only blocked out the four days I was … I was tortured. Instead I have two and a half years missing."

"What?" He was stunned by her words.

No way!

"Are you sure?" he questioned, leaning forward.

Her hands trembled as she raised her mug, sloshing droplets of coffee onto the table. She gave up and placed the cup back down. "Am I sure? Of course I'm sure." She waved her hands around. "Don't you think I want to remember? I've no desire to remember what *he* did to me, but I sure as hell want to remember the rest." The anger she felt was evident in every sharp movement of her hands and body as she became agitated.

"I was found at the end of November. I know that simply because people told me. I don't remember it. All of my memories end at the Easter party my stepmother had arranged for her friends. It was boring, but I was there and remember it. My next memory starts two and a half years later when I woke up in that horrible, private hospital.

"I want and need to remember, but every time I've tried over the years, I get one hell of a headache. Sometimes it's a migraine that makes me physically sick."

He sat back and let her words sink in because she certainly believed what she told him.

"I don't know what to say about that, but if you don't have any memory of what happened, how were you able to make a statement accusing my brother of taking you? How were you able to identify him from a selection of photographs given to you?"

He loved you and you betrayed him.

A barrage of emotion crossed Saige's face—shock being the main one.

"I don't know," she whispered, and buried her face in her hands. "I really don't know. How could I have done that if I don't have any memory?"

Her tear stained eyes lifted to his and Alex found himself swallowing back the harsh words he'd had prepared for the last eight years.

"That's a good question that I think you need to ask your father," he hissed.

Saige dried her tears on a napkin that he passed to her while staying silent. She stared out of the window and drank some of her coffee, her fingers only shaking slightly around the tall cup.

"I tried to ask my father about the trial." She faced him. "He wanted me to leave it in the past."

Alex clenched his jaw in anger. "I heard."

Saige paused and then nodded. "I agreed, but have no intention of letting it go."

"Why? Why would you lie to your father?" He knew she'd lied but he needed to hear the reason from her, and he knew how close she was to her father. She always had been and he overheard enough of their conversation last evening to know that she still was.

"He's protecting me."

Alex wondered if there was something more to her father wanting her to leave it in the past. Did he have secrets too?

Saige's attention went outside the coffee shop again, as though she was seeing something he couldn't.

"If I tell you something, will you tell me if you think I'm crazy?" she asked so quietly.

He nodded, his curiosity piqued.

"When I saw your brother's picture on television that was the first time I recall seeing him. I know I can't remember, but I didn't feel anything like I thought I would if I ever saw the man who took me. I felt safe. I don't understand why I didn't fear him if he was the one responsible for what happened to me. That's what set me off wanting to know what happened." She leaned forward. "And now, are you telling me that it was my statement, and selecting him from a photographic lineup, that got him convicted?"

If she was lying, then she was a damn good actress. He wanted to believe she was lying, except his gut told him she wasn't.

So he decided to be even more honest. "There was evidence at the scene of the crime to suggest that he was responsible. After your statement, they didn't look for anyone else and went after Quinten. Eventually they charged him. As far as they were concerned, they had their man so why look elsewhere."

Saige paled and nodded her head with acceptance.

"I need to see my statement and I need to know what evidence they used to convict him." Saige grabbed her purse and rummaged around before she brought out a small notepad and a pen. "We'll make a list."

"Why aren't you afraid of me?" Alex asked, bemused that she now seemed comfortable with him. She even treated him like they were a team.

She tilted her head to the side. "Should I be?"

"I won't hurt you, Saige. I just want to do everything I can for my brother."

"If I knew you before, then I must have known Quinten too, right?"

He wasn't sure how much to tell Saige because her relationship with his brother had been wrong in a lot of ways. Quinten had been married at the time, even though he'd started to seek a divorce from the bitch, Jocelyn. His brother still hadn't been totally free to be with Saige.

"You knew the both of us. We did the wooden carving on the staircase in your family's home the summer before—" he paused, trying to think of what to call everything before, he finally finished with, "hell happened."

"So I'd talk to you both?"

"Yes."

He could practically hear her thinking, see all of the questions running behind her eyes. He needed to cut them off for now. "I have an appointment with Daniel Sterling, Quinten's defense attorney, tomorrow," he said. "You can come and talk to him with me. He'll probably have a copy of your statement for you to read."

She offered a small smile. "That's who I planned on talking to when I promised my father to leave it all in the past." She shrugged. "I can't do that. I have to know what happened."

Saige stands on the balcony of her apartment, a silhouette in the dark night.

I watch her from the shadows of my own balcony a troubled expression on her beautiful face. Is she pondering over what she's discovered today? Is she wondering what she can do to help Quinten Peterson?

What I'm going to do about her, I haven't decided. All these years I've waited for her to regain her memory. She never has. I wonder why? With the clock ticking on Quinten's life I know what I should do, but I'm not sure anymore.

My cell rings, distracting me from the beautiful Saige.

I answer and listen.

My grin is wide when the call is over.

The first part of my plan, which involved some digging in the dark, has been completed.

In the meanwhile, I will keep a close eye on Saige Lockwood.

Quinten lay on the narrow bed and tried not to think about the end, instead he focused on Saige. He knew Alex thought he was crazy for still longing for the girl who had stolen his heart the summer before everything went to hell, before she betrayed him.

However, his heart still ached every time he thought about her. Their love had been doomed from the minute they had laid eyes on each other.

She'd taken his breath away, and every minute they'd spent together had made his heart race with longing. He hadn't been free to pursue a relationship.

At first, he'd tried to ignore the pull that she'd had over him, but then one day he'd found her upset in the boathouse when she'd thought no one else was around. After that day, they'd managed to spend time together every day. They'd only talked, but she'd kept him going, and it had given him something to look forward to.

He'd struggled to keep his hands to himself, but as long as he was married there wasn't anything else he could have done, and then, that last night when they'd met before she'd headed back to college, he did what he'd promised not to. He'd made love to her, over and over again.

Saige's hands on his body, her lips against his, her breasts soft against his chest. It had all been too much for him, for her. They first came together in a frenzied haze of sexual need. The second and subsequent times that night had been slow and long, until they knew they had to part. Then it had been fast and hard.

His now ex-wife had known he'd fallen for Saige. How could she not when he'd wake in the middle of the night, lying beside her, his head full of the sexual dream he'd had and his mouth full of her name, *Saige.*

He hated his ex, Jocelyn. She'd been unfaithful to him since the day he'd put a ring on her finger. The bitch had constantly lied and cheated, although he hadn't known at the time.

Two weeks before he'd met Saige, he'd spoken to a lawyer about getting a divorce, except before anything could be done, he'd found himself arrested. Jocelyn had lied through her teeth about him and their relationship.

She'd gained a lot of money from her interviews, and she talked to everyone and anyone who paid the booking fee.

The only good thing to come of that was when she'd divorced him. He'd jumped for joy knowing she no longer had a hold over him. Not that it did him any good considering his new living arrangements.

Saige had been his lifeline until it was ripped away. He'd lived on memories of her from the minute he'd been incarcerated. He'd gone crazy not being able to see her. He'd had no idea how she was, or if she'd be alright.

Nothing.

His brother, Alex, had told him what he'd discovered, which hadn't been much. Saige hadn't been raped, but it still hadn't calmed the rage he'd felt toward the bastard who'd taken her. He'd done enough damage to her, but knowing Saige was safe had calmed Quinten. He just wished Alex hadn't grown to hate her because he hadn't been able too. He'd tried once the trial was under way and he'd discovered she'd identified him from a photograph, much to his confusion. Her father had looked at him with hatred.

His heart still held strong and refused to be hardened against her. He loved her too much.

When he felt more down than usual, he'd have his doubts, but then he'd remember how she'd been with him.

Nothing about her had been a lie.

So why did she accuse him of being the one?

His eyes stung with tears as her image

appeared in his mind.

Quinten was hot and miserable with sweat running down his back, and then he spotted the girl he'd fallen in love with on the arm of her father.

She walked with him to the car and when she turned and spotted Quinten, she smiled. The smile she gave him filled her whole face and her body practically shimmered.

Even the anger on Richard Lockwood's face couldn't diminish the moment with Saige.

From behind him, Alex laughed. "You've both got it bad."

Once Saige disappeared into the car, he turned to Alex, a grin splitting his face. Whatever he was going to say died on his lips when he saw Christina Lockwood—Saige's stepmother—in the doorway to the house. She didn't look happy.

Tears fell down his face at the overwhelming longing to see Saige.

Touch her.

Confess his love.

Just one last time.

That's all he wanted.

Just to see her once more.

Day 4

Saige heard Tamsyn banging around in the kitchen before she left for the early shift at the diner. Normally, Saige would be heading out with her roommate, but not today. She wasn't even sure if she wanted to go back and chances were she'd be fired for not showing up. She'd already missed two days. Lou wouldn't be happy, even though Saige had worked for her for a few years without taking any time off sick.

Already awake, Saige rolled out of bed and quickly threw on a pair of sweats and a sweatshirt to join Tamsyn.

She'd make some coffee and hopefully get

some time with Tamsyn before she left. Last night, Saige had hardly said two words to her roommate. Her head had been full of what Alex had told her. He'd left her with more unanswered questions, especially about his brother and her relationship with him.

She noticed that while Alex had answered her questions about knowing him and his brother, he hadn't expanded either.

What hadn't he told her?

Her heart pounded when she thought about Alex and his brother. The feeling of familiarity that she knew Alex had been strong while they'd sat talking. She hadn't felt threatened by him and just hoped he hadn't given her a false sense of security.

Saige wanted her memory back and to help Quinten Peterson if he turned out to be innocent. Alex just wanted his brother free and she had a feeling he'd do and say anything to make that happen.

"Saige?" Tamsyn said, stepping toward her. "How are you holding up? Headache gone?"

"It's not that bad." Saige watched while Tamsyn grabbed two large mugs and poured them both a cup of fresh coffee.

Tamsyn had known the basics of Saige's past for about a year now, but Saige had never sat her down and explained further. They weren't best friends, but Tamsyn had stumbled upon Saige's picture online, so all Tamsyn knew was what had been available to the public.

"I really don't remember anything from before, Tamsyn. I think the other day at work I was more surprised at seeing the man on the television and not feeling anything like I thought I would. It's frustrating not being able to remember anything."

When she paused, Tamsyn offered her a small smile of encouragement.

"I'm going to find out what happened," Saige said, "which is why I'm not going back to the diner. I can't work my shifts and spend my time trying to read everything that I find. This is something I have to do. I'll probably have to head home for a short while as well."

"Oh wow." Tamsyn sat beside her. "But I understand what you're saying. I'm not sure I'd want to remember what happened if it was me, but I can't imagine not having my memories."

Saige sighed as she stared into her coffee mug. "My dad won't be impressed either, once he knows that I lied to him about leaving it all in the past."

Tamsyn raised a brow. "You talked to your dad about it the other night at dinner?"

"Yeah. I asked him about the trial and Quinten Peterson. He wasn't happy that I wanted to drag it all out into the open again, and he asked me to leave it alone." Sighing, she added firmly, "I can't do that."

Sipping her coffee, Saige wondered again about Quinten Peterson and his brother. She knew the work that Alex had talked about. Their carved design didn't only go up the banister. They'd created the same design into molds that went around the light in the foyer of her father's home. The wildlife carved into the bannister had always been her favorite. Each time she had walked downstairs, her fingers would trace along the delicate work, and for years she hadn't had one memory of the Peterson brothers.

"Whatever you do," Tamsyn started, "just be careful." Her friend wrapped an arm around her shoulders. "I know I haven't been around these past couple of days for you, but if you need me, you call, okay? Don't do this alone."

"I'm not alone," Saige blurted out before she

could stop herself. She winced as Tamsyn's attention focused on her completely.

She'd planned on keeping Alex to herself for now because she knew others would warn her about helping him. After all, he was Quinten's brother. They didn't look like brothers. He was broader in the shoulders than Quinten had looked on the TV, and Alex's light hair was a stark contrast to Quinten's deep red.

"I'm waiting for you to explain." Tamsyn moved away and slipped her feet into her shoes. "I need to go so be quick. Who's helping you?"

"Alex Peterson came looking for me."

She frowned. "Should I know who that is?"

"He's Quinten Peterson's brother. We talked last night over coffee."

Her eyes widened. "Wow ... that's, um, strange." Tamsyn picked up her purse and shoved the strap over her shoulder. "Why would he come looking for you?"

"He thinks I lied." Saige looked out of the apartment window to the city below that had started to wake for the day. "Apparently," she whispered, "I gave a statement, which implicated his brother."

Tamsyn moved to stand beside her.

"I don't remember any of that, Tamsyn." Guilt filled Saige as she continued. "So today, Alex is meeting me at his brother's defense attorney's office. I figure it's the quickest way to get the information I need. My father isn't going to be forthcoming and I just need to know."

"Oh!" Tamsyn pulled her close before letting her go. "Try not to be too disappointed if everything turns out to be true." She paused and looked hesitantly toward the door, as though she was debating calling in sick. "I don't want to leave. If you're not going in, then I really need to be on time."

Saige smiled and tried to make it reach her eyes. "I'll be fine. I promise."

Tamsyn stared at her for another minute before she turned, waved, and disappeared out the door.

Saige stared at where Tamsyn had stood and wrapped her arms around herself. She was more nervous than she wanted to admit about what secrets the day would unveil.

❖

Detective Coulter Robinson yawned as he pulled his truck in beside that belonging to the medical examiner. Amber McGregor, ME, had been at the scene for thirty minutes, when she'd called him. He'd then called his partner, Darrin Redgrove. A bit unusual being called to the scene by the ME, but no doubt it would all become clear.

What he'd discovered on his way to the scene was that teenagers had been camping close to the river when they woke early and discovered human bones—a leg and a foot.

He hated cases when the body had been there for years, which was the length of time Amber had estimated. The chances of any evidence being found were practically next to none. The area he'd been directed to was popular with the locals and tourists alike.

Clearing his head, he climbed out of his truck and opened the trunk to grab his hiking boots. He quickly made the exchange and noticed Darrin. His partner looked as tired as Coulter felt.

"I spoke to the boss," Darrin said in greeting. "No big deal. His son had a high temperature so they took him to the hospital. Saved time getting Amber to call us." He grinned. "Bet you enjoyed hearing her voice."

Coulter ignored Darrin and followed Claire, Amber's assistant, through the thick foliage, the odd leaf attaching to his hair.

Annoying things.

"About time you got here Detectives," Amber commented.

Although he ignored her comment, he hadn't missed the quick once over she gave him before she blushed and turned back to the newly discovered remains.

Darrin chuckled and covered it with a cough when Coulter glared at him.

Coulter gave his attention to Amber. "What do you know?"

"Without having her in the morgue, I'm not sure how long. I'm guessing somewhere between seven to ten years."

Her?

Coulter raised his brow at that while Darrin crouched closer to the uncovered grave.

"The size of the bones indicates that she was female. Plus, these were found on the remains." Amber held out three evidence bags. "I removed these because they'd have fallen off when we started to remove the body."

He took the bags and spread them out on one side of the black sheet that Amber's assistant had laid out.

The first bag he concentrated on held a woman's ring—silver with a small sapphire surrounded by either cubic zirconia or the real thing.

Bag two held another ring, a small gold wedding band that he was sure could have only fitted a woman's delicate finger.

It was bag three that made him pause and his stomach churn. The dirty silver bangle with charms hanging off caused a memory to flash in front of his eyes. A woman he'd questioned a few times. She'd had a bangle just like the one he now looked at. She would talk with her hands and the damn thing had jangled, annoying the hell out of him.

It had been one of those cases that had plagued his thoughts for a long time afterwards. Something had been off, but he'd never been able to put his finger on what had felt wrong. The lead detective at the time hadn't listened to his concerns nor had the DA.

In his twenty-eight years as a cop, he'd never been part of a case like it, before or after, where everything was all neat and tidy—too tidy. Too easy.

"What do you see?" Amber crouched beside him.

He met her frown with one of his own, and tried not to let the young woman see that she got to him. Not in an irritable way, but in a way that made him uncomfortable in his clothing.

Coulter cleared his throat and avoided Darrin's knowing smirk. "I recognize the bangle, or I remember a woman wearing an identical one. The charms I remember are the cowboy boot, the cupid's arrow, the diamond, and the skull and cross bone. I'm thinking it's too coincidental for someone to have those exact charms, don't you think?"

"Hmm. It's possible, if it's a pre-set design?" She shrugged. "But I'd love a place to start with identifying her. Save me time if you're right."

He nodded and looked back at the bangle. "Pull whatever records you can find for Jocelyn Peterson."

Because he watched her closely, he didn't miss

the surprise that crossed her face. "Quinten Peterson's ex-wife?" Amber said. "There was an extended news report late last night about the trial."

"Hmm." Coulter straightened to his full height and stretched out the kinks forming in his back.

"What does, 'Hmm', mean?" Amber straightened next to him, a bit too close for comfort.

He moved away and gave himself space to think because having Amber so damn close caused a lack of concentration. He met her beautiful green eyes. "If that is Jocelyn Peterson, then I have no idea where to start. Her ex, who hated her, and yes, the feeling was mutual, was already incarcerated."

He ran his hand over his head and down his weary face. "She was certainly alive for a while after the trial ended because she divorced Quinten shortly after it."

"You really think that's her?" Amber questioned, and stared at the remains neatly uncovered in the earth.

"At least that would explain why no one could find her," Darrin said.

"It's a guess at this point." Coulter glanced at the evidence bag and then Darrin. "I know she wore one of those because I felt like snatching it off her wrist once or twice."

Darrin snickered. "Only once or twice?"

"You have no idea." Coulter sighed.

"Okay, then." Amber cleared her throat. "Let me and Claire finish off here and if we find anything else, I'll call you."

"Why would the killer leave her jewelry on her?" he queried to himself, but smiled when Amber took him up on the question.

"Perhaps he wanted her to be found. I also think that he *wanted* her to be found now, as opposed to years ago or even last week."

His brows furrowed, and then his eyes widened and his gaze sharpened on the burial site.

He knew the answer but he was still going to ask the question. "She'd been partially unburied when the teenagers found her?"

"Yes. I asked them if they had moved anything and they were adamant that they hadn't. They called 911 as soon as they realized what they'd stumbled upon ... but, look here." Amber crouched to where the bones of the victim's feet were visible and Coulter followed her. "See this? Neither my crew nor I dug around the feet. It's too neat for an animal. The boys swore they didn't touch anything, so maybe the killer came back and decided to unveil her. Either he planned on digging her up and moving her or he wanted her to be found, *now.*"

Coulter straightened, continuing to stare at Amber. "You think the timing has everything to do with Quinten Peterson. That's where you're going, right?"

"If she's Jocelyn Peterson, then yes, I do."

"Shit," he cursed under his breath.

"My thoughts exactly Detective."

Coulter sighed and faced his partner.

Well, this meeting was going well.

Whatever high hopes Alex had for the meeting with Daniel Sterling had crumbled within ten minutes of them arriving. Daniel had an excellent court record and even with all the evidence toward Quinten, Daniel hadn't stopped appealing. He fought every step with Quinten and that was why it was so confusing, and annoying, that his brother's only line of defense was being a total dick toward Saige.

Quinten hadn't been the only victim in all of this, which was something Alex had begun to realize last night after he walked Saige back to her building. If she genuinely didn't remember anything, then he wanted to know more about her statement. Had she been coerced? Too many questions where now left unanswered.

Up until now, Alex hadn't had a problem with Daniel. He'd paid the man enough money over the years to file all the appeals, because Daniel sure as hell hadn't done it out of the goodness of his heart. But now, Daniel was acting out of character and was being extremely evasive.

"Enough," Alex shouted, slamming his fist down onto the desk. "We are here to try and save my brother. You"—he pointed to Daniel—"have been paid by me to do just that—to save Quinten. After talking to Saige, I want her to read the statement she gave. I also want her to look at the signature on it to see if it's hers. I've never understood why Saige would accuse my brother. A lot of things have never added up, and that is one of them. So, instead of wasting time, I suggest you dig into your boxes of files and let her read the damn statement."

Once he finished, Alex moved away to the window to calm his temper, which constantly ate at him. It was always there, whispering to him about how unfair every damn thing in his life was. But he needed action and he needed it now.

Saige cleared her throat. "I'm, um, ready when you are."

"Perhaps we did get off to a wrong start, Ms. Lockwood." Daniel held his hand out.

"You think." Alex needed to hold his tongue now that he had the attorney moving along.

"Please call me Saige, and I'm here to read my statement, but I'd also like you to tell me what you remember from the case—the trial."

Daniel deflated before their eyes. "The trial was exhausting and, for what it's worth, I never believed that young man was guilty. I still don't. To begin with, Quinten constantly asked about you and he wouldn't settle. No one would tell him anything because they thought he was responsible for what happened."

Alex watched as Saige listened to what the defense attorney said, but the more he spoke, the deeper her frown became. He could practically see the wheels turning in her head because Alex had only told her about them working for her father. She still had no idea about what she became to Quinten, or him to her, at least he didn't think she did. He was more or less convinced about her lack of memory. After all, he'd overheard her conversation with her father before she even saw him.

"He was a very distraught young man," Daniel continued. "I was there when he was charged. He was in shock and couldn't believe what was happening to him, then word came that you had identified him as your abductor from a lineup of photographs. I think"—Daniel paused and gave Saige a searching look—"he gave up at that point."

Saige wiped her eyes and Alex passed her a tissue. "I don't understand." She looked to him.

Alex moved to the seat beside her. He hesitated before he took her hands into his and closed his eyes. "My brother cared about you. A lot." He opened his eyes and they met hers before he squeezed her fingers, letting go. "The rest I need you to remember on your own."

"No." She grabbed his wrist. "Please tell me."

"Dammit. I can't. I need you to remember without me putting images into your head. Don't you see? If you get your memory back, then I want it to be *your* memory, not something I've put there."

Saige searched his face, but Alex made sure he didn't give anything away. Eventually Saige nodded. "I understand." She sat back and let the silence settle. "Mr. Sterling, would it be possible to get a copy of my statement so that I can take it with me, and I noticed some photographs? If you have any of Quinten around the time he was charged, I'd appreciate a copy."

Daniel looked at Alex for approval. Alex nodded softly. Daniel then made a sound of acceptance. "Let me pass this file to my secretary. I won't be long, and it's Daniel."

They watched Daniel leave when Saige turned to him. "Will you tell me more about your brother? Not the trial, about what he was like. What did he like to do in his free time?"

Alex could do that. "Quinten is younger than me by two years, but he always acted like the one in charge." A wisp of a smile adorned his face as he remembered. "We would have some arguments over the business, but the truth is, Quinten was the business minded one. I'd have screwed it all up.

"As to free time, he didn't have that much, but when he did, he'd go fishing or read. He could spend all day by the river with a book. He loved suspense and I even teased him a few times because he read historical romances." Alex smiled, having forgotten that memory until now. "My brother was a caring guy who should have never married that unfaithful bitch Jocelyn."

Saige rubbed her brow.

A headache?

"When did their marriage end?" She rubbed at her forehead again.

"He talked to a lawyer about getting a divorce a week or so before we started working at your family home. He was saving money to actually proceed with it when his life was turned upside down, so she was the one to eventually divorce him. Good riddance, if you ask me."

"Okay," she whispered. "You know what I'm imagining, right?"

"I know." He turned toward the door so he wouldn't give anything away. "Let's go and see what Daniel is up to." Alex offered his hand, which she took but let go of the minute she was on her feet.

"Let me look through everything and I'll call you, but it will probably be tomorrow now as my head has started to pound. I won't be able to read anything until the pain has disappeared."

Alex hesitated because he wanted to be with her when she read the words she supposedly gave that implicated his brother.

"Or not." Saige looked uncertain. "You don't believe me? About remembering?"

"I overheard you talking to your father, but I won't deny wanting to be with you while you read your statement."

She nodded and wouldn't meet his gaze. "If you want, you can bring breakfast tomorrow and the copies that Daniel is making now." She shrugged and winced, her face pale. "At least then you'll know I'm not reading them without you."

She really wasn't well and he realized she'd made a big concession in trusting him. A part of him couldn't help wonder why. "Don't you fear for your own safety?"

"What?" she asked, surprise filling her eyes.

"You've been abducted before, yet you have no

concern for your safety by inviting me back to your place."

She opened and closed her mouth before her lips pulled tight in anger. "As you put it like that, then I suppose I'll have to call you instead."

Saige gripped her purse and when her hand touched the doorknob, Alex pressed his hand to the door. Once she calmed, and didn't look to be about to leave, he stepped away from her.

"I'm sorry. I shouldn't have pointed that out."

"It's the truth," she said, her voice tight with anger.

"Saige, please look at me."

She turned.

"I was being a dick. I really am sorry, and I promise you'll be safe with me."

"Sometimes you look as though you hate me and I guess knowing that you believe my statement incriminated your brother, I can understand that."

"I won't hurt you," he said as softly as he could manage.

She raised her gaze to his.

"You're probably the only one who can help at this stage. You're all he has. I promise I won't hurt you," Alex said. "You need to go and rest right now. Sleep the migraine away."

She nodded and then winced as they exited Daniel's office.

Alex's attention was diverted when he noticed the man's secretary, Fern, bent over her desk.

He smirked and licked his lips.

Saige caught him and rolled her eyes.

He laughed, motioning for Saige to follow him out, but his eyes strayed back to the legs on display.

Fern knows something.

Has she been investigating?

Saige has started her own investigation—that is unexpected.

I want the truth to come out, but not until the execution has taken place—were would the fun be otherwise? The wrongful death of Quinten Peterson will cause an outcry from the public, but most of all, it will hurt the one person I hate the most in this world.

With help from a very good friend, the remains of another person I once hated have been found today—Jocelyn Peterson. The annoying woman had come very close to ruining everything seven years ago.

No one blackmails me.

She'd paid the price.

Another plan is forming in my mind because what will I do if Quinten should be freed? I need a plan.

If there is anything I've learned over the years it is to always be one step ahead of everyone else.

Day 5

Quinten stared at the blank pieces of paper that sat in front of him, at a loss as to what to write.

Saige hadn't once visited him since he'd been arrested, charged, then incarcerated, so why would she come now?

The warden had asked him if he had any last requests, and the only one he'd been able to think of was to see *his* Saige. The form to have her vetted to visit had been completed, and he'd been assured she'd be granted access, but the rest would be up to her. As much as he tried not to get his hopes up, his heart raced at the thought that he'd get to see her one last time.

Would she really come to see him? Time was ticking and his hands trembled with the reality of what was about to happen to him. He tried not to think about it, but how could he not when he was living this hell?

And what about his brother? Alex was due in a couple of days. It was a visit that he usually looked forward to, but now that he'd been moved and his death imminent, he didn't know how to feel. His stomach was in turmoil, and he feared he'd puke.

He'd escaped a lot of the violence that happened in prison because, as a death row prisoner, he'd had a cell to himself and the security was different, or so he'd been told. It didn't change his longing for the life he'd started to dream about before it was taken away from him.

The dreams had kept him going while Saige had been away at college, and the guilt he felt at being the one to bring her home the weekend she'd been taken still ate at him. He'd been sick and tired of his life, and had needed her badly. She'd heard his need through their connection over the phone and before he could say anything, she'd had a bag packed and was in her car.

That had been the last time they'd talked.

He missed her voice, her smile and, most of all, the feel of her arms around him. Even now, his heart swelled with the love they once shared, and no one could tell him it had all been a dream on his part. He knew that his brother believed the worst about Saige. She'd been the only thing to cause arguments between them over the years.

"You done?" the guard questioned.

They got edgy when he had a pencil in his hands. What they expected him to do with it, he didn't know.

He wasn't a killer.

"I haven't thought of anything to write," he admitted. "I thought the words would come, but now that I have the chance to write to her, I don't know what to say. There's so much." He dropped his gaze to the sheet of paper. "What do you write to the girl you love, who you know you'll never see again?"

Quinten had no idea how long he sat crying with the paper blurred in his vision. He just knew he had to write something because he couldn't leave this life without her knowing how much he loved her.

❖

Saige didn't know whether or not she could trust Alex. One minute, he seemed like Quinten's caring older brother, and the next, he glared at her with hate emanated from him. The only way she'd understand Alex more was to read the statement.

The statement that she'd given so many years before sat on her lap while she gazed out of the window. Saige knew she had to pick it up and read the words she'd supposedly said, but the thought of reading what happened to her made her belly quiver with nerves.

Alex told her that the statement didn't go into too much detail, but if she wanted more details they would be in the hospital report that her doctor had written for the court. She opted to ignore the latter.

Draining the bottle of water that she'd been nursing, she placed it on the table and started to read.

He held me down...
There was so much hate inside him...
He kept talking about revenge...
His voice was distorted...like a machine...
He was so strong...

I don't remember him raping me...Did he?

I just wanted to leave...

I promised him I wouldn't tell...

A short time later, Saige had reached the end of the report, and realized that tears ran down her face. The signature at the end of the report blurred.

"Do you remember?" Alex offered another tissue while he stood to the side.

"My head is full of the report, but I didn't see any mention of your brother by name," she said.

"Then you obviously didn't read the last paragraph." Alex pointed to the bit that she missed because her tears had prevented her from reading it.

Wiping her eyes, and blowing her nose, she took a drink from the bottle of water that Alex passed her, and read the last paragraph.

I, Saige Lockwood, state that the photograph selected, whilst in the hospital, from a lineup of ten photographs given to me by the District Attorney's office, and Detective Jason Harris, is of my abductor, Quinten James Peterson.

She gasped, and managed to look at the signature before her tears started again, not that they'd ever stopped.

"That's mine. Oh, God."

For five days she'd thought that maybe Quinten Peterson was innocent, but her statement obviously said otherwise.

"Saige." Alex crouched beside her, and demanded, "Please stop crying and dry your eyes. I need you to take another look at the signature. Look at it. Don't glance."

She slowly quieted as she dried her eyes. She stared at the signature but she still couldn't see it clearly. She jumped up. "Let me grab a notepad and a pen. I'll sign my name and we'll compare." From the coffee table, Saige grabbed paper and pen, and signed her signature.

"Okay. My signature." Saige laid the paper out beside that of the statement. "It looks the same," she commented after a minute of looking between the two signatures.

"I have to agree." Alex sighed.

Saige felt tired as she sat back and watched Alex trace the curves of her signature. She was disappointed because she hadn't wanted to believe that Quinten was guilty after what she felt when she saw him. Even now, she wondered if she could have signed without actually giving the statement herself. However, she doubted that was the case.

Feeling heavy of heart, Saige picked up the pack of photographs, wanting to see images of a time when Quinten had been free to enjoy life. She curled up in her favorite brown, leather chair and took the photographs out.

Her fingers trembled with nerves as she slowly started going through them. Some of the images were of Quinten with his brother, and others were of him alone. He looked deep in thought, or his gaze had been fixed on something off camera—or someone.

She looked closer at one picture that was a profile of his handsome face. His dark eyes had pure joy in them and as her finger traced along his lips, a memory teased her mind.

She rounded the corner to the entrance of the boathouse and Quinten was there, waiting for her. Her heart felt so full of love at just the sight of him, and when he turned, his face lit up with pure joy.

She gasped and sat straight in the chair, the photographs falling from her lap to the floor.

"What is it?" Alex quickly moved to crouch beside her.

"This picture." She held up the image that had caught her attention. "I saw this and when I traced his smile with the tip of my finger, I remembered him smiling like this, for me, outside of the boathouse." Saige met Alex's gaze. "Did that happen? Did he smile like that for me?"

Alex stayed silent.

"Please tell me. You've hinted that Quinten and I were more than friends, so please tell me if what I remembered was real? Did it happen?"

He nodded and cleared his throat. "It was real." He looked away and then back at the photograph she held in her hand. "I used to tease him for having a sappy look on his face whenever he looked at you. So one day I spotted you in the garden and before I pointed you out, I got my cell ready and snapped that very image when he saw you. I wanted proof of the look on his face whenever he saw you." Alex got up and relaxed back against the sofa. "I'd never seen him as happy. It was as though you gave him purpose to go on."

"What went wrong, Alex?" Saige whispered,

knowing that something had, otherwise he wouldn't be behind bars, facing death.

Alex was silent for a while before he answered. "Your father."

Saige frowned and quickly glanced at him. "My father? What does he have to do with Quinten being in prison?"

He ran his hand over his face. "I've never been able to find out for sure. Your father hated the time you spent with Quinten," Alex said. "I think he was jealous that your affection had moved from him to my brother. All Quinten ever wanted to do was love and protect you."

So her impression of safety with him had been right, but why didn't she feel anything else? If things took a turn for the worst and he took her, tortured her, then surely she should have felt something else at seeing his image. Instead she felt nothing but warmth and safety.

"I must have loved him, or thought I did."

Alex sat forward. "He loved you, Saige. He was so miserable when you'd gone back to school." He sighed heavily. "It was me who convinced him to call you to get you home on that weekend. He didn't need much convincing, mind you. The minute I suggested it, he called you."

Alex smiled and continued. "He was so nervous and I teased his ass for the rest of the night at how bad he'd been on the phone. He'd eventually told you that he missed you. At first, he suggested that he could visit you for the weekend. But you surprised him by telling him you were already packed." He laughed. "He was so in love with you. It was amusing."

"How could it go so wrong, Alex?" she asked, not expecting an answer. "And why are you telling me about Quinten and me now when you refused to earlier?"

Saige thought her head would explode with everything running through her mind, and yet, apart from that small piece of her memory, nothing else had returned.

"I've only really confirmed what you already thought about Quinten and you, anything else you'll have to remember yourself."

Alex sat forward and rested his elbows on his knees. "Because he hurt himself, trying to get you free, all the evidence in the shack pointed at Quinten being the killer."

"No other DNA was found?" Saige asked,

looking at the ground, surprised that she could still think straight.

"The girls, yours, Quinten's … and two unidentified. The unidentified DNA was in a couple of places. With as much blood as Quinten had lost in the shack, it put the other ones on the back burner." Alex sighed. "My brother doesn't have a bad bone in his body, Saige. He'd have given his life for you."

He would be giving his life if she didn't remember.

"And you think I betrayed him?" Saige had to gulp back her tears a few times before she got herself under control. "I don't know what else to say. My statement is in black and white and it has my signature. If what you're telling me about Quinten and me is true, then I don't see why I would lie. I may not remember, but I do know that I'm not a liar. If I loved him, then I'd have wanted to protect him, not throw him to the wolves."

Saige leaned forward to get out of the chair, feeling agitated, but as she did, her eyes caught on another photograph of Quinten. It was an image of him working. He wore protective goggles, and in his hands, he held the tools of his trade while he carved into a piece of wood, which triggered another memory.

"You have the smoothest skin." Quinten *caressed up her thighs while she watched his hands get closer to where she needed them the most.*

She loved his hands and the beautiful tattoos that crept like vines along his arms to finish around the middle fingers of both hands.

And just as quickly another memory shot into focus.

She couldn't move.

Her fear of what the man would do next was strong, but she refused to show him.

He wanted her to cry and scream, but so far she hadn't given him the satisfaction.

She could hear him moving around and knew that soon the pain would begin again.

Everything was black because of the blindfold, but as she strained to see through the gap at the bottom, her eyes widened as she saw his hands move closer to her torso, holding a silver object ... a knife.

"I'm going to be sick." She shot out of the chair and ran to the bathroom, only just making it to the toilet. Bent double, she retched until there was nothing left inside of her.

Saige pulled away from the toilet, her breathing labored while tears streamed down her pale cheeks.

"Saige ... *God*." She heard Alex as he moved around her, but she couldn't stop crying. "Saige, try to breathe and calm down."

Slowly gaining control over her breathing, she accepted the glass of water that Alex passed to her and took a long drink. She met his gaze from where she sat on the bathroom floor.

"What happened?" Alex asked, and held a hand out to help her up from the floor.

She let him lead her back to the chair where she collapsed heavily. "I ... I got two memories back-to-back." More tears hovered on her lashes and slowly slipped down her face. "The photograph of Quinten working." She pointed and Alex picked it up. She refused to even look at it again so Alex took it with him to the sofa.

"I remembered Quinten caressing my thighs. I also remembered how much the tattoos on his arms and hands intrigued me." She finally met Alex's frown with one of her own.

Saige knew that what she had to say would change everything. "Then I remembered being in that shack. I don't remember anything about the place because I was blindfolded, but I do remember catching a glimpse from underneath the blindfold. I remembered his hands moving toward me with something silver in them before I felt raw pain. The man wore clear gloves, and his hands were free of tattoos. I didn't see any sign of ink."

Saige would have thought Alex would be happy to hear that, but instead he looked angry.

"Then why select my brother from a lineup? Why lie? Why sentence my brother to death?" Alex yelled, his gaze stayed unwavering on her, until she felt heat in her cheeks.

Alex was right. Why?

"I'm sorry, I don't know why. I need to find out. There are still so many questions that need answers and I think I need to go home and talk to my father."

"Before *we* go back to Port Jude, we need to talk to"—Alex flipped through Saige's statement—"Detective Jason Harris. He was the lead on the case. An asshole. He had it in for Quinten and refused to even look elsewhere." He paused. "There was another detective. He'd just transferred and I got the feeling he too questioned the evidence."

"Who was the other detective?" Saige frowned and thought it might be easier going to him first.

"Coulter, um," he said, "Robinson. Detective Coulter Robinson. Big guy." Alex ran his hands over his head. "I pissed Harris and Robinson off. I knew my brother wasn't guilty, so I wasn't the easiest person to talk to." Alex sat down again, dropping all of his weight at once, as though he was drained of energy.

"In which case, let me go and talk to Robinson tomorrow. Maybe he'll be more open with me, the only surviving victim," she said softly, trying her best to quell the fire within Alex.

She could see he didn't like her suggestion, but he agreed. "Okay. Call me. Then we'll head to Port Jude."

Saige nodded having no idea what her father would think with her turning up on his doorstep with Alex, but he wanted and deserved answers as well, so she wasn't about to turn him away.

"How often do you visit your brother?" It hadn't even entered her head, but she knew he did, it was obvious with his love for his brother.

"Once a month. I'm due to visit in a couple of days."

"What will you tell him?"

"The truth—as much as I can without giving him false hope. I can't lie about everything that's happened. I need to tell his attorney what you remembered." He glanced at her. "No way. That place isn't for you. And even if I did agree to take you, they wouldn't let you in. The red tape you have to go through to get clearance takes around a month, and even then the inmate has to agree."

He left unsaid that Quinten would be dead before then.

"I don't know about you, but I'm exhausted. I'm going to go home and crash for a bit. Give me a call when you're ready to leave tomorrow."

He wasn't the only one exhausted. "Okay." She watched him leave, wondering if it really would take a month for her to get clearance to visit Quinten.

But if he had loved her, then he'd feel nothing but betrayal toward her now, and she couldn't remember their love, so would it make any difference if she did visit him?

Quinten had finally written the letters that would be given to Alex and Saige after his death. Both of which had been difficult to write because he knew that when they read them, he'd no longer be on this earth.

He didn't know how he was supposed to feel now, as he looked death in the face. His nerves were high and made him jumpy. Every clang in the prison made his heart race with fear that they were coming for him early—that he wouldn't get his twenty-eight days. He was afraid. Anyone who said they weren't at this point in their sentence was a liar.

He was terrified.

"What are you doing here?" Alex raised a brow and frowned when Fern Jordan dodged under his raised arm on the doorframe and slipped into his apartment.

At his brother's defense attorney's office, he'd expected the leggy woman to come and visit, but his horny ass wasn't interested right then—revisiting his brother's trial had a habit of killing his libido.

He slammed the door shut and leaned against it while Fern stopped in the middle of his apartment. She turned and met his gaze and very slowly unbuttoned her dress. His eyes followed the movement of her fingers as they glided over the material, giving him a brief glimpse of what was underneath—nothing.

His mouth watered at the sight of her nude body, and he'd have to be a monk to not be tempted. He just wasn't sure that using Fern for information in this way was such a good idea anymore; regardless of how much his body craved release.

"You're not moving?" she said, backing up to the dining table. "I think you need more of an incentive tonight." Fern leaned over the table, spread her legs, and wiggled her bottom. "Remind me to tell you later what I've discovered." She smirked.

He prowled closer.

❖

I watch the whore park her car, and wonder why it has taken her forty-five minutes to do a fifteen-minute journey. Where else has she been? She's damn carless as well. Who in their right mind parks in a back alley? Doesn't she know thieves and murderers lurk in the shadows?

I grin.

Where I've been waiting, the stink of urine turns my stomach, but I've smelled worse, and no doubt I will again.

She steps out of her car and wears the shortest dress, and the highest heels, showing off an amazing pair of legs. I lick my lips in anticipation while I stroke my rigid cock through the thin sweat pants—perhaps I'll have some fun with her.

"Fern," I whisper, and slowly step out of the shadows.

She stills and then I witness goose bumps appear on her arms. Is she cold? Aroused? Or does she sense my intent?

When she turns, her face splits into a grin, and she gives me a coy smile. "You want more?" Her eyes drop to my cock. She moans and faces the wall; her hands lift her dress above the round white flesh of her naked ass.

She's always ready for me.

Limited on time, I free myself and impale her on me. I want to curse when she convulses, her grip strong.

The whore loudly moans so I cover her mouth with a hand while my cock drills between her thighs.

Faster and faster.

Harder and harder.

"Not a sound," I warn.

She moans, her breath catching as she finally pulsates around my flesh.

I quickly pull free, shove the whore to her knees and demand, "Open wide."

Her warm mouth wraps around me, her red lips spread so wide that the vision alone has me twitching against her tongue.

I'm tempted to let the whore live.

Day 6

Saige took a tentative step into the police station where Detective Robinson worked. From what she'd read, he'd worked here since Quinten Peterson had been found guilty.

Nerves ate at her as she glanced around and noticed the plastic chairs in the waiting area, a water dispenser in the corner, and a corked noticeboard, which overflowed with papers.

A shiver ran down her spine as she approached the glass partition. A cop in her fifties manned the desk and offered Saige a relaxed smile, which went a long way in settling her nerves.

"I wondered if Detective Coulter Robinson is

available to talk to me?"

Officer Reynolds—name tag on her shit—picked up the telephone beside her. "Name?" she asked.

"Saige Lockwood."

The officer mumbled into the phone and while she placed it back in the cradle said, "He's on his way down."

"Thank you."

A loud buzz sounded to her right, and then she heard, "Miss Lockwood?"

He'd startled her and she stumbled in her haste to face him.

"Hey there." The man reached for her arm. "I'm sorry, I didn't mean to startle you."

"It's okay. I wasn't expecting you to be so quick." She frowned at the large man, and then squinted when another memory teased her.

"Are you sure you're okay?" he asked.

"Yes and no. I'm sick and tired of memories teasing me and leaving me hanging."

"I'm not sure what that means." He frowned.

"You're Detective Robinson?"

He opened his mouth and snapped it closed again as though he was going to say something different than what he did. "Yes, I'm Detective Robinson. What can I do for you?"

Saige looked around and felt nervous at being watched by the other cops who hung around in the bullpen behind the front desk. "Um, I wanted to talk to you." She looked around again. "There's a coffee shop a couple of blocks over, are you free to talk to me there?"

He paused and looked to be contemplating something before he nodded. "Let's go."

He ushered her out of the building while he sent a text message then pocketed his cell. "I have to say that I never thought I'd see you again. You've changed, but I'd never forget your eyes."

"I get that a lot." Saige offered him a nervous smile. "I'm sorry to pull you away from work, but I'm not sure this can wait."

They stayed silent for the rest of the walk to the coffee shop. Once they'd ordered and had their coffee before them, Saige sat back and watched the large detective, who watched her silently in return. He was a handsome man and was over six feet tall and built like a linebacker.

❖

After the delicious Fern, I slept like a baby. I hadn't wanted to killer her, but she was a whore, just like the rest of them. She had needed to pay.

In the light of day, I should feel remorseful but I don't feel anything. I never have. My heart is dead just like the whores I leave in my wake.

I lift my face to the sun, enjoying the feel of the warmth on my skin.

Saige leads me to a police station this morning and not ten minutes later she leaves with the detective. He directs her to a small coffee shop.

My memory is just fine and I remember the detective having a bug up his ass about Quinten Peterson. The detective had questioned the evidence. No one listened.

The detective and Saige sit in the window and I watch as two drinks are placed in front of them.

While I know what I plan to do next will be tricky, I know that I can pull it off. I can do any damn thing I want.

Goodbye, Detective Coulter Robinson.

Saige breathed deeply, and asked Coulter, "Did you take my statement?" She bet his brown eyes missed nothing as he ran a hand through his thick, black hair that tapered neatly to his collar. The slight silver around his temples gave him a distinguished look and she guessed he was in his late forties.

He sighed and leaned forward. "My name is Coulter, as your case is closed, I don't see why you can't use it." He frowned. "No, I didn't take your statement. Why?"

Saige swallowed. "How much do you know about what happened to me?" She let her question settle and continued when he stayed silent. "I mean, do you know about my memory loss?"

He looked surprised.

"I remember that you slept a heck of a lot once you'd been found," he said. "It wasn't surprising considering what had been done to you and how long you'd been in surgery. You'd been starved for the entire time you were held captive, so after the trauma, surgery, and everything else, you had no energy to stay awake. On the few occasions that I spoke with you, you didn't seem to know what was going on... I'm guessing you're asking questions because of the execution warrant."

Saige nodded and wasn't surprised he was so

astute. "If I didn't seem to know what was going on, then how could I have given a comprehensive statement? I've read it and it doesn't sound like I didn't know what I was saying."

"I wondered about that when I read it. I was kept out of a lot of the investigation because I asked too many questions. They had their man, and they wanted a conviction. Didn't sit well with me then, hasn't all these years." He sighed. "I do know that you were asked to point out if you recognized anyone from the pictures shown to you. You picked Quinten Peterson."

"Wait!" Saige sat forward. "You said that I was asked if I recognized anyone. Are you sure I wasn't asked if I recognized my abductor? Please try and remember Detective ... *Coulter*."

He frowned and held her gaze. "I was in your hospital room briefly before I was asked to leave as there were too many people in the room. But I did hear, 'Look carefully Saige, and only select the person you recognize.' I do know that day you'd looked confused, but cohesive when looking through the images. What was missed, Saige?" he asked softly.

She cleared her throat. "I've been spending

time talking to Quinten's brother, Alex." She noticed the twitch in his jaw at the mention of Alex, but she continued. "He's convinced that his brother is innocent. I can't remember a lot, but yesterday, thanks to a photograph, brief memories teased my mind. What I remember is that Quinten has intricate tattoos on both arms that finished on the back of his hands with a vine twisting around both of his middle fingers."

"He does."

"The other memory was of the hands of my abductor with something silver in them just before I felt incredible pain. He didn't have any tattoos. None were visible on the back of his hands or his wrists. How can that be if Quinten is the one in prison? I've been told about all the evidence and DNA, but Alex said Quinten had badly cut himself, and bled everywhere."

"That is one of the things that bothered me." He took a sip of his coffee and rubbed at his jaw. "Quinten had a nasty gash along his arm, by the time he was found with you, the blood had soaked through the material he'd used as a tourniquet."

"The shirt from one of the murdered girls?"

He nodded. "Yes. That explained all the blood

124 | TWENTY EIGHT DAYS

in the shack, he also told us what he remembered touching and everything came back positive with his prints. There wasn't anything else with prints on. However, the DA moved to press charges and that was that. The thing is, which I argued at the time, Quinten had stated he'd cut his arm breaking into the shack.

"The evidence from him breaking in was there for us to see exactly like he said. Once he'd been charged and the case was being built against him, no one wanted to look elsewhere. I even mentioned it on the witness stand, which is why I think some of the jury voted not guilty. I'd put the same doubt in their minds, that was in mine."

They sat silently for a few minutes and drank their coffee. Saige really didn't see how everyone would think him guilty. She knew her statement hadn't helped him, but she had a sudden thought. "Why didn't anyone question my relationship with Quinten? I couldn't find any reference to it."

Coulter stilled, and leaned closer. "What relationship?"

She couldn't hide her surprise at his question. "Alex hinted that Quinten and I had something going on. The memory of Quinten's hands was of them on my body." She blushed slightly but continued. "When asked if I knew anyone in those photographs, of course I'd have picked Quinten. Not only that, why wasn't it revealed that both Alex and Quinten worked at my family home?

"They did the wood carving on the stairs and some of the molds around the light fittings. I might have lost my memory but my conscience knew them. Apparently I knew Quinten really well."

"*Shit*!" Coulter cursed and sat back in his chair, shock written all over his face. "Your father swore that you had no relationship with either of the Petersons. I even asked him that specific question. I never even got the vibe he lied."

Saige frowned, wondering why he'd lied. "But, what if we kept it from my father?"

He dropped his head into his hands as he leaned over the table. "Maybe you did keep it a secret."

"Did you ask anyone else about us?"

"I asked both Alex and Quinten and they said no. I'm surprised Alex didn't jump on that because he was desperate to save his brother, and with how Quinten was found wrapped around you, it would have shed new light on that scene. What I don't understand is why Alex and Quinten lied to me about you?"

Saige felt a trickle of hope somewhere deep inside of her. A part of her had known that Quinten was innocent, but she couldn't understand why they'd both lied about her relationship with him.

"I should have listened to my gut instead of *others*. Something has always niggled at me about the case. It's the only case I've worked on since I became a cop that I couldn't stop thinking about. Why didn't I listen?"

"Like you said, all the evidence pointed to him being guilty, plus, if my father and Christina lied, then you had a closed case ... I don't suppose the lead detective from the original case is still around?"

Coulter shook his head. "He died about six years ago."

Saige felt tired and now knew that she had been right to start asking questions, which she would continue with soon. "I'm heading home with Alex. I'm not going to leave until I have answers."

"I wish I could be there when you ask questions, but I have a case that needs my attention right now. I want you to have this though." He pulled a white card from his pocket and a pen. After scrawling something on the back, he passed it to her. "That's my private cell number. If you need help with anything, or if I can answer anything else, call me. Anytime."

Sage absentmindedly took the card from his hand, and asked, "If I wanted to visit the prison, would you be able to arrange it?"

"That's not a good idea, Saige."

"I know it isn't, but I'm serious. Alex has told me that it could take months for approval for me to visit through the official channel. Couldn't you get me in faster?"

He sighed. "If I had to, then yes. What are you thinking?"

"I'm thinking that if I'm with him and can talk to him, then maybe my memory will come back." She lifted tormented filled eyes to Coulter. "I want to remember him, Detective. I want to remember our time together, and I want to remember why I ended up in a private hospital for two years, when I can only remember the last two weeks of my stay there. Why does the scent of antiseptic make me physically sick? There's a lot I want to know and I have a feeling that it all starts with Quinten."

"Your father lied for a reason, Saige. Maybe everything starts with him and his wife. Just be careful, and promise to call me if you need help."

"I will." She shrugged. "I have so many questions and I know the answers are locked away inside of me. I just want to remember."

"Hmm. I once had a case where a young woman lost her memory after being the only survivor when her sister and parents were found dead. Her memory came back in the middle of the funeral. She launched herself at her mother's father ... I'm basically trying to tell you that your memory might come back when you least expect it to. Something will trigger the whole lot and you'll be swamped with nothing but memories."

"As much as I don't want to remember those four days, I want to remember everything else. I need to."

"I understand." He stood after glancing at his phone. "I need to get back, and I know I'll be seeing you again." He smiled. "Take care of yourself."

Saige nodded and watched him walk away, feeling more positive than ever that the truth possibly lay with her father and Christina, but why would they lie? Her father hadn't wanted her to look into the past, but was that to protect her, or for his own selfish reasons? He'd never come across as selfish. In fact, he was the most selfless person she knew. Her stepmother on the other hand—

"Who was the woman?" Amber McGregor asked before he slid into his chair.

Coulter stared at his messy desk and then grinned at her tone and wondered if she was jealous.

Amber, with her riot of fiery orange hair that matched the freckles dusting her cheeks and the bridge of her nose, would cause his heart to race in his chest while in her presence. He spent too much time speculating what that mass of hair would feel like against his naked skin. Would it be silky soft, or rough and springy?

The sound of a throat being cleared made him snap his eyes up to Amber's and he grinned at the blush on her face. He'd been staring at her lips.

He answered her original question, "Saige Lockwood."

Her eyes flickered with recognition. "And the

plot thickens. So what did she want?"

"To talk." He rubbed his face, too tired to carry on with the hundred and one questions, even when he knew that she was there for a reason, and one she could have probably used the phone for.

"Do you have anything for me, Amber?"

She watched him before nodding. "Yes. When we uncovered the breast implants, only a partial serial number remained on them." She smiled. "But, when I gave them a name, that name matched the partial. Jocelyn Peterson had breast implants just over seven years ago."

"I hate being right," Coulter grumbled. "But at least I know who didn't do it."

Amber frowned. "Right, Quinten was already in Harlington."

He nodded. "Jocelyn lied through her teeth once Quinten had been arrested. Nothing that could be proved, outside of the fact that there'd been no official police reports of domestic violence, or disturbances—I had a gut feeling. She wanted to be the wounded party and she wanted people to feel sorry for her. She made some money off of the injured victim act when she charged for interviews. According to her, she'd been married to a murderer."

Coulter offered Amber an exhausted smile. "But the media grew tired of her and no one felt sorry for her. She was accused of knowing and keeping silent about Quinten by the press. As soon as the trial ended, she high tailed it out of town ... This is the first I've heard of her since then."

"I'm still waiting for some test results to come back, but I'm guessing that she's been dead for nearly as long, around seven years."

"I give." He smiled, knowing that she was itching to give him a bit of a science lesson, one he probably knew already, but he loved watching Amber become animated.

"When a body is buried in the ground, and left, once it starts decomposing the chemistry of the soil changes significantly, which means—"

"You'll be able to match up the year of death by how much the soil has changed."

"You got it in one, Detective." Amber grinned, and it was only when his captain cleared his throat beside his desk that he realized he was grinning just as wide back.

Between a half cough and half laugh, he managed to wipe whatever his boss thought he saw from his face. He was too old for that crap anyway, which he needed to be reminded of often when Amber was around.

She was a breath of fresh air to his old ass—mid-thirties to his late forties.

"Where is Darrin?"

"Stomach flu," Coulter said. He kept the opinion that his partner had lied to him, to himself.

"Hmm." The Captain raised a brow, but let it go.

"You have an appointment at the prison this afternoon. Tell him about Jocelyn and when you're done, question the brother next."

Already planned.

"That's on the agenda," he replied.

"You've got a couple of hours until the interview so I suggest you make a move." The man glanced at Amber and then him.

"I'll go back to the morgue." Amber glared at the captain, not giving a shit, and why should she when he wasn't her direct boss.

"Call me if you discover anything else," he requested to Amber's retreating back.

"I will."

Once Amber left, he noticed his Captain stood

gazing after her. "Easy on the eyes."

Coulter slammed his hand down on the desk in anger. "I'll be out for the rest of the day."

He didn't wait for a response and left.

Hopefully, he wouldn't be around for a while longer now that he had to interview the people from Jocelyn's life. Those interviews would happen a few hours away from Tampa, in Port Jude and Harlington.

His gut told him that her death had everything to do with her ex-husband and his trial, but what? The timing was too much of a coincidence for him to not look back at the original players.

He shoved the key into the ignition of his truck, gave it a turn and all it did was choke. He tried again, and nothing. About to try once more, he caught his captain waving to him from the door.

"What does he want now," Coulter grumbled, but climbed out of his truck anyway, slamming the door behind him.

He jogged back to the station door, and was just about to question the hold up, when a loud explosion shook the ground.

Coulter grabbed the handrail on the wall lining the steps to stay on his feet. The shock of seeing his truck completely engulfed in flames made him pause. His pulse raced and the reality of what had happened hit him.

Car bomb!

If his captain hadn't called him back, he'd be dead.

While the shock still gripped him, other officers grabbed fire extinguishers from the building and started to try and hold the fire back. They only stopped when firemen from the firehouse across the street rushed over with two hoses.

Coulter was tugged away from the railing and pulled around the side of the steps by his captain who looked shell-shocked.

"Pissed anyone off lately, Robinson?" If he hadn't been wondering the same thing, he'd have told his Captain where to shove his question.

"I don't know, but you sure have great timing." He met his captain's gaze. "Thank you."

His Captain waved him off. "Forget about it. I can't even remember what I called you back for now," he said. "I need to call the boss." He disappeared inside the building, just as Coulter spotted a slight figure with a head full of bright orange hair come flying out.

He could hear the gasp that left Amber's mouth from where he stood, and then her shoulders started to shake.

Anything he was about to say left his head when he realized she cried—*for him.*

"Amber," he whispered.

She hadn't heard him.

"Amber."

Her head whipped around and before he could catch his breath, she jumped down the steps and was in his arms. Her sobs absorbed in his shirt as she clung to him. Amber's response, made him realize how much she obviously cared for him.

He stroked the hair down her back and buried his face in the curve of her neck, just wanting to inhale the scent of Amber's freshness.

"I'm sorry," Amber whispered as she tried to pull away from him. "I got your shirt all wet."

"Don't be sorry." He kept her in his embrace. "My truck can explode every damn day if it gets you in my arms."

She whacked him on the arm, and dried her tears. "You...you...ugh! How can you say that? Look"—she pointed toward what was left of his truck—"you could have been inside. So don't you dare joke about it." Her face crumpled again, and he tugged her back into his arms, his heart aching with so much longing.

"I'm sorry, Amber." He kissed the top of her head, and met his captain's gaze.

All he needed.

"Will you be okay?" he asked, putting Amber at arm's length, his hands flexing on her shoulders. She felt too good in his lonely arms that he wanted to keep her with him.

She nodded. "Yeah. I'll be okay. I'm not the one I'm worried about." Her shy smile affected him more than it should have. "Are you still going to the prison this afternoon?"

"Probably tomorrow now." He ran his hands through his hair before resting them on his hips.

"Will you call me, Coulter? Let me know you're okay." Amber backed slowly toward the steps.

Before he could think too hard about his next move, he grabbed her hand and tugged her back into his arms. Coulter kissed her pink lips. "I'll call you." His voice nearly failed him, but he added, "I promise." One last kiss and he turned and walked toward the wreckage.

If he stayed with her any longer, he'd be begging her for a lot more, and he wasn't sure he was ready to go there with her. He certainly wanted to. He'd woken plenty of nights with his legs tangled in the sheets, his cock hard and aching.

He needed to clear his head so that he could concentrate on finding the fucker who'd just blown up his truck. He'd pissed a lot of people off over the years, but he didn't think he'd pissed them off that much.

He stared at the flames as they started to die down, his thoughts navigating over all the coincidences. There were too many. Quinten's death warrant, Jocelyn's body, Saige Lockwood visiting him, all the players out on the table and in the open ... now his truck. No way was everything a coincidence, and he would bet his badge that they were all related.

What the hell did I do wrong? I've had enough practice at small explosives. Typical. The only time I make one alone—I screw it up.

With Saige about to head home to Port Jude, no

doubt Robinson will show up there. All the players will be in the same place as before. Pity Detective Jason Harris died in a fishing accident six years ago.

The Detective should never have started looking into Quinten's conviction. I never discovered what had made the Detective take another look. At least I put a stop to it.

Day 7

It had taken Quinten a long time to get used to the shackles going on every time he left his cell. At first, he feared what would happen to him while they were on. Over time, he wouldn't say he'd gotten used to them, but he certainly didn't have to count in his head anymore to keep the panic from completely taking over.

He'd been in them a few minutes when he frowned at the approaching guard, who held the keys to unlock him. "You're having the interview here."

"Who with?"

"A detective. He's been here before. Can't

140 | TWENTY EIGHT DAYS

remember his name. Roberts or something like that."

"Robinson?"

"That's it." The guard motioned for him to enter his cell and then quickly removed his shackles. "You're the only one in this section right now, so there's no reason you can't have official visitors here. Your brother will have to be in the designated area though."

He wondered why Detective Robinson would come to talk to him now. They'd said everything that they had to say during the other visits. The detective had done everything he could to uncover the truth. Quinten knew that.

The sound of the gates opening gave him chills, and the sound of them closing and the locks clicking into place made his heart race with fear. It was yet another reminder of what his fate held.

"Quinten," Robinson greeted, moving into his line of sight.

"Detective. It's been a while," he commented and watched as Robinson tried not to fidget.

Quinten narrowed his eyes and took an assessment of the man. He'd always been professional, cool even, and was always courteous.

He'd been confident, a man that knew his convictions and held firm to them. Today, the large man was different, rattled.

Detective Robinson pulled a chair close to the cell, and sat down. He leaned forward and placed his elbows on his knees before he met Quinten's gaze. "My truck blew up yesterday."

Quinten's eyes widened in surprise before he started to wonder what that had to do with him. There was no way he could have done it, so why had the detective come to the prison. He'd never wished the detective harm.

"That isn't why I'm here." Robinson paused. "I'm rattled, which you noticed."

Quinten lifted his chin in acknowledgement, sitting on the bed.

"When did you last have contact with Jocelyn?"

After a long pause, Quinten said, "I'm not sure why you're here asking questions about her, but I haven't seen her since the day I was sentenced, and I haven't heard from her since then. The divorce was handled by the lawyers." He frowned. "What's this about, Detective?"

"A body was discovered yesterday morning."

Quinten watched the other man but nothing showed even though he knew what was coming.

"At the moment, we are going under the assumption that it's Jocelyn Peterson. What remained of breast implants had a partial serial number on them and that partial matched Jocelyn. These"—Robinson pulled three evidence bags from behind him—"were found on her remains."

Quinten flinched at the detective's words. Everything he'd ever felt for Jocelyn had died long before his life went to hell, but he hadn't wanted her to be murdered. It had to have been murder or the detective wouldn't be here.

He rubbed his hands over his eyes. "Let me see them."

Detective Robinson moved closer under the watchful eye of the guard.

"Make sure he can't grab them," the guard said.

The minute the detective held the clear plastic evidence bag up with the charm bangle, he knew that it was hers. He hated the thing and often wondered whether one of her many lovers had given it to her.

"That was hers," Quinten snapped. "And so

were those. The wedding band had been her mother's, and the other ring had belonged to her sister. They both died, along with her father in a car accident, about fifteen years ago."

"I'm sorry, Quinten."

"Don't be. You know that I hated the woman, more so after the lies she told when I was first arrested, then on the stand during the trial. I didn't want her dead, just out of my life."

"I get that. What I don't like is that someone made sure we found her, after seven years of being buried."

"Seven years? She's been dead for seven years?"

"Yes." Robinson continued, counting off on his fingers. "It isn't a coincidence that your warrant for execution was signed. Then your ex-wife's body was found ... Saige Lockwood came to talk to me yesterday morning. And, to top it all off, my truck exploded in front of the police station not long after her visit."

"Saige?" Quinten heard what the detective said, but it was *her* name that grabbed his attention.

"Yeah, Saige." The detective leaned back in his

chair. "Why didn't you tell me that you had a relationship with her?"

Quinten shrugged, trying to get his head around the fact that Saige had spoken with the detective. "She'd been through enough and I wanted her left alone."

"So you protected her."

Quinten stood and began pacing in his small cell. It suddenly felt smaller.

"I love her. I'd have done anything to protect her, and back then it meant keeping my mouth shut. I'm sure you remember her father. He hated knowing that his daughter wanted to spend time with me. I was nothing to the Lockwoods, and I wasn't someone who they wanted Saige associating with, let alone loving."

"Why didn't I find out any of this back then? I specifically asked *everyone*? How the hell could I have missed all this drama?" Robinson's jaw tightened with anger, and Quinten couldn't blame him.

"I asked Alex to keep quiet about my relationship with Saige when she first went missing. I didn't want you focusing on me when everyone needed to be looking for her. Afterward, there was no reason to come forward without hurting Saige, and I figured you wouldn't believe me anyway … You were investigating the murder of those five girls and Saige's abduction, you weren't investigating a soap opera."

"It sounds like I was in the middle of one … Fuck!" Robinson sat with his head thrown back before he leaned forward and asked, "Did your *wife* know about your relationship with Saige?"

Quinten ground his teeth together at the insinuation. "You know that my *wife* was an unfaithful bitch. Until I met Saige, and started spending time with her, I'd never been unfaithful, regardless of all the times I felt like giving Jocelyn some of her own medicine. I was a possession to her until I was arrested, then I became inconsequential. She moved on and probably found another sucker."

He paused and thought about Jocelyn. He didn't think she had ever loved him, despite their marriage. He continued. "So yes, Jocelyn did know about Saige, but not to begin with. It all really came to a head when Saige went back to school, a week before she went missing. I went crazy not knowing where she was or how she was. I have the scar from Jocelyn's anger down my face. A constant reminder."

"The scar she always said was in self-defense when you were taking your anger out on her."

"I never laid a finger on her, and you know that. You never believed a word she said."

"I believed you, and you're right, I never believed her. But I wish I'd known about all the shit back then."

"It probably wouldn't have made a difference. My DNA was all over that shack. Shit like that doesn't lie."

"It would have explained your protectiveness over Saige when you both were found. It might have made the jurors question the reason you were in that shack to begin with. They might have paid more attention to the unidentified DNA that was found."

"It's pointless dredging all that up now. I'm in here, not for much longer, but I'm in here, and there's nothing anyone can do about it." Quinten dropped his head into his hands.

Silence followed until Robinson broke it. "Your girl's gone home to question her father and stepmother."

Quinten's eyes shot up to the detective's.

"Alex took her," he added.

"What the *fuck?*" Quinten rushed from the bed and gripped the bars that separated Robinson and him. "Why is she with Alex?"

"Calm down," the guard snapped. "And move away from the bars … Now!"

Quinten breathed like a bull ready to charge, but the thought of her with his brother, instead of him, made his head spin.

"They're both trying to help you before it's too late, Quinten. I'm heading to Port Jude as soon as I get the chance, so I'll try and keep an eye on her."

He dropped his ass to the bed. "I'm so goddamn tired, and I won't deny that I'm terrified of what's going to happen across the hall in twenty-one days." He looked up at the detective, unable to hide the tears on his lashes. "How is she? Is she okay?"

Detective Robinson looked away briefly. "She looked healthy." He leaned forward. "Look, I don't know if telling you this will help or not." The detective had his attention now. "Saige has no memory of her abduction. In fact, she has a large blank space that covers two and a half years. I think small pieces have come back to her recently, one of which was your hands on her skin." Robinson offered him an amused smile. "She remembered the tattoos on your hands, she also remembered the man who tortured her having none."

The thought that Saige didn't remember him, or the love he felt for her cut him deep, but he ignored the pain and asked, "Did she remember when she gave her statement and ID'd me from a photograph?" He hoped the answer wouldn't send him to hell.

"Five minutes," the guard warned.

Robinson cleared his throat. "We don't know about the statement."

"I heard a *but* somewhere in there."

"You did. When she ID'd the photo, she was asked if she recognized anyone in the lineup. She chose you."

He felt like he was about to hurl. "Fuck! Of course she would choose me."

"Hence why I wished I'd have known about your relationship. If I had, maybe I'd have realized what was being asked of her. I could have told Harris to make sure she chose her abductor. Not someone she knows. See the difference?"

"Fuck!"

He dropped to his knees, rested his forehead against the bed and let his hands drop to the floor, completely defeated.

"Quinten, I haven't told you all this to make you feel worse. I told you in case there was any doubt in your mind about Saige."

"I never doubted her. I've only ever loved her."

He turned his head to face the detective with tears spilling from his eyes. "Will you promise me that you'll look after her? I need to know that there is someone out there"—he nodded toward the window—"who can make sure she's safe. I don't trust her family."

The detective stayed silent for a while, until he saw the second guard approaching, and stood. "You have my promise, Quinten."

He nodded to the detective and watched him leave.

On his knees he did something that he'd never done before, he prayed, not for himself because he was a lost cause now, but for Saige.

❖

Oh dear!

Poor Quinten has been informed of the death of his wicked ex-wife.

I laugh.

My contact tells me the man hadn't shed a tear. I don't blame him and would have been surprised if he had. After all, Quinten had hated her. Not as much as I had, but close.

Perhaps one day he will thank me for getting rid of the albatross around his neck. The bitch might have lied through her teeth, and divorced him, but you can bet she would have been back now. She would have wanted to be part of the spotlight surrounding Quinten's execution—if it gets that far.

My cell vibrates on the dashboard—the alarm.

I take one last glance at the prison and turn my vehicle away.

My meeting with a very good friend is only an hour away.

I can't be late or he'll get nervous.

Alex dressed in the guest room at the Lockwoods home and felt the walls closing in. He'd been fine when they'd first arrived at lunch the day before, especially when they'd been informed that Christina wouldn't be home until today. He'd dropped his luggage inside the guest bedroom door before he'd driven Saige into town.

That had been fun. No one had forgotten he was a Peterson, and as they'd glanced between Saige and him, he'd sneered.

No doubt the gossip that he was back with Saige Lockwood no less would spread like wild fire through town.

Saige Lockwood's returned home with Alexander Peterson. His brother tortured the poor girl and killed all those college girls. Why she's with him is anyone's guess.

He itched to lay eyes on Christina Lockwood. She was a sexy woman with a body made for sin, and oh yes, back then, he'd looked, and eventually tasted. He'd broken his one rule and let her into his heart only to have her rip it out not long after. He always felt there was more to her last words to him than she wanted him to believe.

Either way, it hadn't made the pain of knowing she didn't want him—he wasn't good enough— any less. So he'd hidden the hurt he'd felt behind anger and arrogance, and started fucking his way through life. No one had come close to removing the longing he still had for her, and that pissed him off.

She was down the hall from where he was, and just the thought of her so close caused his breath to quicken. It was ridiculous after all the years that had passed, but she'd always had that affect on him.

At first Christina reminded him of Jocelyn—conniving bitch—but then he'd gotten to know her and she was anything but.

When they'd first made love, she came across shy and inexperienced, but that had soon changed. She'd taken him to heights of pleasure he'd never experienced before, and then crushed him like a fly.

No matter how ridiculous it was, he'd wanted Christina to stand by his side when Quinten had been arrested, but she'd laid the blame at Quinten's feet, just like everyone else.

Alex yanked his jeans up his legs and fastened the zipper, he nearly broke the thing with how much anger he had inside of him.

He needed to control it, especially when he heard a tap on the door. It could be one of two people—Saige or Christina; his money was on Christina.

He left off his shirt, and undid the button at the top of his pants. He'd let her see just what she'd thrown away.

When he opened the door, he wasn't surprised and stepped back so she could enter. His pulse hammered in his ears as she nervously walked past him, and he allowed his eyes to follow her.

Christina was of medium height with white blonde hair. Her shapely figure was covered in a strappy sundress that molded to her ample assets. He licked his lips and let her imagine the dirty thoughts running through his mind. In fact, if she could see inside his head, she'd run as though her backside was on fire.

He grinned and placed his hands on his hips, drawing her gaze to the erection he'd gotten remembering what it was like to be with her.

He was an idiot.

He'd never had trouble getting hard when she was close. Even just the thought of her would do it for him. But as Christina moved closer, he knew if he chose to *have* her, she would be his for the taking. Seeing her again, Alex knew that it would happen, but this time it would be on his terms.

She stopped in front of him and, lowering her lashes, pouted with her plump, red lips.

He couldn't look away, he was a sucker for red lips, especially when they were wrapped around his throbbing cock—just the thought made him throb.

"No!" he growled and backed away.

"You're going to be inside me, sooner rather than later. You know you will." She matched his movements, constantly staying in touching distance. "You used to love being with me."

"No way."

Sadness briefly crossed her eyes before she blinked and it was gone. "Yes." She quickly reached out and grabbed him through his pants, and his treacherous flesh throbbed. "You can't dispute the *hard* evidence."

It was on the tip of his tongue to blame Saige for his arousal, but he didn't want Christina doing a complete reverse, because then he'd be the one having to chase and he never chased. Ever. But why exactly did he want to be with her again in the first place? Old times' sake? Some sick part of him that didn't care what she'd done? Loneliness? She was a sexy woman, but underneath she could be cold and calculating.

Before the witch-hunt for his brother had started, he liked and respected the Lockwoods, but all that had changed when they'd gone after Quinten. At one point during the trial, he'd gone to Christina to try and convince her that they had the wrong man locked away. She'd listened and had started to tell him something when Richard had appeared. Her whole demeanor had changed, and within seconds, he'd been shown the door.

He often wondered what Christina would have said or done had Richard not appeared when he had.

"You want this"—she jacked him through his pants—"inside me just as much as I want you there. That hasn't changed in eight years." She offered him a sad smile.

"I said no." He knocked her hand away and ignored the hurt that crossed her face at his abrupt dismissal.

What the heck did she expect after how she treated him and his brother?

He fastened the button on his pants and prowled toward her. "No."

Christina was startled by his abrupt rejection, so Alex smiled and backed her into the wall behind her. He trapped her there, his arms on either side of her head. "Richard is a handsome man, he works out, so tell me, why did you come in here wanting me?" He leaned close and breathed her in with a caress down the side of her neck.

She shivered in reaction, and his arousal throbbed behind his zipper as her scent traveled into his system.

"I ... I missed you," she whispered, tears forming in her eyes.

Were her tears for his benefit?

Alex slid his hand over her bottom and cupped her over the material of her dress while he rubbed against her belly.

Christina gasped and then moaned. "You're playing with me," she accused, her complexion pale.

It wasn't a question, more of an observation on her part, but he always had to have the last word. "I haven't even started"—he moved a breath away from her lips—"to play with you yet."

Her eyes darkened and he knew he had her, so he quickly backed off and watched as she sagged against the wall. She stared at him and all he felt at that moment was her sadness.

A tear ran down her face. She shoved away from the wall, put her shoulders back and glared at him. "Nothing will ever happen between us." Her hands trembled as she smoothed the hair from her face, and turned on her heels. "I know that now."

Once she made it to the door, he called, "Oh, Christina."

She paused and turned her head to look back at him, her eyes widened when she focused on the hand he slipped inside his pants.

Oh she'd be back!

"Once you've admitted the lies you told eight years ago, this"—he cupped himself and made sure the tip of his erection showed above the zipper—"will be yours." He offered her a smug grin as she quietly closed the door behind herself, but not before he noticed the sadness in her eyes.

He frowned and wondered. Christina had acted like the wounded party as she left and that troubled him. He'd been an ass, but he wasn't going to be dragged under her spell again.

He was only in her home for Quinten, and his brother had to come first. And then, maybe, he'd uncover what was really going on with Christina, because although she looked the same, she wasn't the same woman he remembered.

Day 8

The alley had apartment buildings on both sides that looked to have been in need of renovation for years.

Coulter winced as the smell of rotting garbage, vomit, and tobacco hit his nostrils. But as he ate up the distance between him and the crime scene he was assailed with the scent of death.

His feet slowed and crunched over a broken beer bottle. He glanced down and noticed an unidentified fluid leaking from a rust-pilled dumpster inches from his feet.

He shuddered, already hoping for a quick escape, and then he heard her voice.

"We really need to stop meeting like this, Detective," Amber mumbled, a secret smile on her lips.

Coulter noticed a softness around Amber's eyes when she met his gaze, which reminded him of an hour before when she'd woken up in his bed, wrapped in his arms.

Amber warm and naked had stretched like a cat as she'd come awake. Her lithe body had slid against him, waking his body in a way it hadn't been woken in a very long time.

Then her cell had gone off.

He frowned and watched as Amber bent and unzipped the black body bag.

He crouched opposite and got his first glimpse of the victim. No matter how many years he'd been a cop, he'd never gotten used to seeing death. Now was no different as he looked down at the young woman.

"What do you have?" he asked, feeling his forty-eight years.

Amber quickly glanced at him, concern etched on her features.

"I'm fine," he mumbled.

"Debatable, but I'll accept that for now."

Amber pointed at the woman's neck. "I was going with ligature strangulation as the cause of death, until we got her ready to go in the bag. But"— Amber pointed to the front of the girl's neck—"he nearly decapitated her."

"Fuck," Coulter cursed, feeling sick to his stomach. He closed his eyes and was about to take a deep inhale—

"Don't," Amber snapped. "Trust me. You do not want to inhale right now."

"These fuckers make me sick."

"I know." She rested her hands on her knees. "He used some sort of garrote, and my guess would be something like a fishing line, which is thin and strong."

"Why are you guessing a fishing line?"

She offered a wry smile and held up her left hand, wiggling her ring finger. "Years ago I got a fishing line stuck around my finger. Very nearly lost half of it, which is how I became an ME instead of a surgeon. Fishing lines are dangerous, and cause more than just superficial damage—they can be lethal. Obviously, I'll know more once I've done the autopsy, but that's my guess."

He nodded, tempted to wrap his hand around

her delicate wrist to bring her finger to his mouth. Closing his eyes, he tried to get his mind back on the case. The victim needed his attention not his distraction.

"Was she raped?" he asked, knowing that would clear his mind.

"She'd had sex within hours of death." Amber wouldn't meet his gaze as she continued. "I don't think she was raped though. There would have been more damage to her genital area if she had been. There would also have been bruising from were he held her down, but there's none. My guess is that the sex was consensual."

"Any identification?"

"She was found naked, and so far no belongings have been recovered. Nothing. You can see where she was found. Whoever did this made sure the area was clean." Amber stood and stretched out the kinks. "We may get lucky, but I'm not holding my breath."

Coulter watched Amber rub at her back, and he longed to be the one to rub out the knots for her.

Amber caught him staring and for a minute, held his gaze, her longing clear to see. He started to reach for her when she stepped back and cleared her throat.

Claire, her assistant, appeared and cast a glance between the two of them. She grinned. "I'll load this up, and come back."

Amber rolled her eyes and grinned. "I'll have a quick look at her when we get her back to the morgue to see if I can give you a definitive answer about what was used around her neck."

"I'd appreciate that."

He watched as Amber bent and zipped the body bag closed, and he felt a sharp pain in his chest at the loss of a young woman, and in such a violent way.

Not only was he weary with the early mornings and late nights, but he was also tired of seeing death. For years, his job had fulfilled him. He was good at following a trail to get the answers he needed, and that was why the case up in Port Jude had always bothered him. He'd always felt that some of his questions hadn't been answered to his satisfaction.

His superiors had shut him down—not to forget that. He could have pushed.

It pissed him off that he was only now

discovering the relationship between Saige and Quinten. It would have thrown more light on to Quinten's actions, even though he didn't think the jurors would have looked at the evidence any differently. DNA didn't lie, but Quinten had always admitted to bleeding all over the shack. When he was found, his arm had required a lot of stitches. The unidentified DNA sat on his mind during the case and trial, but he finally put that to rest years ago.

He rubbed his forehead and let his eyes roam over an equally tired Amber. She stepped close and looked up and met his gaze. The top of her head only came up to his chin.

Without a thought, he curved his hand behind her neck and lowered his head. His lips caressed along the seam of hers, and although he was tempted to deepen the kiss at the sound of the small whimper from her, he kept it light, remembering where they were.

Smiling, he dropped his forehead to hers. "Have coffee with me later."

The sight of her tongue slipping between her lips to moisten them drew his gaze, and a groan from him.

He closed his eyes, and snapped them open when he felt a hand on his chest.

"Seven," she whispered. "I'll message you the address." Amber reached up and pecked him on the cheek before making her way to the ME's van.

Coulter ran a hand down his weary face, and turned back to look at the crime scene. Only then did he notice that Amber and he had had an audience.

David broke away and moved closer, a grin on his craggy old face. The man had been in the department for years before Coulter had started and had aged well. So well, in fact, that no one even knew his age.

"I lost the bet," he grumbled, amusement on his face.

"Bet?" Coulter raised a brow in question.

"Yep. That lot over there had a bet going as to who would be the one to make the first move. We all said she would. Your captain said you would," he said. "I hate losing."

"I hadn't thought it was that obvious."

"Are you kidding me? The minute she was around, your eyes would glaze over before you'd pull yourself together. It's been fun, and I can't wait to see the rest." David wandered off and Coulter was left wondering if he was the only one to not know about the bet. Did Amber?

"You're damn lucky."

Coulter turned at the voice and frowned when Steve, one of the forensic techs approached. "The bomb on your truck had faulty wiring, otherwise it would have exploded the minute you turned the key." Steve shrugged. "The full report is with your captain, but I figured you'd want to know."

"Thanks. Any prints?" he asked.

"No."

He had a feeling that when everything connected together it would lead him back to Quinten Peterson. He just needed to figure out how to connect the dots.

One thing Saige loved about being home was that she didn't have to cook for herself. She wasn't exactly bad at it, but it was nice to take a break, more so considering she was usually around the diner waiting on tables.

Pattie, her father's cook, was a delight and had worked for him for around twenty-five years. She loved to mother Saige, and Saige had never objected, as her own mother had died when she was just three years old. Christina had always felt more like an older sister than anything. Her stepmother hadn't exactly been mean to her, and with age, Saige thought that maybe Christina had just been awkward and not known how to communicate with her since Saige hadn't exactly been welcoming after having her father to herself for years. It had been a shock when, at thirteen, she found herself with a twenty-six year old stepmother.

Saige came back to the present and watched Alex load his plate to bursting with eggs, sausage, bacon, fried tomatoes, hash browns and, let's not forget, the biscuit.

Saige laughed when he caught her watching and offered her a cheesy grin. She selected scrambled eggs and a slice of toasted rye bread.

"Morning," Christina mumbled, taking her usual seat at the table. She looked like she hadn't slept well.

She was still beautiful, even with tiredness clouding her face. Not the kind of tired from lack of sleep, but the kind a person gets when they've completely had enough of life.

Christina served herself a small spoon of fresh fruit.

Saige asked Alex, "Sleep well?"

"Surprisingly, I did." Alex swallowed a mouthful of food. "I didn't think I would, but I had a lot taken out of me last night, so I slept like a baby." He grinned and glanced at Christina.

Saige raised a brow, especially when her stepmother gave him a startled look before she focused on her breakfast and ignored them.

Alex caught Saige's silent question and gave a slight shake of his head, which she'd have missed if she hadn't been looking.

"Christina?" Saige waited for her stepmother to meet her gaze. "Can Alex and I talk to you and Dad about what happened to me?"

Christina's fork clanged back to the dish, disturbing the silence in the room. She glanced between Alex and Saige before answering. "Depends on what you want to talk about," she hedged.

Saige got the feeling that her stepmother was very uncomfortable with the direction the conversation was going, and that caused her stomach to churn.

Her own breakfast in front of her no longer looked appetizing so she pushed it away. "Christina, not only do I want my memory back, but I want to remember my time with Quinten Peterson. I'm sure you remember him."

Christina paled and nodded.

"Nothing to say, *Christina?*" Alex sneered looking angry. He slammed his hand on the table and stood. The plates rattled, and Saige thought her stepmother was about to be sick. "My brother is *fucking* innocent. All he ever did was love your stepdaughter, and refuse to fuck you."

Saige gasped. "What?"

"Forget it," Alex snapped.

She stared at him, her stomach and thoughts churning at the implications of what Alex had just said. She glanced at Christina who was extremely pale, her gaze focused on the melon ball sitting on her spoon and not on them. "I can't." Saige grabbed hold of Alex's wrist to keep him in the room. "What did you mean?"

Christina swallowed a few times and, after she threw her napkin on the table, dashed out of the room.

Alex breathed through his nose and his whole body tensed in anger. "I got angry and spoke out of turn. Leave it, please." Alex smiled, and took Saige's fingers from his wrist and gave them a reassuring squeeze. "I'm going to take a walk near the jetty to cool down."

Saige nodded and watched him leave while she pondered what the hell his comment about her stepmother meant. Had Christina come on to Quinten? And Alex?

Saige felt like she was the last to know everything, and she found it frustrating that everyone who knew her had her memories.

"Saige, honey." Her dad walked into the breakfast room and interrupted her thoughts, but it didn't remove the frown from her brow.

"Morning, Dad. You're up late." She smiled.

"Not really." Her father helped himself to half a plate of food and a small bowl of fruit before he sat opposite her, instead of his usual seat at the head of the table.

He looked tired as he poured a cup of coffee. His usual dusky blond hair had more than a hint of gray around the temples. He'd been lucky that he hadn't shown any sign of going gray until he reached fifty. Her father had always been a strong man, and she knew that he still was, but there was now weariness to him. His square shoulders sagged and the stress around his eyes told her that he worried. Saige had a good guess as to what about, so she decided to get it all out in the open and hoped her father would too.

After Christina and Alex's reaction to each other, she no longer wanted to wait for everyone to come together. Christina, especially, could wait until Saige got her alone. No way did she want Alex setting her off again.

"Spit it out, Saige." He offered her a wry smile. "I've always been able to tell when you had something on your mind, but didn't know how to get it out." He took a sip of his coffee. "You know what I used to say, and you always used to agree with me."

"*You'll feel better once you've had your say, Saige*," she mimicked her father from years gone by.

"That's the one."

Saige glanced toward the bay window with a view of the water, hoping for courage. "I can't leave the past alone."

"I already knew that when you showed up with Alex, which I have to admit, I'm not too happy about." Her father continued to eat while his eyes stayed focused on her.

"I know you aren't happy about Alex staying here, but there's nowhere in town to stay and we're both doing this together, so staying here made sense."

"Hmm," he mumbled and sipped his coffee while watching her over the rim of the steaming cup.

"Why have you never told me about Quinten? About my relationship with him?"

Startled, her father dropped his cutlery as his eyes widened. "You got your memory back?" he asked.

"I wish I did." Saige dipped her head and then lifted it to look at her father. "Alex is convinced that Quinten didn't take me, or killed those girls. There is so much that doesn't make sense to me right now. I mean did I really select him from a lineup of photographs as my abductor? The statement says I did, but that doesn't seem right to me. When I look at images of Quinten, I don't feel fear. Shouldn't it trigger that feeling?"

"Oh, honey. No one mentioned your relationship with him because it could have harmed your recovery. You loved him. As a father, I wanted you well. So I listened to the doctors and refused to let anyone remind you of anything."

Her father pushed his plate away and cradled his cup of coffee in his hands. "I did question his guilt. I spoke with the sheriff, the detective investigating your case, and the district attorney. They were all convinced they had the right man. The prosecutor pushed and pushed until Quinten was found guilty."

Her father held his hand up to keep her silent as he continued. "I honestly don't know what to think, and every now and again when there's mention of Quinten Peterson on TV, I start thinking again as to whether or not he really is guilty."

He took a deep breath and stared into his coffee. "One thing that I've never been able to understand is that he loved you, Saige." Her father stood and walked around the table to sit beside her, his arm going around her shoulders.

He continued. "I knew he was married, which you and I fought over. I also knew that his marriage had fallen apart a while before he met you." He smiled. "I'm a guy, honey, and you only had to watch Quinten when you were around. The guy loved you. So why would he do something to cause you harm?"

"It doesn't make sense," Saige said. "I want to remember him, Dad. I want to remember our time together that you and Alex have now confirmed was real. The not knowing is driving me crazy."

"I guess I was happy to just let everything take its course. While you had no memory, it was fine, it was easier, for you." He paused and looked ashamed. "It was wrong of me, but it was easier for me. I've tried, since then, to forget. To forget the sight of my daughter all bloodied and cut. To forget that the little girl who used to look up to me, and call me Daddy was forever changed. I wanted you to remember. But you never have. Until now it would seem."

"I don't remember him. I remember the tattoos on his arms and hands. I also remember that the man who held me didn't have any."

"What?" Her father was stunned and sat back in the chair, his arms dropping to his sides.

"Quinten didn't take me, Dad. Someone else

did," Saige stated.

His mouth opened and closed as though he couldn't form the words he needed to say.

"I've spoken to Detective Robinson, one of the detectives from my case." Saige sighed. "I only remember hands. That's it. There is still the DNA evidence that convicted him. I can't do anything about that. That's why I wanted to know about the photographs." Saige grabbed her father's hand. "I need to know if I had my memory directly after being found. Was I capable of remembering my abductor?"

Her father squeezed her hand and rubbed his forehead. "At first I thought you did remember. You were on a few different medications at the time for pain and they gave you a sedative to keep you calm and relaxed. The latter was Christina's idea, and I agreed. I never really questioned your memory at first because you knew your stepmother and me. So when I came back into the room after taking an urgent call, Christina told me you'd selected the image of Quinten. I was surprised."

"Dad, Detective Harris asked me if I recognized *anyone* and I picked Quinten. No one, including the DA or the detective, asked me if I recognized my *abductor*. Do you know where I'm going with this? We were in a relationship, so I picked him, or I didn't remember who he actually was, just that I thought he was familiar."

Saige continued. "What about the hospital? I don't remember anything of that apart from the last two weeks of my stay there."

Now her father looked uncomfortable.

He knew she had hated it there, at least, the time she remembered, but her father had left her under the care of Dr. Erikson. Creepy Erik, as one of the other patients had called him.

"They had a reputation of helping victims of trauma," her father said. "I wanted the best for you because, at the time, I wasn't sure you were being truthful about not remembering anything. I'm ashamed of that. It took a few months but then it became apparent that there was more than the attack that you couldn't remember.

"You ended up staying at the hospital too damn long for my liking. When I visited you, you'd just stare through me." He looked away.

Wiping at a tear, Saige tried not to think about the hospital because, every time she did, chills raced down her spine. But that was the first time she heard her father talk about regret.

Saige let her father hold her while she cried into his shirt. She hated knowing that she chose the man she had loved as her abductor. It wasn't just a gut feeling, she knew that she had chosen him for no other reason than he was familiar to her—it had nothing, whatsoever, to do with who took her.

"What went wrong, Dad? I know the police had no clue about my relationship with Quinten. I just don't understand why it was kept quiet." She watched her father, and he winced.

She waited for him as she held her breath in dread ... terrified to know what he'd say but needing to as well.

After a few minutes of silence, he brushed the hair back from her brow and smiled. "It was a confusing time, and because he was married, Christina and I, decided it best to not say anything." He paused. "Alex repeatedly said his brother was innocent. That he was being set up. No one would listen to him. In a way, I felt bad for him because he was a victim as well. His brother had done him wrong, but now his whole trial will be questioned."

"I hope so." Saige wiped at her tears and blew her nose on the napkin her father passed to her. "I need to remember more and we need to talk to someone who might be able to send us in the right direction."

Her father sighed. "Saige, you and Alex aren't the police. What you're doing could be dangerous, especially if what you're saying is true. Because if it is true, then your abductor is still out there."

She jerked her head up and stared at her father as chills raced up and down her spine.

"We'll be careful, and Alex will be around."

"I wish you wouldn't do this. You know that, right?"

"I know. I'm sorry."

"Don't be sorry"—he kissed her forehead— "for wanting your memories back. I feel sick to my stomach that I might have pushed to have the wrong man convicted." He tilted her face up to his. "Promise me, Saige. As soon as you have solid evidence that your abductor wasn't Quinten, you will come to me."

Saige hesitated. "I will."

He continued. "If it turns out that you're right,

and Quinten is innocent, then I will help him. But you still have to keep in mind that he was also convicted of murdering the five college girls. This isn't just about you. It's about those girls as well."

"I'm not sure how, but I'm certainly going to try to untangle the secrets still buried."

"God, it's no wonder I have gray hair," her father groaned, and pulled her in for one last hug.

"Dad?"

"Leave it, Saige."

She wanted to ask more, but her father looked as though he'd had enough, and not just with her questions and talk of the past.

"I love you, Dad."

He smiled at her confession. "It always makes my heart feel lighter hearing those words. I love you, too." He kissed her forehead again, and let her go.

Her dad stood on shaky legs and gave her one more glance before he slowly walked out of the dining room. Saige was left to get herself under control. Not only did she have things to tell Alex, she also wanted answers about the comment he'd made toward her stepmother.

He'd made it in anger, but why?

❖

I want to confront Richard Lockwood for the lies he told to his trusting daughter, but if I do, I'll give myself away. I haven't stayed hidden from the law all these years by being careless.

Not only does that asshole have Christina as his wife, but he also has the most loving daughter. The man doesn't know what he truly has. Maybe one day he will when he loses them both.

Day 9

The sun beat down on Alex while he observed, Main Street, Port Jude. Nothing had changed in his hometown. Tree lined sidewalks, colorful flower boxes or potted plants outside shops. Light posts had hanging flower baskets. Trashcans painted by a local artist to be more appealing sat beside doorways—too neat and tidy for him.

Of course the only dark cloud over the town was that created by the Peterson name. He sneered. The family had been ostracized and snubbed. Ridiculed.

Idiots the lot of them.

A tail pipe backfired and drew his gaze to the four elderly men sitting on the same four rockers that he remembered outside of the barbershop.

And then he spotted Tracy Adams.

Oh! This would be fun.

"If it isn't Alexander Peterson," she drawled.

Alex smirked. "Tracy Adams."

She grinned. "You remember me, huh?"

His gaze swept over her long legs, and he remembered the bare and silky feel of them as they'd caressed his body and wrapped around his waist. Not long after, he'd met Christina, and everything had changed.

Alex realized Tracy could be a needed distraction, help keep him away from Christina. Because no matter what he told himself, he knew that one more signal from Christina and they'd both be naked.

Christina bothered him in more ways than one, and after the other night, he had questions. What happened between them shouldn't have because she was still married and they had a whole lot of lies and hurt between them. The woman had always driven him crazy, and he hated that she still had the power to bring him to his knees.

"You remembering us?" Tracy asked, moving in close.

"How could I forget you?" He lied and offered her a sexy grin that he knew made the ladies weak in the knees. "We need to catch up, for old times' sake."

"I have somewhere to be now," she whispered, and looked hesitant to walk away. "I moved back into my old house after my parents died a few years ago, so come by and see me." Tracy trailed a finger down his chest and dipped into the waist of his jeans.

"Soon," he said, and licked his lips as he watched her saunter away in her tight little shorts.

She'd been the only girl in Port Jude to be a regular port of call when he'd been in his late teens and early twenties … until he'd met Christina.

Sighing, Alex took one more look around and realized that Agnes's son, Paul, had caught the whole exchange before he'd darted back inside the pharmacy. The barbershop quartet also focused on him. He needed to convince Saige to go and talk to them. He knew they wouldn't speak a word to him.

He entered the pharmacy and caught up with

Saige just as she moved deeper into the pharmacy, which was just as he remembered. Old shelves held the items for sale, and the wooden floor creaked in the same place it had when he'd been a child. The wooden and glass display case housing the old, round spectacles and medical journal of the first town doctor was still in one corner of the store.

The town liked tradition, and there was nothing wrong with that. He just wished the current residents wouldn't pass on their prejudices to their children. It hadn't been warranted all those years ago and it wasn't warranted now. But everyone was set in their ways and he couldn't see change happening anytime soon.

"Alex," Saige called, "you remember Agnes?"

He groaned inwardly because he'd hoped Saige would run with the questions they'd planned and leave him in the background to listen in.

Agnes would remember him, and it wouldn't be with fondness.

"Yes"—he stepped forward—"I remember Agnes."

Saige raised a brow at his tone, but turned

back to the smirking woman.

"I'm surprised it wasn't you who ended up in jail. I was so shocked when Quinten was arrested and convicted. That boy wouldn't have hurt a hair on anyone's head." She looked down her nose at Alex. "You, on the other hand. You're the one I thought would end up incarcerated," Agnes said.

Alex clenched his jaw closed so he wouldn't ruin this for Saige.

They both wanted answers, but he didn't want to disappoint his brother's girl by acting before thinking, which he'd always done before.

"I will say that I agree with you about Quinten, but have to disagree about Alex," Saige said slowly, and he could hear a tinge of anger in her voice. "Right now though, we're trying to find something that will clear Quinten or, at least, something that will cause more doubt on his guilt so we can request a stay from the Governor." Saige paused and looked to Alex.

He moved beside her, holding his tongue on his thoughts about Agnes, and instead pleaded, "I know you couldn't care less about me, but what you said about Quinten is true. He isn't guilty and we really need answers to try and get him a retrial, at the very least, before it's too late. Please help us." *You old bat.* He grinned.

Agnes flushed and gazed around the pharmacy. No one else was present, but he did catch her son lurking in the drug dispensing area. Alex had a vague recollection of Paul and remembered him being away at school around the same time that Saige had been. Paul always used to be in the pharmacy whenever he would go in, messing with one thing or another. As a boy, Paul could never be still, but that seemed to have changed as he watched Alex and Saige with his mother.

"I'm not sure how you think I can help. I told the sheriff back then that I hadn't seen anyone with Saige, or Quinten lurking around. I mean, of course I'd see Quinten in town." She waved her hands around and became flustered. "I'd see him grocery shopping or, on occasion, going inside the bar. I didn't see him all that often with Jocelyn. She tended to go off on her own, if you know what I mean."

Alex glanced at Saige and knew she held the answers they sought, but, for now, her memories were locked away. He could see Saige was trying to remember. Her hand went to her forehead and rubbed.

"What about strangers? Did you see any around town before I disappeared?" Saige asked Agnes.

He didn't think it was a stranger. It was someone who knew her, and he had a feeling it was someone who knew Quinten as well. But the big question was who?

"You know we get a lot of tourists through here, so yes, there would have been a lot of strangers. Perhaps"—she looked at Alex and then quickly back to Saige—"the, um, person who took you hadn't even been into town." Agnes shrugged. "I honestly didn't see anyone looking suspicious. I liked Quinten. He was a good man who was trying to build something for himself. If I'd known something, I'd have told the sheriff or that handsome detective, but I didn't know anything."

Agnes caught sight of her son in the background and appeared as startled as he did. Paul tried to disappear and in the process of trying to escape their attention, he knocked a tub of pills to the floor. They fell and scattered like Skittles.

Both Alex and Saige jumped slightly at the

noise and watched as Paul quickly tried to get them back inside the tub while his mother fussed around him. "We'll need to order more. We can't use them now." Paul gathered them up and dropped them into the tub he righted. "What a waste. Be more careful," Agnes berated, and if Alex had blinked, he would have missed the look of hate that crossed Paul's features.

Paul had always been a bit strange but they always considered him harmless. Now, Alex wondered about him and his interest in their discussion and wondered about the look he'd thrown toward his mother.

Alex caught the tail end of the conversation as Saige wrapped up with Agnes, which wasn't much.

"I promise," Agnes smiled, disappearing into the back of the store.

Saige slid her arm through his and tugged him outside where she let out a deep sigh. "God, I get the creeps just being in the same room with him."

"I'm presuming you mean Paul?"

"Yeah," she said. "Forget that for now. What do you think? Does she really not know anything?"

"I missed the last bit, but she was always the best liar in town." He wiped the sweat from his brow and frowned. "He looks familiar." Alex pointed toward a man who was just climbing out of a black Lincoln Navigator.

"Detective Coulter Robinson," Saige said. "He said he might show up around here."

News to him.

Alex followed Saige as she moved toward the rumpled looking detective.

It had been years since he'd seen the man but now that he drew closer, Alex would have recognized him anywhere. Whenever they used to talk, the detective would have a pissed off expression, which he more or less had when he climbed out of the Navigator, until he caught sight of Saige that was.

"Detective," Saige greeted.

Coulter Robinson smiled and took her offered hand, but found he couldn't hold back the frown when he saw Alex Peterson over her shoulder.

He never truly had a problem with the man, and knew that Alex's anger had stemmed from all the evidence piling up against Quinten. Alex had never once doubted his brother's innocence, and now, Coulter started to realize that perhaps he should have listened. Coulter still felt annoyed that no one had bothered to tell him about Saige's relationship with Quinten. Whether or not it would have made any difference, he didn't know. He'd been kicking himself in the ass since Saige had told him.

While he was in town, he planned on talking to the sheriff about Quinten. He couldn't help wonder if Sheriff Hodges knew and had decided to keep it quiet as well.

"Is everything okay here?" Coulter asked.

Saige had discovered something, he was sure of it. He watched as she chewed on her bottom lip, and raised a brow in question.

She huffed and tucked her hair behind her ear. "My dad has only ever seen the video of me selecting the image of Quinten. Apparently, he received a call and left the room." She frowned. "Do you remember Christina's response? Was she excited that I chose that image?"

"Your stepmother"—he cleared his throat— "insisted that you could remember and wanted you to go ahead with identification. She's on my list of people to question while I'm in town."

Coulter shoved his hands on his hips and focused on Alex, who had yet to say anything or even acknowledge him.

"We need to have words about withholding evidence, Mr. Peterson."

"What?" The man had the gall to act surprised and confused.

"You lied in your statement about Saige and Quinten," Coulter accused.

At least Alex had the decency to not deny the fact.

Coulter glanced around and realized that standing in the middle of town with eyes and ears everywhere wasn't the best idea. "Can we go somewhere and talk?"

"In this place, if you want privacy, then you walk." Saige stepped around his car. "C'mon."

Five minutes later, they followed Saige onto a footpath that led into the forest and came to a stop.

"We're hidden from the road here," Saige said.

He glanced around and turned to Alex. "Tell me, how close were you to Jocelyn?"

Again, he caught the man off guard from the look of shock on his face. "I wasn't close to her at all. She made my brother's life hell. I was glad to see the back of her."

"What about you, Saige? Did you have any run-ins with her over Quinten?"

Her brows drew together. "I don't think so. My memory is still elusive, so who knows?" She held her hands out and then let them drop to her sides.

"Jocelyn saw them the day before Saige went back to school. She found out about Quinten seeking a divorce and came by Saige's house steaming. Saige and Quinten had their arms around each other." Alex sighed. "Jocelyn called them a few choice words before she took off, telling them that they'd be sorry. Why the questions?"

Coulter looked between them both. "Jocelyn has been dead for around seven years."

Saige didn't react. Obviously, she had no memory of the woman to put a face to the news. Alex, on the other hand, lost all color and stared at him in obvious shock before he tried to blink it away, but it didn't quite work.

The man moved to a tree stump and dropped his ass down, his hands briefly covered his face.

"Alex?" Saige queried, dropping to her knees

in front of him. "I'm sorry."

"It's just a shock that's all. All these years, I thought she'd left my brother for a more exciting life when in fact she hadn't gotten much of one." Alex squeezed Saige's hand and turned to face Coulter. "Do you know how she died?"

Coulter contemplated what to say without saying too much. "Without getting into specifics, let's just say the ME thinks her death is a homicide. She was dumped, or rather buried, close to the river off Morris Bridge Road in Tampa. Some campers found her five days ago."

Amber believed it was attempted strangulation. Jocelyn's head had been nearly severed—just like the young woman they'd found yesterday. It intrigued him that bones held so much information after being buried for years.

"How do you know its Jocelyn?" Saige asked.

"The ME matched the partial serial number in the breast implants to Jocelyn, and then the dental records. Her medical records also indicated pins in her left arm and leg. They all matched."

"She was in a car accident as a teenager," Alex confirmed what Coulter already knew.

"You're thinking that her death is connected to

Quinten," Saige observed. "Why?"

Alex's head snapped around to Coulter. "Connected? How? Quinten was locked away then."

"I know it wasn't Quinten, and I've never been completely sold on the idea that Quinten was guilty." He nodded toward Saige. "There's always been something niggling at me about the case.

"Getting back to Jocelyn and how she was found, I think whoever put her there went back and uncovered enough so that she'd be found. I don't believe in coincidences."

Saige looked surprised, but Alex became angry. He stood with his fists flexed at his sides before he turned and started pacing.

As Coulter watched Alex walk out his aggression, he debated showing them a picture of the girl they'd found to see if she was familiar. So far, they had no leads on her identification and his gut churned with the knowledge that she was connected somehow to all of this.

With Saige and Alex he was going out on a limb by discussing his doubts and the case, but he was willing to trust them because they all wanted the same thing—the truth.

Coulter unlocked the screen on his cell and before he changed his mind, opened up the image of the young woman's face. Amber had cleaned her up the best she could and the sheet had been pulled up to her chin. His stomach rolled when he thought of the trauma below that sheet—the bastard had been angry and violent. If he did nothing else, he needed to get justice for her—the victim.

"I want to ask you to take a look at this picture." He kept his cell to his chest while he spoke. "And tell me if you recognize her."

Saige eyed him warily while Alex just stared at him.

"She's dead?" Alex asked.

"Yes."

"Okay ... Let me see," Saige said.

He slowly turned his cell, second-guessing his instinct as he did. Her eyes widened. Her face paled and a gasp hissed from between her lips. She slammed a hand over her mouth. "Alex?" She could barely get any sound out. "It's Fern."

Until Saige had identified the victim, Alex hadn't looked all that interested, but he did now as he took two long strides and took Coulter's cell from his fingers.

"What the fuck?" Alex met Coulter's gaze, shock clear in his eyes. "When?"

"She was found yesterday morning—dead for four days. Who is she?"

"Fern Jordan," Saige offered. "She worked for Daniel Sterling, Quinten's defense attorney." She swallowed and Coulter wasn't sure if she was fighting down bile or tears. "I can't believe she's dead." Her voice wavered. "We only spoke briefly when we went and met with Daniel."

Coulter's eyes snapped to Saige. "She was part of Quinten's defense team? I don't recognize her."

"No," Alex added. "She started at Daniel's firm about twelve months ago ... How did she die?" Alex gulped, which told Coulter more than he thought Alex wanted him to know.

"The same way as Jocelyn."

"What?" Alex whispered. "Why? I don't believe Jocelyn and Fern knew each other."

"How well did you know Fern?"

Alex hesitated. "Not well."

"But you *knew* her." He held Alex's gaze, making no mistake as to what he meant.

Alex stepped away and tugged at his hair. "We

fucked around a few times. Nothing more."

Just as Coulter thought.

Saige stayed quiet, seemingly lost in thoughts of her own, so he carried on questioning Alex.

Coulter didn't believe Alex had anything to do with Fern's death, but he'd been wrong before.

"When was the last time you 'fucked around' with Fern?"

Alex looked tormented but then answered, "Three weeks ago."

And now Alex had lied to him. Why? He'd let it go for now, but not for long.

"Fern's connected as well. First Quinten's ex-wife, and now a woman from his defense attorney's office is dead. What if there are other women who have died that have some sort of connection, but you never got their case?" Saige asked, interrupting Coulter's interrogation.

"I already have someone working on that back in Tampa," Coulter answered, staring at Alex.

Saige worried at her lip. "I've also been thinking, and I was wondering if you can arrange for me to visit Quinten." She paused. "I know I asked before, but I need to see him."

"Are you sure?" Alex crouched beside Saige.

He was the one who seemed unsure. "Once you've seen him in that place, you won't ever get it out of your head."

"I'm sure, Alex. I want my memory back and I'm hoping that seeing him will help it return. I need to see him." She bit her lip. "But what if he doesn't want to see me? I named him as my abductor."

Coulter held Saige's begging gaze. "I've spoken with Quinten, and I know he wants to see you. The warden already has paperwork from Quinten requesting you have visitation rights."

"Really?" Saige smiled.

"Yes, really. It will be a few days, so hang in there."

Saige nodded, and that's when he felt the first drop of rain on his head.

"I still have questions about Fern." Coulter glared at Alex so the man knew he wasn't off the hook yet. "But I think we need to get out of the rain."

The storm hit before they reached their vehicles.

❖

Why did Tracy have to wiggle her ass and shake her tits in my face? The whore flirted outside of the pharmacy. It will only be a matter of time before I have to take care of her and that angers me.

Killing in my hometown is dangerous, but with careful planning, I'm sure I can manage it. I think I will have some fun just like I did with the delicious Fern.

The detective came all the way here to find out what was going on. I bet he never expected the beautiful Saige to identify the victim especially as Fern Jordan. It was one more connection to the Peterson's that the detective will have immediately made.

I'm not sure how I feel about that.

Saige moved fluidly toward the bed where he sat, allowing him time to savor the sight of her nude body. She was exquisite and made his blood thrum through his system and pool in one place, and one place only.

Quinten's shaft was hard and pulsed with a life of its own at just the sight of the beautiful woman he'd fallen in love with. She was everything to him and, if he had his way, she'd be his everything for the rest of his life. Only when he was with her did his heart feel full and his soul at ease.

They'd met secretly at the boathouse on her father's property for a month and the thought of her going back to school, and them being separated, had caused him to break the one rule he told himself not to break—he'd made love to her.

He hadn't been able to think straight when he pulled her into his arms and sealed his lips over hers. Pure desperation had run through him, and he'd needed to love her. He'd needed her to know just how much he loved her and had decided to show her.

Saige had been just as desperate and Quinten had been humbled to realize that he was her first. She had no idea, but he planned on being her only.

Reaching for him, her palms went to the sides of his face as she straddled his thighs. His hands caressed her hips and slipped around to her soft-as-silk bottom. He gently tugged her closer and lowered his head to kiss each hipbone.

They'd already made love three times, and he knew that by morning, they'd have made love numerous more times.

Sliding his hands up her torso he cupped each round breast in his hand and gently rubbed the hard buds of her nipples. He smiled when he heard her breath catch.

He'd discovered how sensitive her breasts were the first time he'd been inside her. She released the second his mouth had closed around the hard nub and he suckled against it.

And, just as expected, when he brought a breast to his mouth and rubbed her nipple between his tongue and the roof of his mouth, her legs quivered and she dropped to his lap.

"Mmm," Saige moaned. "I love the feel of you against my softness." She wiggled closer and he arched his hips when she settled against his balls and ground down.

"Saige," he hissed. "Rise up a bit. I need to be inside of you."

"Yes."

When the welcoming lips of her sex started to enclose him inside her snug channel, he didn't think he'd last another minute.

He was fully seated inside her as Saige wound her arms around his neck, her breasts pressed against his chest, and she kissed him. "I love you,

Quinten, and before you know it, I'm going to be home and in your arms again."

"Damn straight, baby." His arms went around her waist, holding her tight. He flipped them over on the bed and with a desperation he hadn't felt before, his hips rhythmically moved against her until he felt the woman he loved quiver in his arms and then fall apart on a loud, long moan.

Her core pulsed tight around him, he lost it, and spilled his warm release deeply inside her. Tiny aftershocks tugged and massaged his cock as his legs trembled from the power of his climax.

Panting, Saige started kissing him all over his face, neck, and back up to his face. Finally finding his lips, she whispered, "I'm yours, Quinten. I love you," before she sealed their lips in such a powerful kiss that he felt it in his toes.

Suddenly awake, Quinten panted and tried to get his bearings.

Like a cloud lifting, reality struck his heart and caused it to lurch in pain. Saige wasn't there. He was alone. He was still in prison, dreaming of her. But it had felt so real that he'd come hard in his briefs.

His breath caught in the back of his throat and tears fell from his eyes for the love that never had a chance so long ago.

Day 10

Saige watched Quinten sleep softly on his back beside her, the covers long since shoved to the floor.

Sated from a night of loving, Saige smiled as she remembered how beautifully he'd made love to her the first time, and she vowed to never forget it. She'd fallen in love with him and wanted nothing more than to spend all her time in his presence.

They had never made love before that night, but she knew he'd thought about it, like she had.

Usually they'd talk until the early hours of the morning then go their separate ways before anyone else was up for the day. That part she hated. She wanted to be able to sleep in his arms every night, and to wake up with the sun streaming through the windows while they made slow, sweet love. She wanted to take him to breakfast with her family and shout to the world that they were in love, but they couldn't do that, at least, not yet.

Needing to feel his hands on her once more, Saige couldn't resist waking him in a most delicious way. A way he hadn't wanted her to feel she had to do to him, after he'd used his wicked mouth on her.

Her eyes moved to his penis and widened when she saw how swollen he was in his sleep. Her heart pounded with arousal as she reached out with a hand and slowly traced around one of his nipples before she let her fingers tickle down his hard stomach and along his shaft.

Becoming bolder, Saige ran her fingers back and forth along Quinten's throbbing flesh. Warm and smooth beneath her touch.

Her small hand wrapped around his girth, her thumb rubbed over the leaking tip, and that's when she heard a loud groan before she found herself on her back with Quinten looming over her.

She met his glittering, hunter green eyes seconds before he dropped his head and kissed her taut nipples, rousing a melting sweetness within her.

"I love these," he whispered, cupping her breasts in his large hands before blowing warm air over them.

He smiled and slowly moved his hands downward, skimming either side of her body to her thighs. They trembled at his touch and she whimpered when he placed her legs over his shoulders and nibbled along her flesh until he arrived at her pelvis.

He nuzzled against her and she felt her face heat with embarrassment.

Quinten chuckled, and opened her up to his eyes. All it took was a teasing pressure against her clit with his tongue and she was ready for him.

"Inside me," she begged.

He met her gaze, his face buried between her legs. "I love being down here." He breathed against her.

"It's morning," she felt tears choke her. "I have to leave—" she didn't finish her sentence.

Quinten quickly rose up, took hold of his hard flesh and slowly sank into her welcoming heat.

He gathered her against his warm, pulsing

body. Her breasts tingled against his hair-roughened chest. Her hands caressed the planes of his back before her fingers dug into his buttocks.

"I love you, and I don't want to leave," Saige confessed.

He kissed her, hard and long. "You'll be back in my arms before you know it, Saige." He kissed her on the tip of her nose. "I love you. Only you."

Quinten slowly moved his hips.

Tears streamed down her face and Saige felt the wet pillow under her seconds before her eyes opened. She knew, without a doubt, that her dream had been a memory. The love she'd felt coming from Quinten had been tremendous, and to think that she'd thrown all that away because she hadn't remembered. How had she not remembered being with him before now?

And the chair that she had in her apartment in Tampa—her favorite one that they would cuddle up on and talk. It had been their chair. Somehow she'd known that the chair had meaning to her, and now she knew what it was. Saige just wished that she had the rest of her memories. She was so desperate to remember. The fact she couldn't left a hard lump in the pit of her stomach. How did Quinten feel knowing that she couldn't remember him or their time together? Saige knew, deep in her heart, that he hadn't been the one to harm her.

Saige turned over in bed and laid on her side, using the quilt to wipe at her cheeks. Her heart hurt and she felt utter misery. Only having that one vivid memory of Quinten made her crave to have him lying beside her with his arms holding her snuggled tight against his strong chest.

The chains grated on Quinten's nerves as he entered a small room to visit with his brother. The visiting rooms in the building he'd been moved to were more private than what had been used when he'd been in a death row cell. And while he liked the new rooms, reason as to why he'd been moved caused his heart to beat recklessly in his chest.

As the guard indicated for him to sit, he wondered whether or not a stay would be given. Until he'd been convicted, he believed in the justice system, but not anymore.

Quinten knew that he was innocent—of the murders and hurting Saige. He only had himself to blame for screwing up the crime scene with his blood. His only concern at the time had been getting Saige and getting the hell out of the shack.

Eight years later, he still had trouble getting his head around the fact that he had been convicted while the real fucker was out there somewhere. That had been his fear at first—the real bastard would go back and finish off Saige because she'd been the one to get away—to survive.

No one would listen except Detective Robinson. The detective hadn't completely been on his side, but Robinson had been the only one to question the evidence at the scene. In the end it hadn't mattered, he'd still been given the blue pants and orange shirt to wear for the remainder of his life.

When the door creaked open, he turned and watched Alex walk into the room. His brother looked the same as always in his jeans and heavy rock T-shirt. But he had cut his normally unruly hair.

Once a month, his brother would visit and Quinten knew that it always took a lot out of Alex. It took a lot out of him—this time it would be different.

Alex cleared his throat and finally met his gaze. "You okay?" Alex asked.

"I haven't been okay in eight years." Quinten sighed. "Sorry. It's not your fault I'm in here."

"It is." Alex's eyes flickered to the side before he said, "I should have done more." Alex as the older brother had always taken on the task of watching his back.

Quinten changed the subject. "I've heard you're helping Saige. That's good." Even saying her name out loud to his brother caused his heart to hitch in his chest.

"Yeah." Alex let out a loud breath and laughed. "I'm an idiot. I spent all this time being angry with her for not helping you back then when she had no clue about any of it. Even when I first talked to her I was slightly skeptical about her loss of memory, but there was no faking her reaction when I told her that she had a relationship with you."

Quinten flinched, dipping his head so Alex wouldn't see how much it hurt. Not only couldn't she remember him, but she was out there right now trying to get her memories back. He hoped that she did. He wanted and needed to see her just one more time before—

"If it helps, she dreamt about you last night."

That got his attention and his eyes snapped back to his brother.

"Go on." Quinten waited impatiently for Alex to tell him.

"Saige was tired at breakfast and wouldn't go into detail, but she looked visibly shaken. She finally admitted to dreaming about you. I got the impression that it was, um, one of those dreams." Alex cleared his throat and offered him an embarrassed smile. "I think Christina is hiding something as well."

Saige hadn't been the only one to dream last night. He'd lain awake for hours before he'd managed to fall back asleep. In a way, he hated having dreams about Saige because it made him realize all the more what he'd lost.

"Christina hated me being with Saige. She also hated the fact that you'd tease her before knocking her back."

Alex wouldn't meet his gaze. "She'll talk."

"Alex," Quinten growled, "don't go doing something you'll regret." His brother was hot headed and had a habit of acting before thinking.

"The last thing I want is for you to end up in jail and for Saige to be alone out there."

Alex smirked. "Are you only concerned about Saige, bro?"

"Dammit." Quinten tried to control his temper at his brother. "You know damn well that I love you. You're the only family I have, but I love Saige as well. Hell, God knows what can of worms she's going to open by doing what she's doing, you as well."

"You mean trying to save your ass?"

"Yes." Quinten hated knowing that Saige was out there and vulnerable. "Whoever took her is still out there and if the wrong person finds out what she's doing, I don't even have to say it. It's obvious. Just watch her back as though it's mine."

Guilt filled Alex's gaze. "I didn't do such a good job with yours."

"There was nothing you could have done." And wasn't that the truth. He'd been guilty in their eyes regardless of what he'd said. Jocelyn, his ex-wife, hadn't helped with her lies. He didn't think she'd have known the truth if it had jumped up and bit her on the ass.

"You heard about Jocelyn?" Quinten asked, and

watched Alex wipe a hand down his face as though he was exhausted.

"Yeah. Detective Robinson showed up in Port Jude and told Saige and I—" He glanced around the room, his eyes falling on the barred window that overlooked an exercise yard. "A woman was murdered five nights ago as well," he added, his voice raw with emotion.

Quinten frowned. "What does that have to do with me?"

"I don't know. Her name was Fern Jordan and she worked for Daniel Sterling. Detective Robinson thinks both Jocelyn and Fern's murders are connected in some way to you. I don't see how." Alex raised a questioning brow to him.

"I never met Fern, and I don't think I've heard her name before."

"Didn't think so," Alex admitted but avoided his gaze *again* as his eyes swept the room.

"What's going on with you?" Quinten asked, wondering if his brother lied to him.

He used to be able to tell when Alex lied because he'd avoid looking at him, and he'd twitch, which he did now.

"Nothing," Alex replied and laughed.

"Seriously, I'm okay. But I do need to talk to you about Saige."

"Five minutes," the guard said.

Quinten nodded.

"What about Saige?" Quinten asked.

"I'm not sure it's a good idea that she comes here." Alex waved his arms around. "Are you sure you want her to see you in this place?"

He closed his eyes because he wanted to be selfish and say yes.

"I don't think it would do her any good coming here. This place takes it out of you. I wouldn't want any girl I cared about seeing me in here."

Quinten's anger rose as he listened to his brother. At least Alex could leave when he wanted. There was only one way Quinten was leaving.

"I don't even know if she wants to come and visit me," he said, his anger leaking out.

"Robinson agreed to bring her. He'll be able to get her in, but I want you to refuse."

"Why?"

"She's too damn sweet to be in this place," Alex admitted.

"If she wants to come, then I look forward in seeing her." Quinten stood and shuffled toward the guard.

He refused to look back at his brother. He was angry and wondered what the fuck was going on between Alex and Saige.

"Well...well...well, if it isn't the whore..."

Saige dropped to the grass on her hands and knees as pain echoed in her head and she wondered what the hell that memory had been about. Someone with long dark hair had taunted her with those words.

She had no memory of ever talking to the woman. Saige had felt a shiver of fear slide down her spine at the taunt that had been delivered by a very angry woman.

"Saige?"

She heard the voice but it sounded like it came at her from faraway.

"You'll never have him."

Rapidly blinking, Saige tried to shake more of the memory free as hands grabbed her arms and helped her sit on the grass.

"Saige, look at me."

Her eyes moved and met those of Detective

Coulter Robinson.

"What happened?"

She raised a shaky hand to her forehead but, feeling weak, gave up and let her hand drop to her lap. She rested her forehead against her raised knees. "A sudden vision of a dark haired woman"—Saige swallowed, not wanting to admit who she thought it was and held Coulter's gaze— "was before my eyes." She sighed. "She said, 'You'll never have him' so I'm presuming she meant Quinten? Could it have been Jocelyn? I didn't see her properly, more like a fuzzy image."

"That would make sense, I guess. But Quinten and Alex said they didn't think she knew about you two until the day you left for school." Coulter frowned.

"Even though we lived in the same town, I don't ever remember talking to Jocelyn, and her appearance would change with the wind. I knew who she was. I think the whole town knew of her, but it would only make sense for her to say those words I heard." Saige turned to her hands and knees and scrambled to her feet.

Coulter followed and stood in front of her. "I don't like any of this, Saige. None. Something happened eight years ago and I'm now, more than ever, convinced an innocent man was sent to prison. That's the first thing that needs correcting." Coulter placed his hands on his hips and stared out across the ocean.

It would normally have a calming presence on her, but not anymore. Not while her mind was in turmoil.

"I'm scared, Coulter," Saige whispered. "What if we can't help Quinten in time?"

Coulter watched her carefully. "I'm taking you to the prison with me in two days."

Saige gasped and turned to the detective. "It's been approved?"

He nodded. "The warden will be present."

Saige raised a brow as Coulter continued to explain, "Although it isn't unheard of for a victim to visit her abductor in prison, it isn't everyday that one wants to visit one on death row. I spoke to the warden and told him about your memory loss, so he's as interested as I am in seeing how you react in Quinten's presence." Coulter offered a small smile. "He has a soft spot for Quinten."

"I'm really going to see him?" Saige whispered the question as her body was wracked by a whirlwind of emotion—excitement, need, fear, apprehension, and worry. She was scared of going to the prison. She was terrified of what she might remember.

"Yes. You really are going to see him." Coulter watched her. "The prison isn't for the fainthearted, Saige, so remember I'll be with you every step of the way, okay?"

Saige nodded. "Alex won't be happy."

Coulter frowned. "Why?"

"He wants me to stay away from the prison, but I can't. I need to see him, and I won't lie, I'm hoping the rest of my memory hits me when I'm in Quinten's presence."

"Try not to get your hopes up. The mind doesn't always do what we want."

"I know." Saige started walking toward the house. "Can I get you a coffee or a cold drink?" she offered, and smiled when he fell into step beside her.

"I'll pass this time. I want to head back into town and talk to some of the townsfolk."

Saige smiled. "I hope you have a better luck at it than Alex and I did." She shrugged. "Agnes at the pharmacy knows everyone and everything, except what happened to those girls or me. She genuinely seemed disappointed that she didn't know anything."

"I'll call in and say hello." Coulter smiled.

"Mmm, using some of that hidden charm, Detective?" Saige's eyes lit with amusement, more so when Coulter blushed.

"Maybe," he agreed, and then changed the subject. "The sheriff is out of town and due back this evening, so I'll visit the sheriff's office tomorrow morning."

"What about my father and Christina? You're still going to talk to them, right?"

Coulter nodded. "I hoped to catch them while I was here, but Pattie informed me that neither are around."

"My father has a meeting with a client, and I've no idea where Christina is."

"What about Alex?"

"I haven't seen him since he left to visit Quinten." Saige couldn't meet Coulter's gaze any longer. It hurt that Alex had gone to see his brother but had refused to take her with him. It would have been pointless as she wouldn't have been allowed in to see him, but, at least, she would have been closer to him. Alex had made it clear that he didn't want her anywhere near that place, but thanks to Coulter she would be going.

As much as she wanted to trust Alex and talk to him about her upcoming visit to the prison, Saige decided to keep it to herself for now.

"I need to go," Alex said.

He could stay and play all night but Tracy was different, and he sensed that she wanted a lot more than he was willing to give. Nearing forty like Alex, he didn't think Tracy was too picky about whom she ended up with—it wouldn't be him.

But he was a bastard and had only used her to make a point to himself about Christina. The woman had him tied in knots just like last time. He was running scared and needed to grow a set of balls and face his fear—fear of being with her only to have her trample all over his heart again.

He rubbed his chest where his heart ached.

"Are you sure?" Tracy asked, her eyes hooded and her lips painted red in a pout. She obviously thought it was sexy, when in fact she looked ridiculous and he tried his best not to laugh.

He ducked his head. "I'm sure," he answered and climbed from the bed.

For the first time in a while, he felt like a heel leaving a woman the way he was about to, but he quickly lost interest.

He tugged his clothes on and let Tracy lead him through her small house to the front door. She opened it and, once he stepped outside, she smirked. "Pity you're leaving. I thought that you might have wanted to know who really took Saige."

She slammed the door in his stunned face.

"Tracy?" I call, not wanting to scare the woman.

Time for that soon enough.

She stumbles to a stop, pressing a hand to her chest as she faces me, the light from her flashlight dazzling. "You scared me." She gives a nervous laugh, dipping the head of the flashlight. "Why are you walking around out here?"

I raise a brow and laugh, trying to put her at ease. "I could ask you the same question."

"True," she admits. "I needed a walk."

"In the dark?"

"Yes, in the dark. Obviously." She rolls her eyes.

There is no reason to continue arguing with the whore, she'll be dead soon enough.

I allow my eyes to caress over her body so that there is no mistaking what I want. When the heat in her eyes flares to life, I step into her space, and grunt when she grabs me through my jeans.

Unexpected.

"I knew you'd want more." Her hand clenches around my dick. "I want it rough," she confesses, and I have the thought that she doesn't really want it as rough as I'm tempted—then again, maybe she does.

Seconds later, her jeans are around one ankle and her legs are spread wide as I pummel into her pink flesh.

The slap of flesh-against-flesh sounds loud in the forest, as I sate my lust.

I might not rape my victims but what I do after the sex by killing the whores—I consider my kind of justice.

Weary from his day of questions without any real answers, Coulter pulled his car in beside the sheriff's. The last thing he expected was the call he received fifteen minutes ago.

The body of a woman had been found half a mile outside of Port Jude—a random call to direct them to that particular spot.

Coulter tried to keep an open mind, but with the discovery of Jocelyn, followed by Fern, it was difficult not to imagine that they were all connected—only one way for it to be confirmed.

With his hiking boots already on his feet, he climbed out of his car and followed the path toward the lights he could see through the trees.

The road alongside was isolated, so chances of a witness coming forward would be next to nothing.

"Sheriff," Coulter greeted, the only sign of his frustration with the whole Quinten Peterson case was the tightening of his jaw.

"Detective." The sheriff dipped his head and moved closer. "I heard you've been looking for me. I didn't think we'd be meeting under these circumstances."

Coulter let the sheriff's words settle, and asked, "Why did you call me about this?" He'd ask the sheriff about the Lockwood family at a more appropriate time.

"Like I said, I knew you were around. My curiosity was piqued, especially when Tracy Adam's was found." Sheriff Hodges took off his hat and wiped at his forehead with his arm. "I've known Tracy all her life and no matter what she's done in the past, she didn't deserve to die the way she did. I'm just glad her parents aren't alive to see this."

"What's my connection to Tracy?" Coulter couldn't let it go. There was a reason the sheriff had called him to come to the crime scene and he needed it spelled out.

"Tracy Adams and Alex Peterson used to be an off again, on again, *couple*."

"Couple?" Coulter hadn't missed how he used the word couple rather loosely.

"It was probably more like itch scratching if you know what I mean." He turned back toward where Coulter could see the body. "Alex is back in town, and now Tracy is dead." Sheriff Hodges seemed to let his unsaid accusation sink into Coulter's mind. "I read about the young woman in Tampa who worked for the defense attorney, Daniel Sterling. I remember him, and the fact that he was Quinten's defense. With you being in town asking questions, I put two and two together. So what's going on in my town, Detective Robinson?"

Coulter wiped a hand down his tired face and knew he couldn't keep the sheriff out of the loop, or at least he'd have to tell the sheriff something. "I'm thinking now the warrant of execution has been signed, someone feels like he can move freely. There are suddenly dead bodies piling up and I think it has something to do with the Petersons.

"Quinten has always maintained his innocence. I've always had my doubts about his guilt, which you know. The recent deaths and other information I've received make me believe that there was a lot more going on back then. I believe Quinten Peterson was set up. Perhaps not intentionally, considering he always admitted to bleeding all over the shack—the blood turning out to be the evidence that convicted him. I think the real killer saw the opportunity of escaping, and has maybe laid low all this time."

He paused and stared down the path where he could see people moving, "Serial killers have been known to lay low for years, but the modus operandi has changed from eight years ago. Maybe he doesn't want any connection to the past, which is why he changed the way he killed. We'll have to capture him to find out what really is going on."

Silence followed Coulter's assessment of the old case, and hearing his thoughts out loud made him realize that he was probably on the right track. He just needed a direction to go in and, right now, he had zero leads.

"I'm not sure what to think," Sheriff Hodges mumbled, sounding exhausted. "Let's get this over with."

Coulter slowly followed the sheriff, and silently cursed when he saw the nude body sprawled out on her back. She appeared to be asleep until you looked closely. Then you could see the bruising on her arms, and the side of her rib cage.

"She put up more of a fight than Fern." Coulter knelt closer and could see the congealed blood around her neck and face. "I'm not sure what that means." He looked at the ME.

The ME glanced at him and then stared at the victim. "I read about your victim, Detective, and although my victim was nearly decapitated, I think it was post-mortem as opposed to yours being pre-mortem. My guess is that she died of asphyxiation. There are obvious signs of a struggle, and the bruising on her jaw and nose were pre-mortem. It looks like whoever did this grasped her face from behind." The ME paused. "See the way the bruising is spread? The assailant looks to have held his hand tightly over her mouth while pinching her nose closed."

The ME sighed and looked back at Coulter. "If it's the same person who killed your victim, Detective, then I'd say Tracy here wasn't surprised to see him and wasn't afraid of him to begin with. When she realized what he intended, she fought and he overpowered her. Whether or not he intended to kill her the way he did is anyone's guess."

Coulter stared at the victim and wondered if there were two killers running around, or just the one. It was too much of a coincidence for his liking, especially when both recent victims had a connection to Alex Peterson. Not to forget Jocelyn.

He ran a hand down his face and moved away. "Can we talk at the station tomorrow?" he asked the sheriff.

The sheriff nodded.

Coulter took that as his cue to leave.

Trudging back to his car, he decided the private talk with Alex would happen sooner rather than later.

Invigorated.

After every kill I feel better for a short period of time, but then the craving for vengeance against those who have done me wrong creeps closer and closer to the surface.

Fern and Tracy hadn't been planned in the beginning, but as soon as I discovered Fern worked for Daniel Sterling, the plan had formed and I'd gotten to know the young woman. Tracy had been different. I'd known her for years, and maybe I do have some remorse for killing her. I wouldn't have made the call otherwise. For some reason I wanted her to be taken care of immediately and not days later like with Fern who'd meant nothing to me.

In the end they were both whores and had needed to die.

I've gone years without spilling blood, and now I've gotten another taste for it, I'm not sure I will be able to stop.

Day 11

Saige had tossed and turned for most of the night, and as she glanced over at Alex, realized that he looked to have slept about the same.

Not quite able to hide the yawn behind his hand, Alex dropped into the chair beside her and, after helping himself to coffee, sat back and drained his cup.

"I needed that," Alex commented and grinned.

"Rough night?" she asked.

"Yeah." He yawned again. "I'm not usually so tired."

"I know what you mean. I slept badly. Too much going on inside"—she tapped her forehead—"for me to settle." She shrugged.

"I've been thinking," Alex paused, "I think I'm going to give Daniel Sterling a call and ask him to start getting the paperwork together to present to the governor. I think we have enough to request a stay. He can put the bits you've remembered into the paperwork, and, at least, the majority of the work will be done and ready for when we find more evidence to prove that Quinten is innocent."

Saige rubbed her forehead. "I have the feeling that all the answers are locked inside of me." She took a minute to compose herself. "I need to remember, Alex."

"I wish you could remember. I wish you had your memory when it happened so that Quinten wouldn't have been convicted. But it is what it is. You can't push it, and I'd be a liar if I wasn't hoping that you seeing Quinten will jog your memory."

"So, you're really okay with me going to see your brother?"

Alex sighed and poured them both more coffee. After taking a sip, he said, "The prison is no place for you. The first time I went to visit Quinten scared the fuck outta me, and it took a while to get used to the visits. I don't like the idea of you going, and I told Quinten that. He won't listen. He's desperate to see you. Talk to you."

He grasped her hand. "He never stopped loving you, Saige. He never stopped hoping that one day you'd visit him. He confided in me a while ago that his one dying wish was to see you just once more."

"Oh," she sniffled, and reached up to wipe a tear.

Alex wrapped an arm around her and tugged her against his chest. Saige raised her face to him and realized that he shared her sorrow. She leaned her head back on his chest and they stayed like that for a while until her father's faithful housekeeper and cook came bustling into the room, followed by the detective on her heels.

"Detective," Saige sat and greeted Coulter, realizing she was genuinely happy to see him, although troubled when she realized he looked tired. "Is everything alright?"

"Yes and no."

"Have you eaten breakfast yet?" she asked.

"I'm fine," Coulter replied, but the growl from his stomach made a liar out of him.

Saige grinned. "Please sit and eat. There's a lot

of food, and fresh coffee."

Coulter hesitated before he sat opposite them. "I guess I can't refuse coffee after the night I've had."

Saige frowned. "What happened?"

He glanced between them and, after taking a drink of his coffee, announced, "Another body was found last night."

Saige glanced at Alex but he held Coulter's gaze, so she asked, "Who?"

"Tracy Adams."

"*Fuck*," Alex hissed between his teeth.

"You know her?" Saige asked.

Alex breathed deeply and glanced at her. "Yes, I *knew* her." He dropped his forehead into his hands. "We went to school together and used to be...to be,"—he sucked in a breath—"fuck buddies for want of a better description."

"The sheriff told me that last night, but what else can you tell me, Alex? You had a connection to Jocelyn, Fern, and Tracy. All three are dead."

"I honestly don't know." His eyes bore into Coulter's and he looked physically sick. "Could the person who took Saige be the one doing all this? I don't know why women I know are being targeted, but it sure as fuck isn't me."

"I'm not accusing you of anything, Alex. I'm just pointing out that you're connected to all three victims." Coulter added, then corrected, "The three we know about."

Saige had gone cold as she listened to the men talk about death and connections. She was so tired of thinking, of trying to remember something significant to help save Quinten. Her brain just wanted to rest.

"Why would someone go after Alex?" Saige questioned. "Quinten is the one in prison so I don't understand why someone would go after you." She met Alex's gaze before looking at Coulter. "Do you have a theory?"

Coulter leaned forward and frowned, resting his arms on the table. "I have my theories," he said quietly as he assessed Alex.

Saige wondered if he thought Alex was the killer. She stared at the man but she couldn't see it in Alex. She trusted him, even though she didn't really know him.

"There was a difference to both Fern and Tracy's murders, but because of the connection to Alex, it's too much of a coincidence for it to be more than one killer." Coulter said quietly. "I just don't know the why. If it is a serial killer, why change the modus operandi now. I assume that the killer went to sleep ... went back to his life until now. But why not attack college girls again in the same manner? Why have his victims changed and how he kills them? Why start again when the man convicted of *his* crimes is about to be executed? Unless we have a copycat, or someone who is tied to Alex in some way."

It was clear that Coulter had forgotten they were in the room and was just spit balling his theories in an effort to see which one sounded plausible. It was horrifying and exciting to watch at the same time. The man's mind was sharply tuned for his profession.

He said to Alex, "That is, presuming it's the same person. The more questions asked, the more tangled this case becomes."

Saige felt her stomach drop to her knees at Coulter's assessment of the situation. She wanted to hold on to the killer being the same person, but what if his end game was to finish what he'd started?

Coulter watched Alex, and Saige turned to him,

offering her hand.

"Have you seen Tracy since you've been in town, Alex?" Coulter asked.

There was a slight twitch in Alex's body at the question.

She frowned.

Alex answered, "I bumped into her outside the pharmacy in town the day before yesterday. She flirted. It was a brief exchange before I followed Saige inside to talk to Agnes."

"I didn't see her." Her frown deepened.

"You'd gone inside the pharmacy. Paul Lewis saw us talking, and the barbershop guys did. The old guys don't miss anything, plus I saw them turned in my direction after she left and I went into the store."

Coulter was an observant man so Saige knew he wouldn't have missed the fact that Alex hadn't been completely truthful.

Her head ached with everything churning around. Saige rubbed at her forehead. "Do you think that we have enough to go to the governor to get a stay?" Saige asked Coulter, wearily. "Alex thinks its worthwhile asking Daniel to get the papers ready."

"Hmm, maybe." Coulter mumbled as he quickly added sausage to a piece of toast and made a sandwich. "You have my cell number, Saige, so message me Daniel's email address and I'll send a formal report to him to be included."

"I'll send it to you," Saige agreed.

Coulter nodded. "Thank you for breakfast but I need to go." He stood and shoved the chair back under the table, his sandwich in the other hand. "I'll pick you up tomorrow morning. I'll text you a time when I know I'll be free."

"Thank you." Saige stood to walk him out, but Coulter waved her back into her seat.

"I can find my own way out ... stay together. Safety in numbers." Coulter disappeared and, a minute later, she heard the front door close behind him.

"God! What a mess." Saige turned to Alex. "What do you think is going on?"

"I have no idea, but I agree with Coulter's assessment. If this killer is the one who let Quinten take the fall, then why is he back now? It doesn't make sense. For years he's let Quinten sit on death row, which allowed him to be free ... so why would he start again unless he couldn't help himself.

"I just hope that I'm not on his target list." Saige met Alex's gaze. "I'm the one that got away. I also have a connection to you and Quinten."

"Let's not go there, Saige. But I guess it won't hurt for you to have someone with you if you leave the house."

Saige shivered and felt cold right down to her toes.

Coulter observed the sheriff while he spoke with a couple of officers.

Every encounter he'd had with Sheriff Hodges, including last night, Hodges had been professional and had never given Coulter reason to doubt him, until now.

Saige's statement that held the sheriff's signature gave him reason to question the man, and he knew it wouldn't go down too well. Questioning someone in law enforcement about something they may have screwed up just wasn't done. But Coulter wanted answers and he'd get them.

"You wanted to talk. Follow me." The sheriff led him into his office. "Take a seat."

Once comfortable, Coulter waited and watched, just like Hodges did him.

"I'm too tired for this." Coulter rested his arms on his knees. He wasn't up to playing games and he had too much to do and very little time left if he was going to be able to help Quinten, and find the actual killer before he killed again. "What do you remember about Saige Lockwood from when you took her statement?"

The sheriff's eyes widened as he sat back in his chair. "That has to be the last thing I expected." He shifted forward, arms on his desk.

Coulter didn't have long to wait for his answer.

"What I remember is that Saige was a very lucky young woman. She spent hours in surgery and it took forever for the plastic surgeon to stitch her back together. As I took her statement, some of the words made me think they came out of her stepmother's mouth."

"As though she'd been coached?" Coulter interrupted and cursed himself for making the sheriff lose his flow.

"Yeah," Hodges sighed. "Her statement was flawless, and no matter how many times I asked her if it was a true statement of events, she constantly said yes."

"Was her father in the room when she gave the statement?"

The sheriff rubbed at his brow. "I don't think so. He was busy arranging the private hospital if memory serves me right. He stayed with Saige for just over a week while she was in the hospital and would only leave when his wife visited, and only for a short while. After that, he went back to work, but he would always be there in the evenings. Out of the two of them, I'd have said her father was the more caring. But that's an assessment that probably goes back years before Saige was taken."

That was the impression Coulter had gotten back then. Christina had always come across as self-centered, and he'd felt what happened to Saige had been an inconvenience to the woman.

"Just to clarify—Saige was the one who told you what was written in that statement?"

The sheriff's gaze hardened. "I don't like your insinuation, Detective."

Coulter ground his teeth together to swallow the words he wanted to say. The man was being intentionally obstinate.

Coulter held up his hand and showed his index finger. "So far, there have been three murders. Three women who all connect in some way to the Petersons."

He held up a second finger as though he was making a tally. "My truck was blown up outside of the station in Tampa."

The third finger went up. "Saige Lockwood is remembering things and she's trying to remember who took her."

The sheriff's eyes widened and it was clear that he was starting to see the pattern. "Is there a connection? I don't know. Quinten Peterson has seventeen days left on this earth. I questioned his guilt back then during the investigation and trial, and I'm questioning it more now. I don't believe Quinten Peterson should have been charged or convicted. Something else happened back then and I'm going to find out what it was. I don't care who I piss off in the process as long as an innocent man gets his life back."

Coulter stood, his anger eating at him and he wanted to unleash it on Hodges. "Saige Lockwood and Quinten Peterson were in a relationship." Coulter rested his hands on his hips and held the sheriff's sharp gaze. "Love was involved, which explains why Quinten was found wrapped around Saige in the forest. I'm beginning to realize that Saige had already lost her memory in regards to Quinten and what happened to her before she 'supposedly' gave that statement." He walked to the window. "Damn." Coulter dropped his head and concentrated on getting his temper under control as he stared outside.

Minutes later, he felt movement close to him. "I'm not going to state the obvious, Detective. I've already told you I felt it was more of a rehearsed statement than a real one, but what could I do? Saige insisted it was hers and that everything she said was true. She signed it and passed it back. I didn't think it necessary to query anything, especially once the DNA results came back and Quinten was charged."

It appeared he wasn't the only one to have questions during the initial investigation. Coulter had been vocal about his misgivings at the time, and now he wished he'd pushed a lot harder than he had.

"Did you talk to Saige again?" Coulter asked. "I mean directly after she'd given her statement, before she was transferred to the private hospital," he clarified.

"Not that I recall. I remember talking to her father, and he seemed torn about whether he was doing the right thing or not." Hodges shrugged. "I'm a father, are you?"

Coulter wasn't sure he would ever want a kid after the stuff he'd seen in the department.

Hodges continued. "Well, I can't imagine the hell he was going through. If it had been my daughter, I'm not sure I would have been able to keep myself from hunting the bastard down and shooting him myself. Richard wasn't like that. He wanted the bastard caught, but his focus was completely on Saige. He was a man worn down by what had happened and I know he felt like it was his fault—like he hadn't been a good enough father and protected his daughter."

Hodges stared outside the window Coulter was perched beside. "Not long after Saige was transferred to the private hospital, Richard hospitalized with pneumonia. Christina was involved in a car accident, but luckily, she walked away pretty much unscathed. It was a rough time for all involved. The family was in ruin and I thought it best to give them some time to heal."

The sheriff moved away and sat back behind his desk. "I asked a few times as to Saige's wellbeing and was always told she was 'improving'." He shrugged. "I left them alone, which I'll admit was easy to do considering how short tempered they were when I'd talk to them."

Coulter sighed and dropped into the chair. "It isn't our job to follow up when a case is closed, but, I went after Jocelyn once Quinten was sentenced. She'd already cleaned out."

Hodges frowned. "Why'd you look for her?"

"Because I never believed a word out of her mouth, and I wanted to push her buttons and push her into admitting she'd lied … she may have already been dead by then."

"We both did our jobs Detective, and the evidence was there, otherwise Peterson would never have been convicted. We both need to forget what happened and concentrate on sorting through the mess we have now because if what you believe about Quinten is true, then time is running out."

Coulter agreed. "Seventeen days."

I wish I were a bug on the wall in the Sheriffs office. I can see how annoyed the detective is. I can also see how much he is pissing off the Sheriff. The detective is like a dog with a bone. He won't give up this time. I can see that clearly now.

I guess I'm going to have to help him along.

My slip up with the car bomb can be forgotten now the detective is of use.

I find it a great deal of fun killing the whores and playing with everyone involved in the Peterson case.

"The detective is bringing your friend with him tomorrow."

Quinten's head snapped up to look at the guard. "What?" he whispered.

"You heard me. The warden has approved her to visit you. Your detective friend had something to do with rushing it through. Been told to tell you they'll be here sometime before lunch."

He nodded at the guard and rested his back against the wall.

Saige really was coming to visit him. Just the

thought and he felt sick with nerves. What if she really didn't remember him? When he remembered everything.

Her smile could bring him to his knees, and the way her eyes would light up when she looked at him always made his heart thump wildly in his chest. Saige had given him a reason to get out of bed every day. Before he'd met her, he'd felt his life spiraling out of control because of the disaster of a marriage he'd been in.

His business with his brother had just started to get off the ground, and he'd finally managed to hide enough money to go ahead with the divorce and then his life had shattered.

He'd given his heart to Saige, something that Jocelyn had never had. He thought back to his marriage. It had happened quickly and he realized, even before he'd sought a divorce that he'd confused lust for love. When he'd met Saige, however, he had finally understood what it meant to love someone unconditionally.

Saige was a breath of fresh air in his miserable life. She'd given him something to look forward to. Meeting at the boathouse, he'd spent hours with her in his arms as they'd talked.

At first, he'd felt guilty for being with Saige while still married. The guilt hadn't been for Jocelyn—that woman had had so many affairs he'd lost count. His guilt was for Saige. He wanted to be with her freely, without all the baggage that he had. He'd planned to make that happen before everything derailed.

Slowly shaking his head, Quinten made his way to the metal desk in his room and sat down heavily. The only item on the desk was a dog-eared book, *City of Bones*, which had been Saige's favorite. She'd given it to him for safe keeping when she'd gone back to school. It was the only thing Alex had brought to him once he'd been shown his new home in Harlington.

Opening the book to the center, his fingers rubbed against the worn leather bracelet that Saige had given him. He never wore it because it was too small for his thick wrist, but he'd taken it and treasured it always.

When he was first incarcerated, it had been his security blanket of sorts. Eventually, he'd hidden it away in the middle of the book. No matter how much he'd been asked by the guards to lend the book to other inmates, he'd always refused.

Smoothing his hand over the page, he smiled, remembering the rosy blush that would coat Saige's cheeks when they'd get to more of a romantic part in the book. He'd nuzzle into her neck to hide his amusement. Her voice would go all soft and husky and it had taken a lot of self-control to not take advantage of the situation. He'd craved a taste of her but he'd always held himself back—until that last night.

Dreaming about that last night a couple of days ago and waking, not having Saige in his arms, had crushed him all over again.

He was desperate to see her in the flesh instead of in his memories, and tomorrow he would.

❖

"Bring me a beer and yourself, woman." Quinten smirked and laughed.

"Getting demanding aren't we, Mr. Peterson?" Saige grabbed a beer that Quinten had brought with him, and flounced over to the sexy man.

He'd showered and changed into a long-sleeved, navy t-shirt and workout pants. The long sleeves had been shoved up to his elbows, showing off the amazing artwork that he'd had permanently inked into his skin, which she thought was sexy. Not that he needed anything to add to his manliness.

Placing the beer on the table, Saige straddled his thighs and wiggled closer. Quinten sucked in a sharp breath when her breasts pressed into his chest. She grinned and wrapped her arms around his neck.

"Saige," he groaned as she felt something growing hard beneath her. Saige pressed closer. "Fuck." Quinten hissed as he held her hips still and closed his eyes before opening them to look into hers. "I want you. More than I've ever wanted anyone, but until I'm free, we can't."

Saige knew he wanted her, he couldn't exactly hide it and, unfortunately, she agreed with him when they'd talked about it.

The time in the boathouse was so they could be together, and Quinten had often told her that it was out of love and respect for her that he couldn't make love to her. He wanted to come to her free of everything. She understood that. It just left them both frustrated.

Taking pity on him, Saige rearranged herself on

his lap and snuggled into his welcoming arms.

Quinten kissed her on the forehead. "You know how much I love you, Saige. How much I want everything with you. As soon as I'm free, I'll claim you and never let you go. I hope you know that."

She smiled. "I can't wait for you to claim me, Quinten, and I respect you for wanting to wait."

"But?" He rested his head against hers.

"I want to be closer to you," Saige admitted.

"You're closer to me than anyone else. You know more about me than even Alex. I respect you too much to take what I crave while I'm not completely free."

"As frustrated as I am, as I think you are, I love you all the more for that." Saige cupped his bearded jaw and placed a sweet kiss to his lips. "I love you, Quinten Peterson, and I've never been more excited about my future as I have been since I met you."

"God, babe." Quinten kissed her hard before he pulled back and rested his head against the back of the chair and stared at the ceiling. "Talk to me because you sitting on my erection is killing me."

Saige felt butterflies fly around in her stomach at his confession. "When?"

Quinten blinked at her but she could see he

knew what she meant. "I told you that I already talked to a divorce attorney before I even met you, right?"

Saige nodded.

"I called him at the beginning of last week. I paid the deposit he requested and he's starting on the paperwork. I quoted irreconcilable differences as to the reason for the divorce. Figured it would be simpler then her adultery." He sighed. "Jocelyn will be mad as all hell when she finds out I'm actually going through with the divorce."

He shifted so that she was half on and half off his lap as he loomed over her. "She's vindictive and I really don't want her knowing about my feelings for you." He leaned down and kissed her. "But make no mistake, Saige. Nothing and no one will be able to stop this divorce from happening. I should have listened to Alex, but I didn't and I've paid the price. No more though." He caressed along her lips with a finger while licking his own lips.

"I love you," he whispered softly before sealing their lips together.

Saige jumped and her eyes snapped open seconds before she rolled from the sofa with a thump.

"Oomph ... ouch," she moaned but remained on her back while she got her bearings, and slipped back into reality.

Tears seeped from her eyes in a strange mixture of longing and desperation. She wanted to be with Quinten and she wanted to remember all the times they'd spent together.

"Saige?"

Alex.

"Saige, what the fuck?" he stated and stood over her. "Shit. What's wrong?" he added.

"I didn't sleep so well so I decided to lie down on the sofa and I had a dream." She shrugged, but Alex could see through her confession.

"Let me help you up." He reached out and, with a tug, had her up and back on the sofa. "What did you dream?"

She paused and then admitted, "About Quinten and our time in the boathouse." She offered him a shy smile. "I want to hold on to him, Alex. There's this need inside of me to hold on and never let him go. It scares me. Every night I go to bed with another day behind me. I'm so scared that I'm going to remember everything once it's too late."

Saige wiped her tears from her face with the sleeve of her sweater when she got a good look at Alex. Her eyes narrowed. "What's wrong?"

He laughed but there wasn't any mirth behind it. "That was my line."

She nudged him. "We're a sorry pair." She grinned. "Spit it out."

"It bothers me about Fern and Tracy. I'm almost afraid of so much as talking to another woman."

"I'm alive," Saige added.

"I think you're safe. It only seems to happen to women I've had, um"—he blushed—"you know with." He cleared his throat.

"You had sex with Jocelyn?" Saige asked, shocked.

His brother's wife!

"Fuck, no! She was Quinten's wife for one thing." Alex stood and ran his hands through his hair. "I never touched that woman." He shuddered in revulsion. "Don't get me wrong, she was one hell of a looker, until you got to know her, or got on her bad side, which I was always on."

"Then maybe there isn't a connection," she

commented, hopeful that the killer wasn't targeting women Alex had slept with.

Alex said, "Sorry to burst your bubble, but I think there is. I'm connected to Jocelyn through Quinten, and Fern and Tracy through sex. There has to be something, or someone, missing from all of this. It's driving me crazy."

Saige grabbed a cushion and wrapped her arms around it for comfort, her knees curled under her while she rested her head on another cushion. "I don't know what to think anymore. But I do know that Quinten is innocent. He didn't take me. I know that with every fiber of my being. And even though I don't relish the thought, I wish I dreamt more about my time in the shack. Maybe if I did, then I'd remember hearing or seeing something that could be added to Coulter's report for the governor."

"I don't know why your dreams are centered around Quinten rather than the shack, but I think with Coulter's report, and your new statement, Quinten will get a stay. The governor is up for reelection and will want the support of the public, which he won't get if he executes an innocent man." Alex didn't look worried. He looked annoyed more than anything.

"I hope you're right," Saige whispered.

Alex was angry and worried. There had to be a reason why the killer would take both Fern and Tracy's lives mere hours after he'd been with them. That was no coincidence. Then why hadn't he admitted that to Detective Robinson?

You know why.

He didn't want Coulter's investigation centering on him. Now that Quinten was close to being free of the crime, they would need to go looking for another killer. And he was terrified that it would all fall back on him—the brother of a killer, leaving a trail of dead women behind him.

He dropped his ass to the foot of the bed and cradled his head in his hands. Exhaustion seeped through his body and he ached with it. For once, he felt real panic well in his gut for Quinten. Alex had always hated his brother being locked away, but now that time was running out, he had never felt so helpless.

Hearing a tap on his door, Alex froze, and heard it again.

Christina?

She was back and, with the mood he was in, he wasn't sure it would be wise to have her in the same room as him. That didn't stop him from walking the short distance to the door and letting her in.

Christina's gaze slid over him, her eyes widening when she really looked. He had a feeling she didn't miss anything, which could be dangerous.

He rested against the closed door, his arms crossed in front of him. "To what do I owe the visit?"

Christina nervously paced, her fingers tugging together. "You were right."

"About?"

She stopped and faced him before she closed her eyes and inhaled. Exhaling, she met his gaze. "After a few days in the hospital, I suspected Saige had no memory of you or your brother. She wasn't talking about anything or to anyone. Richard figured it out."

Christina backed up and sat on the edge of the bed while he stayed by the door. He didn't trust himself around her, and heaven knew what else she wanted to confess.

"A few days after Saige had been found, the sheriff and detective wanted a statement from her, but Richard put them off. She wasn't talking. I hated how the witch-hunt took off after Quinten. I wanted to help but didn't know how.

"I saw the way he'd look at her. He loved Saige, and she him. I was jealous." She shrugged and wiped at a tear. "No one had ever looked at me that way, but I never would have done anything to split them up. No matter what anyone thinks, including Saige, I love my stepdaughter, Alex." She shuddered and Alex realized she was struggling to keep her emotions in check.

"I know what you think of me because of what I was like with you and Quinten, but the truth is, you and Richard are the only men that I've been intimate with since I married him. And it's been a very long time since he and I have—"

His eyes snapped to hers in surprise, not believing a word she said.

"Hard to believe, huh?" She fidgeted. "Richard," she hesitated, "isn't the kind and loving husband he would like everyone to believe. My life isn't what it seems and never has been."

What was she saying? And did he believe her?

"When ... when the sheriff took Saige's statement after selecting Quinten's photograph, I helped her through it. The evidence had already piled up against him by then." Christina started to cry softly. "I'm sorry, Alex. So sorry. I want to help you get your brother free. The detective is in town and wants to talk to me, so perhaps he can take my statement and that will be enough to cast doubts over Quinten's guilt.

"I just wonder whether there is a way of doing it without Richard knowing." She bit her lip, something that Alex had noticed Saige did when she was nervous.

He frowned and moved to crouch in front of her. "You really are afraid of Richard?"

Her eyes skirted away.

"Look at me, Christina ... please."

When she did, he realized she'd told him the truth. Her misery was clear to see on her face and in her eyes.

It wouldn't be the first time he'd been played, but he really did believe her.

His heart raced when he realized he had the beautiful woman sitting in front of him. No matter how much he tried, he'd never been able to erase Christina from his mind or heart, and he wanted to lose himself in the warmth only she could give him.

The other night, he'd treated her badly. He couldn't take that back, but he could make it right.

"Where's Richard?"

"Jacksonville for the night on business."

He watched her and after a minute or two started to slip his hands up her silky thighs—

What is Christina up to? She's stayed silent all these years because of Richard.

The man isn't what he seems but only a handful of people know that. It has been so easy for Richard to manipulate his wife, and his daughter.

I wonder what Saige will do when she finds out the truth about her dear old daddy. At least I'll be around to witness the betrayal in her eyes.

If she doesn't work it all out for herself then perhaps I will need to sit her down and explain it all to her in detail.

I'll tell her after Quinten's funeral.

Day 12

Saige had new meaning to the saying, cold to the bone, as she gradually came awake. She shivered and her teeth chattered together in the frigid temperature. Her eyes blinked open but darkness was her only companion.

"About time you woke up," a man hissed, and Saige's situation came rushing back to her.

She was going home to Quinten.

Flat tire.

The side of the road.

The rain lashing down.

The woman who appeared from nowhere...

Saige tossed and turned in bed wanting to remember more, but too afraid as she slipped back into sleep.

"Saige, honey," Alex drawled as his gaze raked over her. "You're going to bring my brother to his knees in that dress."

Saige smiled and twirled around for Alex. "I hope so."

Alex groaned and laughed. "I need to witness this."

"Where is he?"

"He went to the car for some tools." Alex continued to chuckle as he indicated for Saige to follow him.

Saige hurried down the stairs and caught a glimpse of Quinten on his cell, her heart turned over with love for the man. It would be their last night together before she left for school. Only one semester left and then she'd be back in his arms forever.

It had taken a lot for her to pack up her clothes because her heart wanted to stay home where the man she loved would be, but he wouldn't let her. He was right that she had to finish her education. It didn't make her heart hurt any less at the thought of not seeing him daily.

Alex flung the door the rest of the way open and stepped outside, calling out to Quinten.

Saige followed him out and stopped. Quinten turned to his brother and then did a double take when he caught sight of her. His mouth fell open and his hand holding his cell dropped to his side.

Moving closer to Quinten, his mouth snapped closed and she watched as seconds later his tongue slipped out and moistened his lips.

Saige didn't stop until her arms were around Quinten's neck, her body pressed up against his harder one, and her lips caressed along his jaw.

"Mmm," Saige moaned when Quinten gripped her hips, holding her tight against him.

"How am I supposed to work when you're dressed like that? All I want to do is peel this dress off you and get lost in your body." Quinten groaned and tossed his cell into the car, his call obviously forgotten.

He cupped her face between his hands and slowly kissed her. His lips caressed along hers, his tongue traced the seam before his mouth claimed hers.

"I love you," he whispered, wrapping her up in his arms. "I can't let you go."

"I'm yours, Quinten. Even when I'm away at school, I'm yours. Always." Saige buried her face in his neck and sighed.

"I hear a car," Alex commented.

Saige snuggled deeper into Quinten's arms, no longer bothered by who knew about her relationship with him. She loved him and wanted to shout it to the world.

"Christina is due back. She knows about us and I don't want to hide what I feel for you anymore, that's if you're okay with that?"

Saige met Quinten's delighted gaze. "I'm more than okay with that." His hand slipped to the nape of her neck as his lips met hers in a brief kiss.

"Oh fuck," Alex cursed. "It's not Christina."

Saige shot up in bed.

Her heart pounded in her chest as she stumbled to the desk in her room for the bottle of water she'd left there. Taking a long swallow, she breathed in deeply in an effort to calm down.

She couldn't remember anything after Jocelyn had arrived, but she knew that seeing her and

Quinten wrapped around each other hadn't gone down too well. What did she expect though? Jocelyn had still been married to Quinten then, even though the woman had cheated on him from the start. One thing Saige felt was that Jocelyn wanted to own Quinten and didn't like him being with anyone else.

Jocelyn had been a very jealous woman where Quinten was concerned, regardless of how many lovers the woman had had.

The woman had hated Saige and from what she'd previously remembered, she must have hated Saige very much, because she'd been the woman on the side of the road when Saige had been taken.

Saige's question was who had Jocelyn been involved with back then? There had definitely been someone else there that night.

Alex was so screwed.

No matter what he said, he'd had no intention of ever fucking Christina, but last night had turned into something else.

Christina's confession had caused something

266 | TWENTY EIGHT DAYS

inside of him to shift and instead of fucking her he'd made love to her. A combination of missing her, and having her gorgeous body beneath him, had caused his orgasm to crash through him more powerful than it had in a long, long time.

She slept beside him, the curves of her nude body outlined in the moonlight from the window enticed him to start all over again, but in truth, after last night she scared him. He'd had a hard on for her years ago and he obviously still did. She wasn't that much older than him, but realistically she was so far out of his league that he tried not to think about it. He'd used the excuse that she slept around, just like Jocelyn, to keep his pecker zipped in the end—except her sleeping around had been lies. Deep down, he'd known that then, and he knew it now.

As he caressed down her side and over her hip with his hand, his heart leapt in his chest. He tried to calm himself before the panic could really well inside of him. The night would be all he'd allow with her.

He turned her onto her stomach and tugged her bottom up into the air. She moaned and spread her legs ready for him—his tongue woke her body.

❖

Saige had nerves in her belly that were caused by a mixture of fear and excitement as she waited beside Coulter to go through another security gate.

The thought of being locked inside the prison walls, never to have freedom, caused her breathing to hitch in her lungs. Sweat beaded on her forehead.

She turned and nervously looked around. The place chilled her to the bone. Footsteps echoed along the walkways. Whistling and humming could be heard in the distance. The loud buzz of a gate opening in front of them made her jump.

Coulter offered her a wry smile and squeezed her arm. "You okay?"

"Nervous."

He nodded and led her through the door. "This part of the prison is a lot quieter. I think there's only Quinten in this section right now," Coulter tried to reassure her, but it didn't work.

It made her realize that she walked close to where it would all end. She wanted to cry and wondered if she'd be able to hold it together until they left the dismal place.

"Peterson's waiting for you," a guard informed as he buzzed them through yet another secure door at the end of the corridor.

Her steps faltered the closer she got to the door. Coulter entered first, and Saige slowly followed, keeping her head down.

Coulter wrapped an arm around her and ushered her into a chair. She couldn't put it off any longer and lifted her head.

Quinten sat across the room his eyes fixated on her with an intensity she knew she'd only ever felt with him.

Her eyes welled with tears as she looked at him. His hair and beard had been trimmed. His shoulders and biceps filled out the orange t-shirt that spread across his chest. But her eyes kept moving back to his.

She wasn't the only one with tears on her face and it hurt not being able to feel his arms around her, or to be able to offer him comfort—something that she didn't think he'd had since the last time they were together.

"Ms. Lockwood."

The man standing behind Quinten pulled her gaze away and stepped forward. "I'm Warden

Jonathan Roscoe."

Saige nodded, afraid to talk in case she burst into tears.

"As you probably imagine," the warden continued. "I don't usually meet with visitors, but I was curious about this meeting. You're the victim, but wanted to meet with Quinten. We get this occasionally, but I've always wondered as to Quinten's guilt."

That got Quinten's attention as he turned abruptly to stare at the warden before his gaze landed back on Saige.

"I know about your memory loss, but I have to ask you, is Quinten guilty, Ms. Lockwood?"

Saige ignored the tears that had started to run down her face while her gaze stayed on Quinten. "No … Since I saw Quinten on television—twelve days ago—I've been getting bits of my memory back. The man who took me had white hands. No markings. Quinten's hands were"—she glanced at his hands—"and still are, large, and he has the vine tattoos that wrap around his two middle fingers."

The warden didn't seem surprised. "Have you told anyone else? The governor?"

"Yes." Saige wiped at her tears. "Detective

Robinson, and Daniel Sterling, Quinten's defense attorney. He's writing a report for the governor to request a stay."

Saige held her pleading eyes on the warden. "Can I ... can I please move closer to Quinten."

The warden looked between them, and just when she thought he'd refuse, he nodded. "For a minute, but Quinten stays seated."

She nodded, and slowly stood on legs that she wasn't sure would hold her up. Quinten didn't move, but watched her intently as she approached.

When she was within touching distance, Saige dropped to her knees and reached for his hands. She slowly caressed over his tattoo on the back and felt his quiver in response. Her eyes moved back to his face that was covered with tears.

Her tears flowed freely as she reached up and cupped his bearded jaw. He leaned into her touch and, with her other hand, threaded her fingers through the soft hair of his beard. "I remember doing this," she whispered, her vision going blurry with tears. "I remember." Her hand slipped from his jaw to the nape of his neck as she leaned closer, her other hand grasping his.

Quinten dropped his forehead and Saige could

see the fight going on inside of him. She knew he didn't want to break down … knew that he wanted to reach for her like she reached for him. Then his watery eyes met hers. "I love you, Saige. Don't ever forget how much I love you. Promise me."

Saige had no fight left in her and sobbed at the desperation behind Quinten's words. "I love you too, and I promise I won't ever forget how much you love me, but you have to promise me that you won't give up. We're trying to get you a stay, and Alex and Coulter both think that we have enough to put doubt on your original trial to get a new one. We're trying."

"I'm sorry to do this," the warden interrupted, "but Quinten needs to be escorted back to his cell."

How was she supposed to let go of him? Even without all her memories of their time together she felt the connection that had obviously been there before.

"Saige," Coulter lifted her to her feet, but Quinten kept a tight hold on her hand, as though he couldn't let her go either.

When Quinten stood, Saige leaned into him and wrapped an arm around his waist to hold him close, her face buried in his neck. "I'll be back. I promise." She raised her face to his and placed a tender kiss to his lips. "I love you."

"It's time," the warden interjected.

She felt Coulter behind her. He wrapped an arm around her waist, tugging her back and away from Quinten, her fingers reached to hold on to him even as he was led out of the room.

"Saige, you have to calm down." Coulter turned her to face him and cupped her cheeks. "Look at me. Now, Saige." She met his concerned eyes, her sobs slowed at the urgency in Coulter's tone. "That's better. Listen to me. You need to calm down before the warden refuses you entry again. Do you hear me? He can do that."

The shock of Coulter's words penetrated and her sobs turned to hiccups as she took the tissue from him.

"I'm okay." She sniffled, and turned for the door.

"You're not," Coulter mumbled. "But I'll accept that until we get out of this place."

Quinten stopped outside of the room and stumbled into the wall. The guard went to move him along but the warden stopped him. "Give him a minute."

While he'd waited for Saige to walk into the room, he hadn't known what to expect, and that in there, wasn't even like anything he'd imagined. His heart had nearly pounded out of his chest when Saige had entered. Although she'd changed her hair color, she was still the woman he loved. She was still *her*.

Her touch had unmanned him—the first touch from someone who cared about him in eight years. He knew touching was prohibited between prisoners and visitors, so he'd been surprised that the warden had allowed it. A part of him wished that he hadn't because he now craved more.

Why had the warden been so lenient with him, not that he was about to complain, but he needed to know. His eyes sought out those of the warden. "Why did you allow that?"

Warden Roscoe nodded to the guard. "We'll talk in your cell."

Quinten let them lead him back to his small space and tried to control his breathing so he didn't panic. The shackles came off and then he dropped to his bed and placed his head into his hands.

"Is there anything else you can tell me to help your case? Anyone who seemed out of place during the trial?"

Quinten met Roscoe's gaze. "Why now?"

"I've always wondered about your guilt, something a man in my position is not supposed to do. I see people confessing their innocence every day and it has never been my job to question what the courts have decided. But you are different. I've been around killers for years and never have I met anyone like you before. Hearing Ms. Lockwood, the victim, made me realize that something isn't right."

"You don't get a say in what happens to me now the governor has signed the … *warrant*." He could barely say the word.

"I can write a letter in support of a stay."

Quinten's eyes snapped to him. "You'd do that?"

"It's unethical to get involved this closely, but I couldn't live with myself if I didn't try to help you." He gave him a sad glance as he stepped away from the bars. "I can't promise you anything other than I'll write the letter. The rest is up to the governor, and the committee."

"Thank you."

He nodded and went to step away before he stopped and looked back at Quinten. "In the meantime, try to think about people who were around back then ... people who were around you immediately before and after your arrest ... in court during the trial. It would give the detective more leads and get him closer to finding the real culprit." With those words the warden nodded again, and disappeared.

Left alone, Quinten knew that he shouldn't hope, but he'd been offered a lifeline and he wanted to grab it and hold tight.

He should never have been arrested or convicted. The conviction had been a shock because he truly believed that they'd see the truth. Instead, they'd seen what the prosecution had wanted them to see.

But, after seeing Saige, his body was wrung out emotionally and the anger had left him for now. It would be back before too long, but all he felt was sadness for what could have been with Saige.

Regardless of her family status within the community, he knew deep in his heart that they'd have made it work, because he couldn't think about anything else.

As he lay down on his bed, he prayed that she hadn't been scared off and that she'd be back.

I really shouldn't have followed Saige and Robinson to the prison—too risky—but I hadn't been able to resist.

It shouldn't have been a surprise when I discovered that Saige was being allowed to visit Quinten, but it had been. It made me wonder what she'd remembered about her lover.

While I wait for them to come back outside, the heat makes my clothing stick to my body, but an hour later makes the discomfort worthwhile. The tears on her pretty young face as Coulter leads her to his car are real.

I wince and rub at my chest before I can sensor the movement. What am I doing? I really don't feel anything for her. Why should I? She fell in love with a Peterson.

I'm angry but I admit to myself that I do feel for Saige Lockwood because she's been a pawn in whatever game her father is playing for a long time.

If anyone deserves to be happy then it's her.

With his head down, minding his own business, Alex felt the eyes of the barbershop quartet watching his every move. He paused and glared back, but not one of the old guys flinched. Mr. Matheson, at the end, used to own the hardware store, which now belonged to his son and grandson. His left eye twitched when Alex turned and crossed the street toward them.

Movement out of the corner of his eye caught his attention as he stepped off the sidewalk. He turned and frowned when he realized it was Christina. She sat in the car with her forehead pressed against her hands on the steering wheel.

He was tempted to turn and ignore her. She'd gotten to him before, and more so now. Her confession had been a surprise and he knew, without having to ask, that Saige had no idea that her stepmother was anything but self-centered.

Alex should be running in the opposite direction, but he found his feet moving toward the woman in the car. The woman who looked like her world was being destroyed with every second that ticked by.

He didn't wait for an invitation and opened her door to her shocked surprise. "What happened?"

Christina lifted her tear-stained face up to his. "Someone tried to run me off the road." Her lips trembled and he could see by the way her body folded in on itself just how shaken she was.

"Come with me." He didn't give her a choice and helped her out of the car. "Are you hurt anywhere?"

"Other than shaken, I'm fine."

Alex wrapped an arm around her shoulders and pulled her between two stores, away from prying eyes of the townsfolk. Once hidden, Alex tugged her into his arms and held her, letting her cry her shock out. "I have you," he mumbled, and rolled his eyes when he realized how he sounded—as though he cared.

He let Christina pull away while she searched in her purse for a Kleenex. Seconds later, she met his gaze. "Thank you. You surprised me."

He laughed. "I surprised myself." He frowned. "You're married and I'm an asshole."

Christina said, "Don't say that. I know our

previous meetings haven't gone so well, but last night was, different." She blushed. "I know even if I wasn't married that you wouldn't look at me as permanent. For what it's worth, thank you. And thank you for today as well."

Alex heard the words and then heard the vulnerability in her voice. He knew that she thought her words were the truth, but he wasn't too sure anymore. There was certainly something about Christina that had held his interest over the years—something there that caused his heart to ache at her obvious distress.

He pulled her close. "Listen to me, okay. I want you to stay with me until I can get you home."

"Alex, you're worrying me."

"I know." He touched his forehead against hers and wondered whether or not she could handle the truth.

Alex knew she would hear it from elsewhere, so he briefly closed his eyes, and said, "There have been murders." Christina gasped and fear filled her eyes as he continued. "Jocelyn was the first to be discovered, but it appears that her death was not long after Quinten was sentenced." He rubbed the nape of her neck with his thumb. "Since then, two other women have been killed within hours of me *being* with them."

She winced at his bluntness.

"I didn't think last night and I should have. But this morning I did and realized that it was morning and you were still alive so I breathed a huge sigh of relief."

"I don't know what to say." Christina quivered against him, and moved closer into his loose embrace, which tightened. "I guess I should count my lucky stars, huh?"

"I'm not sure what's happening, but I'm wondering if there's a reason why he didn't come after you."

Her eyes widened. "Aren't you forgetting something?" She pointed toward her car.

"I have a feeling that if he wanted you dead, you would be." He grabbed her shoulders. "Did you see the plates on the car that went after you?"

She bit her lip. "No. I didn't think about it. I was stupid." Her forehead dropped to his chest.

"Christina, you have to be careful, okay?"

She nodded. "So what is going to happen now?"

"I don't know." He sighed. "What I do know is

that you're staying with me and I'll drive you home after I've spoken to Coulter. He isn't that far out. Saige texted me not too long ago that they were almost back ... we'll work it out." He kissed her forehead, squeezed her hand and stepped back.

His gaze swept the area and he spotted Paul Lewis in the doorway of the pharmacy, staring right at them.

Alex narrowed his eyes and watched as the man scurried back inside, and then Coulter drove up with Saige riding shotgun.

Alex could only hope the detective wouldn't be too annoyed with him for originally lying about when he'd last seen both Fern and Tracy.

Christina ran scared this afternoon. The fear on her face when she thought I actually wanted to cause her harm should have filled me with excitement, but it hadn't. I don't want to hurt Christina. No way will I ever harm a hair on her blond head. If I could love anyone, it would be her.

"I love you, Saige..."

"You'll never have him..."

"He's not good enough for you..."

"I'll help you..."

"Don't tell..."

"He's not who you think he is..."

"It's killing me to watch you leave..."

"Come back to me, babe..."

Darkness started to engulf her. Her body was chilled, her limbs heavy, sluggish. A sixth sense told her to run, but she couldn't move. Icy fear clutched around her heart as her senses started to disappear and her eyes fluttered closed.

Day 13

"Saige, what's going on?" her father asked, coming into the living room with a very rumpled looking Detective Robinson on his heels.

When she'd woken up screaming, Alex had been the one to come barging into her room, and he ended up calling Coulter to come to the house.

As she watched Coulter pour coffee into a mug from the sideboard, she answered her father, "I got my memory back."

Coulter burnt himself with coffee and cursed. Saige turned toward her father and watched him drop into a chair beside Christina, who sat huddled into a thick bathrobe on the sofa. Alex sat at the opposite end and Saige caught his quick glance at her stepmother, which confused her all the more. She thought they were at war with each other.

"Alex hinted at something when he called me. Do you mind if I record what's said?" Coulter asked.

Saige bit her lip and nodded. "It's okay."

Coulter moved forward and after they tested that his cell picked up her voice clearly, he then placed it on the arm of the chair Saige curled up in.

"Go ahead, Saige," Coulter encouraged.

Saige closed her eyes to settle herself and then started her story from that night.

It had been a warm day, but from the minute she'd started out to Port Jude, the heavens had opened and bombarded her car with rain, which made visibility bad. Night had started to fall halfway into her journey because she'd been late leaving after talking to Quinten. At first, she hadn't wanted him to know that she was on her way to him for the weekend, but she'd ended up giving it away. Just the sound of his excitement told her how right her decision had been.

Although it was only a two-hour drive between

Tampa and Port Jude, a four hour round trip wasn't feasible all the time. They would have to work it out because she realized earlier in the day that she couldn't go weeks without seeing him. Quinten had been just as miserable without her.

Leaving the main route, Saige started to wonder about the wisdom of the trip. She should have waited until early morning and set out at first light instead of driving in the pounding rain.

Her fists gripped the steering wheel and her stomach clenched with nerves as she peered out of the windshield. Driving past the sign welcoming tourists to Port Jude, Saige sighed in relief. She only had another twenty minutes or so before she hit the turn to her father's house, and the boathouse where she knew Quinten was waiting for her.

A pop, and another pop, startled her. Her car started to slip across the slick road, followed by more popping noises.

Saige shrieked as she wrestled with the steering wheel. She managed to bring the car to a stop along the side of the road without any damage to it or herself.

Her hands trembled and blood rushed through her head and ears. She rested her forehead against the steering wheel and concentrated on breathing in and out to steady herself.

"Oh boy," she moaned, realizing the predicament she was in, and it wasn't good.

She couldn't see anything through the lashing rain and the darkness that surrounded the car.

Turning, Saige tipped her purse onto the passenger seat and grabbed her cell to call Quinten. But as she swiped her finger across the screen, she stared at it in shock and panic.

She gave it a shake and kept trying, but nothing. The battery was dead. Even as the realization sank in, she kept trying in hope that it would come to life.

Nothing.

Tears slipped down her face as she glanced through the windshield once again. She'd have to walk into town, which lucky for her was only a thirty-minute walk away. But it was dark and, if she was honest, the thought of walking along this stretch of road scared the crap out of her. She didn't have much choice unless she wanted to spend the night where she was.

She leaned her head back against the seat and tried to get herself together.

She could do this.

She really could.

"Here goes nothing," she mumbled and grabbed the flashlight from the pocket in the door. She climbed out and the minute she did, she was drenched to the skin. She hadn't thought to bring a jacket even though the weatherman had warned of a surprise cold front hitting the area—earlier in the day it had been in the high eighties.

Shivering, Saige switched the flashlight on and felt the nerves in her stomach take flight. The forest surrounding her was dark with lots of places for someone to hide.

Saige gulped, her heart thumped wildly in her chest as she pushed away from the car. She'd only gotten a foot in front when the beam from her flashlight landed on a pair of boots. She froze, her heart hammering in her throat as she slowly moved the beam upwards, and screamed. She fumbled with the flashlight but managed to keep a hold of it and shined it in Jocelyn's face.

"Well...well...well, if it isn't the whore," Jocelyn sneered, her eyes hard and evil.

Shocked, Saige shouted back, "What the hell are you doing out here?" She waved her arms around.

"Normal people don't lurk around in the woods," Saige yelled, fear lacing her words.

"I'm waiting for you, of course," Jocelyn told her, and pointed back toward the road. "Shine your light over there."

Saige didn't know whether or not to trust Jocelyn enough to take her eyes from her, but she was curious. She turned slowly, and gasped when the beam of light landed on spikes in the middle of the road. A shiver of panic shot through her.

She felt as if a hand had closed around her throat while her mind ran in different directions at what was really going on. One thing she was certain of was that Jocelyn was crazy.

Shocked, Saige stared and gaped at the deranged woman standing in the rain. Jocelyn's dark hair was drenched and hung like spikes around her face. Saige tried to open her mouth to say something but couldn't find the words. She said, "Are you crazy? Oh my God! I can't believe you'd stoop to this level."

"You're trying to steal my husband, but I can tell you now that it won't work. He loves me and just wanted to sample innocence for a change."

Saige clenched her jaw knowing that Jocelyn

spoke nothing but lies. Quinten and Alex hated the woman, and the only reason why Quinten was still in the house with her was because he owned the house. It had been his mother's until she signed it over to him when she went into the residential care home, and no way did he want Jocelyn to get a hold of it.

"You don't believe me?"

"No. Maybe, if I didn't know your reputation around town. But no, I don't believe a word out of your mouth. I wouldn't unless it was Quinten standing in front of me, telling me."

Jocelyn's face twisted in anger and, for the first time, real fear slithered down Saige's spine.

"You'll never have him," Jocelyn growled, seconds before Saige felt a presence behind her.

A hand covered her mouth and nose; a sickly, sweet smell slowly crept into her system, causing her stomach to roll.

She fought and tried to elbow the person behind her, but they were too strong. Her hands reached over her head and yanked at hair, which earned her a curse. The hold around her stomach tightened and, as she started to lose the fight, she heard Jocelyn say, "I'll deal with Quinten."

Saige tried one last struggle and heard Jocelyn laugh. "You'll never see him again, bitch."

When Saige came back to the present, Coulter was sitting on the coffee table in front of her with her hands inside of his. Tears trickled down her face, and she felt the anger that radiated off of Alex.

"That bitch is lucky she's already dead," Alex fumed. "All along it was her." He paced. "Obviously someone else helped her, and it wasn't Quinten."

Coulter placed her hands on her lap and stood to face Alex. "Getting worked up now isn't going to help anyone, but I'm going to head to the sheriff's office and type up the report. I'll need everyone's signature as witnesses and then I'll get it to Daniel Sterling."

"Do you think Quinten will be released?" Christina whispered. The question had all eyes on her.

"Don't be stupid. Of course he won't be released," her father snapped.

"What the fuck," Alex exclaimed. "Eventually he will be released ... and don't fucking talk to her like that."

Saige blinked, startled at Alex's outburst.

"She,"—her father pointed at Christina—"is my wife. I will talk to her as I please."

"Let's calm down," Coulter advised. "Arguing isn't going to help." He turned to Christina who had a stunned look on her face. "To answer your question, he won't be released immediately, but there shouldn't be any problem getting a stay. He was still convicted for the murder of those girls, which is a problem, but now we can get Saige on the stand to tell her story."

"I hate this," Saige mumbled, resting her head in her hands. "It's like waking up in the middle of a nightmare."

Her father cleared his throat. "Do you remember anything else?"

"Yes, but everything is jumbled and a lot of it is personal. I'll let you know if I remember anything else about that night and the days after I was taken." Saige wanted to keep some things to herself and not just about her and Quinten.

She stared at her dad and tried to look at him differently than she'd done as a little girl and up until she'd lost her memory. Her memory was at odds but she knew everything she'd remembered was real. She could hear his raised voice in her ears and Christina's soft words as she struggled to keep him quiet.

It had been after a party at the house. Her father was livid and had hit Christina across the face, knocking her to the ground. He'd stood over her accusing her of having an affair with Alex.

Her father hadn't known Saige was still awake, and she'd heard their argument. At the time, Saige had been brokenhearted to discover what her father was really like. She knew Alex thought Christina had been like Jocelyn, when the truth was Christina had more or less been a nun compared to her unfaithful father.

She had no idea what life had been like at the house for Christina. Saige had always presumed her stepmother tolerated her rather than liked her, but she couldn't have been more wrong. Christina had told her father she'd never leave him as long as Saige still lived at home because she didn't trust him with her. That had shocked and confused Saige back then, and it confused her all the more now. She wondered what Christina meant by not trusting her father with her.

"Saige." Coulter snapped his fingers in front of

her face.

She blinked and her gaze slid from her dad's face before she focused on Coulter. "Sorry," she mumbled. "Memories of Quinten are bombarding me."

Coulter offered her a wry smile. "Walk me out." He held her gaze, conveying he wanted a minute alone with her.

Saige glanced at the others and followed Coulter into the foyer where he wasted no time and asked her, "Is all your memory back?"

"I think so." Saige rubbed at her temples. "I don't remember much about being held in the shack." Her heart thumped hard as she gulped down the fear that rose when she thought about it. "I think they must have kept me drugged. There are snippets of pain, and white hands and wrists." She stepped outside and moved with Coulter toward his car.

Coulter turned to her. "I talked to the sheriff and he felt your statement was more rehearsed than what had actually happened. He thought perhaps Christina had coached you. Do you remember, Saige?"

Saige felt the blood leave her face, and then

Coulter had a hold of her arm as he shoved her into the car, and crouched down beside her. "Sit and breathe."

"I'm okay. My memory is still trying to slip into the correct timeline. It was Christina who told me what to say, but she kept looking at her cell. Thinking about it now, it was as though she was reading from her phone, and I remember that I noticed her hands trembled. Perhaps someone else had told her what to tell me." Saige frowned. "My father influenced my decision over the photograph."

"How? He wasn't in the room."

"No, he wasn't. He woke me up before you all entered and told me to only choose the man I recognized. He stressed that so many times that I remember biting my lip so I didn't yell at him to stop." She didn't want to believe her father would do something like that. "He gave Christina an intense look and told her to make sure I selected the right picture." Saige balled her fists in anger.

"Why the hell would my father do that, Coulter? Why would he want Quinten in prison and the real person to walk free? That doesn't make sense." She dropped her head into her hands in frustration.

"I don't know."

Saige looked up and met Coulter's gaze. "You have an idea."

Coulter glanced away quickly before holding her stare. "Did your father know about Quinten and you?"

Saige nodded.

"Was he happy that you were together?"

"He wasn't happy because Quinten was still married. We argued about that. I refused to stop seeing him."

"That would explain your father's hang up with Quinten, but if that was the case, why didn't he want the real culprit behind bars? If you were my daughter, I'd want the real bastard put away. I'd want to rip his throat out."

"I can't think about that right now," Saige said, and she realized she was exhausted. "The real man who partnered with Jocelyn is still out there, and I'm not going to lie … I'm afraid he's going to want to finish what he started with me." She stood from his car. "Thank you for believing me, and for helping Quinten."

"No thanks needed, Saige. I swore to uphold

the law and that's what I'm doing. I just wish there had been more help back then so Quinten hadn't been convicted." He let out a sigh. "You go on back inside and try and get a few hours of sleep. I'll talk to Daniel Sterling later and I'll let you know when there's something to know."

Saige nodded and walked back inside.

Alex rubbed his chest and wished that things had been different for him and Christina. Even as he craved to have his arms around her, he knew that they weren't meant to be because of the main obstacle keeping them apart—her marriage. It didn't stop his heart from aching though.

He watched a tired Saige walk back into the room and glance around. "Where's Dad gone?" she asked as she slumped down into the chair she'd occupied since she brought them all together.

"He's gone to dress," Christina replied, her legs folded under her on one end of the sofa.

Watching Saige fight a yawn behind her hands, Alex suggested, "Why don't you both go back to bed."

"If I thought I'd be able to get back to sleep, I

would, but I think I'm awake for the day now." Saige yawned again and settled back down.

"I'll go back to bed soon." Christina glanced toward the stairs and then at him—she was avoiding Richard.

Alex cleared his throat and paced. "I need to tell you both something." He glanced from Christina to Saige and back again. "The night Fern died she told me she knew something—hinted that it was about Quinten's case. I could have misunderstood but I don't think I did."

He continued. "Tracy also told me the night she died that she knew who had taken Saige, and then she'd slammed the door in my face. I don't have any idea as to what either of them knew."

Saige sat up and focused her gaze on him.

Alex ran his hands wearily over his face. "According to Daniel there is nothing new that has come to light." He dropped onto the sofa beside Christina, who'd stayed silent throughout everything. "What do you think?" he asked her.

Christina's eyes flickered around the room before landing on Saige. "I think that Quinten is innocent and that someone wanted him out of the way for a reason," she whispered. "I'd try and figure out why." Christina stood the minute the words left her mouth. "I'll see you both later."

Alex frowned as he watched her leave the room, but Saige's next words made him swivel to stare at her.

"What's going on between you and my stepmother?"

He thought about lying but there were enough lies running around, and that had to stop. "I was in love with her a long time ago, and seeing her again has thrown me off. I'm like Quinten, unable to switch my feelings on and off like a faucet."

"I'm guessing that means you're still in love with her, huh?"

"I wish I wasn't, but there you have it." Alex shoved his hands into the pockets of his sweats and moved to the window.

Saige followed.

Standing together they watched the sun start to rise over the ocean when Saige said, "You had an affair with Christina before."

Alex felt his heart drop to his toes.

"I overheard my father shouting at her for being with you. He told her it had to stop, otherwise there would be consequences, which doesn't make sense considering he didn't fire you."

"I'm not sure why he kept us working at the house, although it would have been hard to find someone else to finish what we'd started." He shrugged. "I don't want to talk about Christina, although, I do think you have the wrong impression of her."

Alex turned Saige to face him. "So why don't you find a time to chat with her and see what she has to say. If you push her, you might get her to talk more than I can."

Saige chuckled. "I'm sure you'd be able to get her to talk if you really tried."

He tilted his head to the side, studying her. "Why aren't you bothered about Christina and me?"

Saige bit her lip. "I didn't only find out about Christina's affair with you that day. I also learned about my father's *numerous* affairs. Apparently, he only married Christina for her money, which I have to say, I had no idea she came into the marriage with any. I feel sorry for her really. I'm also upset that I'm discovering a different side to my father." She shrugged. "I always thought he was a pleasant, caring guy. I'm not sure who he really is anymore."

Alex wrapped an arm around her shoulders and tugged her close, wanting to offer her comfort, and maybe, have some comfort for a change.

Sighing, Saige settled against him and he wondered what she was thinking ... or remembering.

He'd had a soft spot for her when they first met, and more so after she'd put a smile back on his brother's face. She'd made Quinten happy, and Alex had finally started to believe that she would again. He had hope for the first time in a long time that everything would work out for his brother.

He also had an idea on where to start looking for the man who assisted Jocelyn with Saige.

"Hey, Quinten."

He looked up as the guard stood in front of the cell but stayed silent.

"The warden has been called to a meeting with the governor, first thing tomorrow morning while they consider a stay." The guard shrugged. "Thought you'd want to know." He walked away.

Quinten clutched Saige's book in his hand and

held it against his chest while he absorbed the shock. As much as he'd hoped, he didn't really believe that his case would get as far as being heard.

He moved slowly to his bed and laid down, the book still clutched against his chest.

A stay didn't mean he would be free. It meant that he'd have time, and the doubts that were being cast would put things in the right direction toward a new trial with a new jury. The case had been a mess. The supermajority vote shouldn't have happened. He always believed there should be an all juror vote on a death penalty case. Something that still wouldn't happen unless the law was changed within the state.

He'd think about all that later and just pray that the governor's decision was in his favor.

Saige had been restless for most of the day, which was why she'd decided to take a walk to the boathouse. The narrow wooden dock behind had always been one of her favorite escapes.

Her feet dangled in the water while the gentle lap of the waves calmed her. Sun sparkled on the water as she prayed Quinten would eventually be given the chance to start a new life—hopefully with her.

If only—

The creek of the first wooden plank drew Saige's attention back toward the boathouse. She watched as Christina hesitated and then slowly moved closer. A slither of guilt crossed her mind, causing Saige to frown. She'd always had a love-hate relationship with her stepmother, but since she remembered what Christina and her father's relationship had been like, she felt guilty for not giving the woman a chance, regardless of her father's thoughts on the matter.

"Mind if I join you," Christina asked, her hands fluttering nervously in front of her.

Saige nodded.

Once Christina sat beside her, silence followed until Saige couldn't take it anymore. "What's going on?"

Christina sighed and glanced back toward the main house. "Lots of things." She swiped at one of her eyes.

"Christina?"

"You know about Alex and I, don't you?"

Christina looked at her.

"Yes."

Christina smiled, ignoring the tears that ran down her face. "I married your father to get away from my controlling family. I was in my twenties and still jumped when they told me to do something. I hated it. Except I jumped from the frying pan into the fire." She gave a mirthless laugh. "Then I met Alex. He was everything I wasn't supposed to be attracted to, but I couldn't stop it and, for the first time in my life, I was in love. I was stuck between being with him and staying here for you." She shrugged.

"I don't understand. Why would you stay because of me?" There was no reason that Saige could think of.

"Your father is very possessive, Saige. I didn't think that he'd ever hurt you physically, but he wanted you under his control to do what he wanted. When I was around, he wasn't as bad with you, but, other times, he would irritate you and you'd fight back. That frightened me."

"I remember you always trying to defuse the situation when we'd argue. What you've said throws it all into a different light."

"I'm sorry to be the one to burst your bubble about your father, but I can't stay around any longer, Saige. I will until all this with Quinten is over with, but then I'm leaving."

Saige took hold of Christina's hand, and rested her head against her shoulder. "I wish we could have been friends."

"Me too." Christina sniffled and grabbed a tissue from her bra.

"Can I ask you something?" Saige asked once Christina cleaned herself up.

Christina frowned. "You can ask me anything. I hate that I was never there for you."

"My father kept you away from me. I heard that from his mouth when neither of you knew I was around." Saige shrugged. "What I wanted to ask was about Alex. Do you still love him?"

"I don't even need to think about the answer because I do. I always will. I said some pretty bad things to him back then to make him leave. I was so worried about what Richard would do if I continued seeing him. I was afraid. At the time, I had no idea Richard had already talked to Alex. He'd told him that he was one in a string of affairs. It really hurt that Alex believed him. In the end, it was easier to let him think it was true because that would mean he'd stay away from me. My heart broke that day."

Saige pulled Christina into her arms and let her cry as her anger with her father grew. He'd been the guilty one for having numerous affairs, not Christina. Saige's heart broke now that she was learning and remembering another side of her father that she'd forgotten about.

He'd certainly been loving, especially since she was in the hospital. But before she was taken, they'd argued and had many a disagreement about how he thought Saige should live her life, as opposed to how she wanted to live it.

Her father hadn't agreed with her choice in men either. To their face, he'd been polite, but she remembered hearing him ranting on and on to Christina about every boyfriend she'd brought home. She remembered how violent those arguments had become when he talked about Quinten and how he wasn't good enough for her.

She'd hated that.

About to ask Christina about Quinten, raindrops landed on Saige's bare shoulders. She glanced at her stepmother, who'd glanced back at her. "We better hurry," Christina suggested.

Scrambling up, they jogged along the dock toward the boathouse as the drops became a lot heavier.

"I have to be somewhere soon so I'll see you in the morning," Christina said as she continued jogging up to the house. She'd be soaked by the time she got there.

"What were you talking about?"

Saige jumped a mile and laughed. "You scared the crap out of me, Alex."

"Sorry." He grinned, although it was clear from the mischievous look on his face that he wasn't sorry at all.

"Hmm." Saige stood under the overhang above the door to the boathouse and watched Alex as he watched her. She smiled. "She told me what my father told you about her, which was a lie in case you were wondering."

Alex blinked and his eyes had lost all humor. "She told you that?"

Saige tipped her head to the side and realized Alex had been hurt just as much as Christina had. "I overheard it, first out of my father's mouth. He hit her and told her to end your affair and if she didn't, he'd end it for her, and not in a way that she'd like. He threatened you, and at that point, Christina agreed to end it. She loved you, Alex, and wanted you safe. It hurt her that you believed what my father had told you."

Alex shoved his hands into his pockets. "It was obvious that she needed me to leave her alone, so I chose to let her believe what she did. I went away and got drunk. Just when I decided I wasn't willing to give her up and intended to fight for her, all the shit with you and Quinten happened."

Saige waited until he met her gaze. "Don't let her go this time." Once her words had been received, she decided against the boathouse and went back up to the house.

Her memory is back, but so far she hasn't identified me as being the one to have taken her—to torture her.

I enjoyed having her under my control. She'd made me ache, as she lay naked, and tied down, on my table. To this day I've never understood why I hadn't fucked her like I had with the others. Or maybe I did know.

It doesn't matter anymore.

Quinten would be released in the end I know that now. Maybe the man has been punished enough. I'm not angry that my first plan failed. After all he has served eight years behind bars while others have suffered on the outside knowing Quinten is innocent. That will have to be enough for now.

I certainly haven't finished with my revenge. It will just get more interesting.

With Christina in the picture a new plan has formed, and it will start tomorrow. There will be no turning back.

I can't wait to see the confusion I will cause, or the shock when I'm finally discovered.

Everything has always been black and white for me: good vs evil.

I am pure evil, and for that I blame the choice my family made before I was old enough to understand anything.

Revenge will continue to be taken on those who have done me wrong.

Day 14

Unable to sit at home any longer, Saige headed into town with the plan of going into the pharmacy again. With a bit of luck, Paul would be inside stocking the shelves. She wanted to talk to him because the last time she'd been inside she'd gotten the feeling he was nervous and she wanted to know why.

She'd gone to school with Paul but had never really spoken to him. He'd been a loner and others had been cruel with the name-calling. Back then, his mother, Agnes, used to make the best milkshakes anyone had ever had.

A lot had changed in Port Jude over the years and the town was more geared toward tourists passing through than for the people who lived in the area. It was a shame to see some of the changes from what she'd held as fond childhood memories.

Some things would probably never change and that was the barbershop quartet. Mr. Matheson was the eldest and had held his chair from when she'd been in high school, and he never missed a thing. As she started across the street, he watched her—so did the others.

"You stepping inside?" Rosa asked, pulling Saige out of her reverie.

Rosa was forever fifty, probably closer to ninety now. Her hair was pure white and her brown wrinkled face had aged well, and she always had a welcoming smile. Although she smiled now for Saige, the elderly woman had a frown marring her brow.

Saige smiled. "I am. How are you today?"

"Just fine."

Saige went to step past Rosa but paused when the other woman took hold of her wrist. "I never believed that young man had anything to do with your abduction," she whispered before skittering away like a scared mouse.

Saige frowned after her as she continued into the pharmacy. Did Rosa know something?

Rubbing her brow, Saige turned and met Paul's gaze. The minute she did, Paul looked away and continued with his work. His hands trembled the closer Saige got to him.

Saige glanced around and noticed he was alone, which was good. If Agnes had been there, then Saige's chances of talking to the man would have been zero.

"Afternoon, Paul," she said, hoping to put him at ease. "It's too warm to be outside and I started reminiscing about the milkshakes that your mother used to sell here. Do you remember? They were so popular that the kids would grumble when she closed that down during the winter months."

Paul smiled. "I remember," he mumbled. "You used to like the strawberry and peanut butter one." He screwed his face up. "I remember trying that one and it made me sick."

"It was my favorite back then. I don't think I could drink it now though. Now I'm more of a coffee drinker than anything." She smiled. "How are you doing?"

He hesitated. "I'm doing well. Still hoping to get away from small-time life, but it isn't easy," he whispered. "Everyone knows something about someone else that can get them into trouble. I know it's what happens when you live in a place like Port Jude, but I hate that. At least, no one knows my secret." He grinned but it didn't reach his eyes. A chill raced down her spine forcing her to take a step back.

"Paul," Agnes snapped, coming through the front door, "get back to work."

Saige hesitated before she moved further away from Paul and turned to Agnes. "I'm sorry. That was my fault. We were just talking about the milkshakes you used to make. I'm sorry, again." Saige made her way outside and sagged in relief.

Paul had looked at her strangely and the chill she'd felt had been real. Which begged the question as to what secret did he have that no one else knew about?

She bet at least one person knew his secret, and she knew where to start as she glanced across the street.

Mr. Matheson watched her watching them. It was a surprise when he stood and said something to his friends, then disappeared around the side of the store.

Saige darted across the street and down the side of the hardware store, heading toward where Mr. Matheson had disappeared.

"You're going to get into trouble if you keep asking questions, especially if you keep going over there." Mr. Matheson pointed toward the pharmacy.

She ignored him. "You wanted me to come after you?"

"I couldn't very well talk to you with the others around, now could I?" he said. "Please stay away from there. Paul isn't right in the head. I don't trust him and you shouldn't either."

"Do you know what's going on? How I can help Quinten?" He looked around and started to back away from Saige. "Tell your detective friend to look closely at the locals—"

"But who?" Saige asked.

He glanced toward the pharmacy and said, "Paul." With his final word, he returned to his friends.

Slowly walking back the way she came, Saige was confused about Paul. He had given her chills, but surely she'd know if he had been the one to take her. Wouldn't she? She'd gotten the sense that Quinten was innocent when she saw him on TV, so why wouldn't she feel something was more off than normal with Paul?

She would go crazy before this whole damn thing was over with.

Back on Main Street, Saige was about to step off the sidewalk to head toward her car when Coulter pulled up in front of her. "I've been trying to get in touch with you," he said, climbing from his car.

Saige quickly checked her cell and realized she somehow managed to switch it to silent. "Sorry. Have you heard anything?"

He nodded, his face solemn. Her heart sank.

As she felt the tears burning her eyes, Coulter grinned, and said, "The governor and the rest of the committee agreed on a stay. The official stay for Quinten James Peterson was signed about an hour ago."

Saige burst into tears and felt Coulter's arms wrap around her. "I didn't mean to make you cry."

"These are happy tears. I think," Saige said.

He laughed. "C'mon, get in. We're going to the prison to break the good news to Quinten. The warden has agreed to hold off."

She didn't need telling twice and practically jumped into Coulter's car. When she was strapped in and Coulter was navigating his car toward the prison, she told him about what Paul and Mr. Matheson had said.

"From what I remember, Paul wasn't around back then. He certainly wasn't questioned like the rest of the people in town. I think he was away at school."

"That would make sense because so was I. I'd have stayed there as well if I hadn't missed Quinten so much."

"I'll check out Paul when we get back from Harlington. The sheriff has been helpful and is allowing me to work out of their offices, which is better than the car." Coulter grinned. "I promise if there is something to find, then I'll find it." He paused. "I asked the Sheriff to call in the Feds. He agreed."

Saige nodded. "Extra help." She frowned. "Weren't they involved before?"

"It was kept local as far as I'm aware, although I have a vague recollection of Harris arguing with a federal agent."

Saige nodded. "Harris had a very strong opinion and wouldn't let anyone sway him off of it."

"I shouldn't speak ill of the dead, but that man should never have been a detective." Coulter glanced at her then back to the road. "Tell me about Quinten."

Saige rubbed at her brow, which seemed to be in constant pain these days, but she smiled at Coulter's question.

"Quinten used to fish a lot to get away from life in his house. He owned that house and refused to let Jocelyn have it, which was why he still lived in it with her even though he'd started the divorce process. I used to go fishing with him sometimes." Saige chuckled. "I wouldn't go anywhere near the bait and Quinten was good about that. He didn't tease me or anything, and he'd leave the bait a few feet from where we sat on the bank."

"He loves you, Saige, and I hope, really soon, that you both get that life back."

"Me too."

❖

He had a belly full of nerves as he waited in the visiting room for Detective Robinson. That was all he knew—the detective was on his way. Quinten had been too afraid to ask the guard if he knew why, which was something he'd usually have asked.

Sweat glistened on his forehead when footsteps could be heard moving closer to where he waited, and then, when the door opened, he felt as though his heart had stopped altogether. *Saige.*

Her eyes swam with tears as she tried to control her *unhappiness.* He couldn't look at anyone or anything else. She filled his vision and he knew that he'd love her until the day he died.

"Quinten," Detective Robinson drew his attention, but almost immediately it was back on Saige. "The governor granted you a stay."

He blinked and snapped his gaze back to the detective who nodded and smiled. "You heard me right. The governor has granted a stay. Your defense attorney put your case before the governor and the committee this morning."

Quinten had no words and even if he tried, he

didn't think anything would come out of his mouth. He was thankful to be sitting down because his legs felt like jelly as his whole body started to tremble, and then he cried.

In the next breath, he felt soft hands that could only be Saige's cup his head and bring him against her chest. She cradled him against her and cried with him. He felt her body shake and he'd give anything to be able to wrap his arms around her to keep her close. But that wouldn't happen today, if ever again.

Her fingers were gentle as they massaged his scalp and now that he started to calm down, he could smell the floral body lotion she always used. It teased his senses and started to make him uncomfortable in all the places that had ached for her since he'd been incarcerated.

He coughed and lifted his head to meet her watery gaze. "I love you," she whispered, causing his eyes to fill again.

He was an emotional wreck from the news they brought him but more so because of Saige's touch and closeness.

"Here," Warden Roscoe said, passing him and Saige each a tissue.

Saige stepped back and dried her face, which he also did, and only then did he allow his eyes to go to the warden. "What happens now?"

"You'll be moved back to a death row cell in the morning, but I'm hoping you won't be a resident here for much longer."

"How?" He had no idea how that could be possible. Saige could speak on his behalf about her abduction, but he had still been convicted of murdering the college girls.

Saige kneeled and took his large hands into her much smaller ones. "Don't give up hope. I love you, Quinten."

Rising up, she pressed a light kiss to his lips and smiled. "I promise to come back."

He nodded, and whispered, "I love you."

"I know."

Detective Robinson wrapped an arm around Saige's shoulders and led her from the room. It hurt not being the one to comfort her, but if he weren't in prison, then she wouldn't have needed comforting.

His head dropped to his chest with exhaustion. The stress and worry that he wouldn't be alive to see day twenty-nine was finally over, but his mind wondered what next. Would he really be cleared of all charges?

There had been a lot to take in during the course of the day, and Saige longed to be closer to Quinten, which was why she'd decided to spend the night in the boathouse. It had been their secret place and she still planned on keeping it that way. Tonight, however, she felt that she needed to be where they'd been at their happiest because having to leave him in that place had hurt her deeply.

Slipping through the door, she paused when she saw the shape of a man sitting in a chair facing her. She gasped and his head snapped up at the sound, giving her a clear picture of his features as the moonlight cast him in its glow.

Paul.

Her heart thudded wildly in her chest as she stood, watching him. Paul clutched something in his hands. It looked to be a wooden box and when she flicked on the light, she realized it was a jewelry box.

"I thought you would be in bed," Paul stated,

unmoving.

"I couldn't sleep." Saige stayed by the door and slowly started to back out.

He seemed cool as a cucumber while he clutched at the box with one hand and tapped the lid with his fingers. "I often come and sit in here when I've had enough of my mother going on and on about gossip. I have no interest in her gossip when mine is much more interesting." Paul smirked. "Bet you're curious."

Her first instinct was to turn and run, but she wanted to know what he knew. What if he knew something that would help set Quinten free? Did she want to take that chance? She'd never feared Paul before, like she did now.

"Okay, I'll bite. What gossip is more interesting than what your mother has to say?"

"Murder of course."

Her blood ran cold and shards of ice slithered down her spine. "Whose?" she asked, not sure she really wanted to know.

"Poor Quinten, the clock is running out for him. I can see him, sitting in a death watch cell, watching the clock, feeling every second slip by until he'll have no seconds left. It must crush him, especially since he didn't do it." He grinned. "Quinten wouldn't have harmed a fly and I'm sorry that he was the *Peterson* brother to end up in jail. That shouldn't have happened."

"What are you talking about?"

"Saige"—he stood—"you know exactly what I'm talking about. Jocelyn knew about me and that's why that bitch managed to talk me into taking you."

Saige took an involuntary step back and sagged into the chair by the door.

Paul ran his gaze over her. "Jocelyn was pissed as hell when Quinten found you. But I was relieved that you were free. I hated doing what I did, but I promised Jocelyn that I would do it. She wanted you dead. Did you know that?" He cocked his head to the side as though he was seeing something Saige couldn't. He gave her a sorrowful smile. "But I couldn't kill you. Growing up, you were one of the only kids to never call me names or ignore me. I liked you."

"How did Jocelyn talk you into taking me?" Saige asked, but she had a feeling she already knew.

"She said she loved me, taught me all about

sex. Told me that we'd be together once you were dead. I was stupid. She never would have given Quinten up for the likes of me. I grew to hate her." His mouth curled into a smile that was so sweet it was terrifying. His eyes glowed as though he was remembering a fond memory. "When I came for her, she begged me, told me she really did love me, but I knew the truth. And then she screamed ... and screamed ... but no one came to help her. She got what she deserved."

Oh God! Oh God!

Strength drained from her legs. Despite the warm night, she felt cold and her legs were heavy, unable to move. "The others," she barely whispered. He heard her though as he tilted his head to the side.

"I don't want Quinten to die, so I uncovered Jocelyn from where I buried her. It was close to where I went to school. Did you know that?" He didn't give her time to answer and carried on, "Then I watched to make sure everyone found the right clues."

No matter how she felt about Jocelyn, she hadn't deserved to die that way. "What about Fern?"

He smiled. "She was a bonus." His hand slid down his thigh and then back up as though his fingers were remembering the women he'd killed. "I found her when I was lurking outside of her apartment. I wanted the police to take a hard look at Alex, and what better victim than a girl he'd just fucked. She didn't fight. Rather fragile. Like a fawn." He chuckled at his own joke and Saige felt the bile burning her throat.

"The cops are stupid. They didn't look at Alex at all, which was why I needed to get to Tracy. She was different. Somehow, she knew that I'd taken you. I don't know how because she wouldn't tell me, but she knew. When she hooked up with Alex again, it was the perfect opportunity for me to shut the bitch up." He rubbed his jaw. "She was even more enjoyable than the rest. She fought hard and, at some point, I thought that maybe she'd get away, but she died eventually, just like the rest."

Saige tried to clear her head from the horror that Paul admitted to. Her lips felt numb as they formed around the word, "Why?"

Paul tilted his head to the side as he considered. "All I wanted this time was for Quinten to be set free. He's innocent in everything. He didn't murder anyone."

Saige's mind scrambled over all of it. She'd never have expected Paul Lewis to be the killer.

Paul stood and moved closer. "I have their jewelry." He grinned and it sent chills down her spine. "Do you want to see?"

She dreaded the answer, but asked, "Whose jewelry is it?"

"The college girls, of course." He said it as though she should have known, and placed it on the table not too far from where she sat. "I'll show you."

"I can't believe you killed them, or anyone ... Paul?" She met his gaze. "Please tell me you didn't do all this."

Something flickered in his eyes before he stared down at the jewelry box. "I can't do that, Saige. Enough is enough, and I realize now that the only way to help Quinten is to tell the truth. They won't give me the death penalty because I have mental problems." He smiled and it reminded Saige of a child on Christmas morning. "And I'll finally be free of my mother. I can live away from her and be taken care of. Eat regular food. Exercise. Read books that she hates. That's all I want."

Saige stared at him incredulously and sputtered, "But ... but ... Paul, why? You sound like you're talking about a dog."

"Because I am nothing but a dog," Paul snarled, the switch to anger was so sudden that Saige felt her breath catch in her throat. "That's what Mom calls me. A worthless dog who deserves to live in a dog house."

"Paul, please tell me the truth. Did you kill all those women? Please don't say yes just to get room and board away from your mother," Saige begged him.

"I killed them and I tried to blow up the detective's truck. That was a spur of the moment thing, and I'm kinda glad that it didn't work. Relieved actually. I wasn't thinking at the time. If I'd killed him, then they probably wouldn't have bothered about my mental problems with him being a cop." He waved his hands around.

It was at that point in Paul's confession that Saige heard rustling outside of the door at the same time Paul did. He jumped, startled, and looked at her and back to the door, and then back at her.

"Paul Lewis, keep your hands where I can see them," Coulter called as he came through the door, his weapon raised.

Paul laughed, the sound was high and strange in the quiet of the boathouse. "I won't fight. I promise. Please just take me away from here," Paul begged and then his laughter turned to sobs. He dropped to his knees and allowed Coulter to cuff him while he read Paul his Miranda rights.

Saige felt the blood flowing through her, warming her, so she struggled to her feet and made her way to the table with the jewelry box on it.

"Don't touch it," Coulter snapped, and winced. "Sorry. I don't want your fingerprints on it."

"Oh. I should have thought about that." Saige couldn't stop staring at the box though. "Is it really the jewelry from the girls?"

"Yes. It's been buried for years. I dug it up to add things from Fern and Tracy." Paul started to cry again. "I didn't want to hurt Tracy but she threatened to tell Alex. I was hiding alongside her house. He told her that he'd be back for answers, and then left. That's when I knew I had to shut her up. I wasn't ready to be arrested then."

"And you are now?" Coulter asked, a brow raised.

"Yes." He sobbed and his eyes burned with hatred as he said, "I was ready to kill her—my mother—and as much as I hate her, I would never forgive myself if I acted on it. It was time to turn myself in to protect her, and to finally be free of her."

Saige met Coulter's gaze and saw the same doubts shining in his eyes. Was Paul really the killer or was he lying to escape his mother?

"I know what you're both thinking. All you have to do is send my DNA for testing and it will be a match to one of the unidentified ones from the shack."

Coulter nodded and pulled his cell phone out of his pocket, calling in the arrest.

The sheriff arrived with the cavalry, and once they hauled Paul to the station, the sheriff, Coulter, and a deputy medical examiner carefully opened the box.

Sheriff Hodges cursed and Coulter's face tightened with anger before he met her curious gaze.

"It's the missing jewelry from the murdered

girls."

Blood thundered in her ears and her vision started to dim.

Quinten would be freed.

Coulter caught her as she passed out.

The excitement at watching the Oscar worthy performance by Paul Lewis still holds me in it's grip. The man had been so much better than I thought he would be.

What a surprise.

There had been a moment when I thought Paul would hurt Saige. I would have had to intervene, but as luck would have it, Paul backed down and I'd stayed hidden from sight.

I hope Paul remembers what else he is supposed to do. My plan will only fail now if Paul suddenly gets a case of cold feet.

In eight years Paul has never once let me down so I am confident he won't now.

Only time will tell.

Day 15

I really should have found a way to bug the Sheriff's office because not knowing what exactly is going on is driving me insane. The hub of activity now that I have spotted two Feds is getting more interesting than I thought possible.

I also wonder who the woman with bright orange hair is as she disappears inside the building? She appeared to be carrying a medical bag?

Rubbing my hands together, I glance around to make sure I'm alone, and then I pull out from my hiding place and head to my temporary home.

❖

Coulter had one hell of a headache when he came out of the interview room. Not only had Paul Lewis told them enough about each and every crime scene, going back to Kelsey Louise Ingram, the second college girl killed, he'd also told them how his own parents had treated him. Nothing should surprise him anymore, but he was.

He pressed a finger and thumb to the bridge of his nose and closed his eyes, praying the headache wouldn't turn into a migraine, and then … he smelled coffee—real coffee and not the junk they dished out at the sheriff's station.

His eyes snapped open and his heart fluttered in his chest.

"Amber?" he whispered, thinking his eyes were playing tricks on him. "It is you."

She smiled while he stared at her like an idiot. Her riot of fire-orange hair was loose down her back and she looked like she was fresh out of college in her jeans, t-shirt, and sweater. But just the sight of her made him wake up.

"Figured you'd need this." She handed him the cup. "I decided to drive up to take his DNA myself. I missed you."

"I shouldn't be glad you're here in the middle of the night, but I am."

"Good." Amber turned and smiled at someone to her right, but he couldn't take his eyes from her as his libido took on a life of its own.

Amber slipped her hand into his and gave a tug. "Saige is waiting for you."

Well, that snapped him out of his lustful thoughts. "She's still here?"

"She is. Wanted to wait and talk to you before she left."

"Okay."

Amber led him down the hallway and toward the waiting room where they found Saige. He offered her a tired smile when she met his gaze. "Have you given them your statement yet?"

She nodded. "Yeah. I have a copy and one of the FBI Agents faxed a copy to Daniel Sterling." She shrugged. "Daniel hadn't been too happy to be woken this late, but when I told him why it couldn't wait until morning, he was awake and waiting for the fax. He has it now and will wait to talk to you tomorrow, um, later today before he goes to the governor."

Coulter slumped down in the chair opposite

and smiled when Amber sat next to him, her hand slipped into his. He'd never had anyone to offer him comfort before, and he liked it. A lot.

He turned his attention back to Saige. "Saige, this is Amber McGregor. She's the ME in Tampa. She's here to administer the DNA test and see if it is a match with the DNA in the evidence file. I'm trying to cover all bases, but we have a confession. He's told us things that only the killer would know. Even though we have all that, I can't help feeling I'm missing something." He rubbed at his brow again, his headache becoming intense.

"You don't think he's guilty?" Saige queried.

"Oh, he's guilty. I'm just not sure if he's guilty of everything he's confessed to, or if he just wants us to look after him because he can't take care of himself and is tired of his mother having that control."

"Yeah, it's the whole food and exercise thing that has me worried," Saige agreed.

"You're both over thinking it." Amber pointed out, watching him with concern in her eyes. "I'm going to quickly get the DNA sample and then one of the Agents is going to drive it to the FBI lab in Tampa where his sister works." Amber grinned.

"She's going to do it straightaway … then I'm going to drive you back to the motel."

"Alex is picking me up. He should be here by now," Saige said.

"Get some sleep, Saige, and I'll call you when I'm awake. We'll sort out where to meet up." He stood and tucked Amber into his side. "Hopefully, later today we'll know more and have a strong case to get Quinten released and his record expunged."

"You really think that can happen?" Saige asked, and he didn't miss the hopeful note in her voice.

"I think it's a strong possibility." Coulter hesitated. "We have a confession, evidence that links Paul to the victims. Once we have the DNA results, if they link Paul to that shack, we'll take it from there."

Saige was silent and bit her lip. "Thank you."

Coulter walked outside with Saige and watched as she climbed into Alex's car.

"Was that the truth?" Amber asked.

He didn't need to ask her what she meant, he knew. "Personally, I think that Quinten will be released within the next few days. The governor is up for reelection and there is already a lot of protesting going on at the prison over the death penalty, especially Quinten's case. So I think the governor will want the Peterson case to disappear quickly. I didn't want to get her hopes up just in case I'm wrong."

Amber hugged him close. "You're a big softy, Detective Coulter Robinson."

He blushed at her observation and he did what he'd been itching to do from the moment they'd partied company; he ran his fingers through her hair. "It's so soft," he mumbled.

She moaned. "Let me get the sample then we can leave, and if you're good, I might let you feel how soft the rest of me is."

Headache or not, he was certainly up for that.

Alex talked Saige into having a pre-dinner drink in town, and he wished he hadn't bothered.

From the minute they had walked into the small bar, the occupants hadn't taken their eyes from them. Saige sat with her back to them, but not Alex. He needed to keep his eye on them.

Saige watched him gaze around the old bar

with its wooden tables in need of a fresh lick of paint, and the chairs worn so thin from years of use that they looked ready to fall apart underneath any poor sucker who sat on one wrong. He'd been coming to this bar since he turned twenty-one and not one thing had changed.

"Have they stopped staring at us yet?" Saige took a drink of her beer and let the bottle dangle in her hand.

"No." Alex sighed. "Ignore them."

She chuckled. "You mean like you are?" Raising a brow, she sat forward and asked, "What do you think is going on with my father?"

He raised a brow. "About the evasive answers he keeps giving you about the hospital?"

"Yeah. I remember everything but that now, at least, I think I do." She shrugged and although she tried to act as if it didn't bother her, he knew that it did.

"I think once Quinten is free you both need to take a trip to the hospital and ask questions. I'm guessing you'd be able to request to see your medical records from your time there. Maybe ask Daniel if he can get some sort of legal paperwork to give you access just in case the hospital doesn't cooperate."

"Hmm." Saige sat back, thoughtful for a few minutes. "That could work."

"Why do I sense a but in there?"

Saige set her bottle of beer down on the table and played with the spare beer mat. "It bothers me a lot that my father won't answer the simplest of questions about that time. I get that he was worried about me and wants to protect me, but something isn't right. My curiosity is piqued and that's his fault," she said, tiredly.

"Do you think he's hiding something?" he asked her outright because Alex sure as hell thought he was.

"Only because he won't answer my questions." She drained her bottle and eyed him before she smiled.

He recognized that smile. She was about to put him on the spot.

He narrowed his eyes.

Saige threw back her head and laughed, which made him smile. Alex knew that his brother had loved to watch Saige when she laughed and he could understand why. Quinten used to tell him that he could watch her laugh all day, every day, and not just because of her infectious laugh, it was because she laughed with her whole body and soul.

"Spit it out, Saige. I'm dying of curiosity," Alex drawled, while he watched her and drained his warm beer, which he did with a wince.

Saige smirked. "I was about to ask you about Christina."

His heart thudded in his chest. "What about her?"

"Are you going to take her with you when you head back to Tampa?" Saige looked nervous and he wasn't sure if it was because Christina would be leaving her father or something else.

"Would it bother you if I did?"

"A few weeks ago I probably would have said yes, but now, I'm not sure that it would. My father and Christina haven't been happy for years. I knew that before my memory even returned, now that it has, I remember things I'd rather forget." She grimaced at the memory. It wasn't pleasant and really made her see her dad in a new light. "Perhaps Christina will be happier with you, and my father will find someone else to love this time around. I guess I just want everyone happy—

Quinten and me included."

Alex wanted Christina with him because she'd been inside of him for years and still was. He loved her and had gone off the rails when she ended things between them the first time. This time though, he had no intention of letting her walk away from him because she kept him grounded.

"She's coming with me."

"Good." Saige offered him a smile. "Are you ready to leave? I think I need some of Pattie's cooking in my stomach, which is currently full of alcohol."

"Let's go." He stood and led her from the bar.

"Detective, I'm beginning to think that you like Pattie's cooking just as much as I do." Saige smiled as she walked into the room and found the detective there.

Coulter smiled. "I did enjoy the breakfast the other day, but I'm afraid I've just eaten."

"With Amber," Saige teased quietly, and was delighted when he blushed. "I'll let you off the hook. Come and sit"—Saige slid her arm through his and tugged him into a chair beside hers—"and have dessert and coffee." She grinned, not knowing anyone who could refuse dessert and coffee.

"Well, if you insist."

Saige was happy to see him and, regardless of what he'd come to tell her, she enjoyed his company. She'd been surprised last night when she saw him with the medical examiner. The woman had looked younger than Coulter, but it was obvious how Amber felt about him. Saige had a feeling that the other woman's feelings were returned just as strongly.

Coulter cleared his throat and gave her a pointed look. "You're staring," he commented.

She chuckled. "So I am. So, not that I'm complaining, but to what do I owe the pleasure?"

She caught his small smile when she placed a slice of lemon meringue pie in front of him and poured his coffee.

He still looked tired and she knew he must have had a difficult day of questioning and following leads to see if Paul's story checked out. In truth, she was impatient to find out how his day had gone, but she wanted him to tell her in his own time.

"This is really good," Coulter began around a

bite of the pie. "The best I've ever tasted."

"I know. It's my favorite dessert." Saige watched him, but her impatience grated on her and she finally gave up. "Please tell me?"

"I wondered how long you'd wait to ask." He offered her a wry smile, and after he drained his cup, he held her gaze.

"According to the polygraph test, Paul Lewis is telling the truth. The test isn't always accurate. However, he was arrested with the jewelry belonging to the college girls—both his and Tracy's fingerprints were on them. He has also given a detailed account of the murders, the description of the girls, how they were taken and several other details that only the killer would know. With all of that evidence, the DA has charged him with eight counts of first degree murder, and the abduction and attempted murder of you."

"Then that means ... wait, Tracy?"

"Tracy's prints were found on the box. I don't know why yet, as Paul wouldn't say. As for Quentin," Coulter paused. "The governor is well aware of what's going on. He has agreed to a full pardon and immediate release of Quinten, providing the DNA test comes back a match to the unidentified blood found along with Quinten's eight years ago."

"What about the other? Won't the fact that there would still be one unidentified cause problems?"

Coulter sighed. "One of the FBI Agents now involved is hung up on the DNA. Even if Paul Lewis has his DNA confirmed, there is still the puzzle of who does the other one belong to. Paul when asked, grinned, and commented that perhaps there is another victim to be found.

"So far there is no other evidence to say that he is being truthful. All the jewelry matched each known victim.

"It's a puzzle that I hope will be solved. The evidence and confession is enough to free Quinten."

Coulter took hold of her hand. "Everything Paul has told us so far has shown that he's telling the truth. He couldn't tell us anything about the first murder. He says his memory about the first one is hazy—that it had been a crime of passion and he just reacted. He woke up covered in blood and had some images in his head of it, but that is it.

That really isn't unusual for a serial killer. Something set off the chain of events before that first kill. But he told us everything else, Saige." Coulter took her other hand. "Did you know that he went to the same school as two of the girls?"

"What?" Saige said, shocked. "Why wasn't that looked into at the time?"

"I honestly don't know. The fact was he wasn't around during the investigation, so I'm guessing the officers who questioned the town residents weren't even told about Paul."

"I have to say that I never saw that coming with Paul," Saige said. "I get the feeling that there is a whole lot more going on."

Coulter stood and squeezed Saige on the arm. "You've tapped into my worry. Leave it to me. I'll call the minute I know something about Quinten."

Saige nodded. "Thank you."

Day 16 '

Saige paced restlessly in the living room with her cell phone in hand. Coulter was certain the DNA results would be back today as the FBI had used their resources for speed. So far she hadn't heard anything. The temptation to call him was getting stronger, but she really didn't want to bother him if he was busy.

Turning at the end of the living room for what felt like the millionth time, Saige stopped dead when she found Coulter leaning against the doorjamb. She waited as he walked toward her not giving anything away with the blank expression on his face.

As he approached his lips twitched and finally he smiled. "The governor has ordered his release and his record expunged."

Saige blinked.

"Really?" she whispered.

Coulter nodded. "Really."

The next minute she was wrapped around the detective with great, big sobs wracking her body. Saige knew that he tried to soothe her but, no matter what he said or did, her tears wouldn't stop.

Even when a commotion outside of the room startled her, she stayed secure in the detective arms.

"You have to watch this," Christina shouted, running into the room with Alex and her husband following closely behind.

Christina switched the television on and flicked the channels until she found what she was looking for.

The image was of Governor Stewart Sheffield at a press conference, and then he started to talk.

"I can confirm that Quinten James Peterson will be released from Harlington with all charges dropped and his record expunged later this week.

"His release comes after the arrest of Paul Lewis, who has confessed to the murder of the five college girls and the abduction of Saige Lockwood, which Quinten Peterson was wrongfully convicted of eight years ago. In addition, Paul Lewis has confessed to the murder of Jocelyn Peterson, Quinten Peterson's ex-wife and two recent murders—Fern Jordan, who worked for Quinten Peterson's defense attorney, and Tracy Adams, a one-time friend of Mr. Lewis.

"Mr. Lewis has been questioned extensively and is aware of things that only the killer would know. His DNA is a match to a previously unidentified DNA sample found in the shack eight years ago.

"At this time, we would like to extend our sincere apology to Mr. Peterson and his family and we are grateful that we were able to locate and apprehend the real killer before an innocent man lost his life."

Saige turned to Coulter. "He's being released this week?"

Coulter leaned close and whispered, "We have

to be at the prison at four in the morning to pick him up." He smiled down at her. "Tell Alex when he's alone."

Saige nodded.

"When?" Alex asked.

"I'm not sure yet," Coulter replied.

Saige glanced up at him. "They're just going to forget everything that has happened?"

Coulter offered a wry smile. "No, they aren't going to forget. It would appear that a lot was kept hidden in regards to Quinten's case and the governor has asked for a formal inquiry to be made. He is up for reelection, but this makes the law look like idiots, so he wants answers. As do I."

Saige frowned as she watched Alex slip from the room.

"I'll pick you up around one-thirty in the morning," Coulter whispered as he gave her one last hug. "Be strong."

Saige nodded and smiled through her tears when Christina wrapped an arm around her shoulders.

Quinten would be free, but where could she take him? His house had been sold years ago by Alex, and she sure as hell didn't want to bring him to her father's house.

Which meant that she really needed her own car. She didn't want to rely on Coulter to drive them around. "I need to borrow a car," she blurted.

Christina hugged her close before she let go. "You can have mine for as long as you need."

"What? You hate anyone driving your car," her father snapped at Christina.

"Dad, I'll soon have Quinten back, so please don't get annoyed at Christina for helping me out. I'd have thought you'd like the fact they're getting along."

Anger flashed in her father's eyes and his jaw tightened before he visibly tried to relax his features. She felt, rather than saw, Christina backing away from her.

"I'll see you later," Christina said, and disappeared out of the room.

Saige moved to stand in front of her father, tears in her eyes. "I love you, Dad." She wrapped her arms around his waist and held him. Minutes later, she finally felt his arms hold her just as tight.

"I'm sorry, honey." He kissed her on the top of her head. "I'm so sorry."

"Please be happy for me."

He hesitated. "I'll try, now I have to go out."

Her father pushed away and quickly left. Not five minutes later, she heard his engine rev before he tore out of the front drive.

Alex sat on the dock with moonlight shining on the ocean in front of him when he turned to Christina who'd quietly moved toward him.

"Are you okay?" Christina asked.

She took Alex's offered hand and he tugged her into his lap, his arms wrapped around her. "I am now." He breathed against the side of her head, his chin rested on her shoulder and he felt more content than he had in a very long time. "I missed you."

"I missed you, too." Christina turned and met his lips. "Talk to me, Alex. How are you really feeling now that Quinten's going to be released?"

"Shocked, surprised, damn glad, worried." Alex held her closer. "Nervous."

Christina watched him closely and he knew she could see through him. "I'm damn happy that I'm going to get my brother back, but I'm worried as well. What does he have to come out to?

Everyone knows who he is, so he'll struggle for work. God"—he dropped his forehead to Christina's—"I sound ungrateful that his life has been spared. I'm not. I love him and never wanted to see him in jail."

"You don't sound ungrateful." Christina cupped his face. "He's your younger brother and you're worried about him. What you're forgetting though is that he loves Saige and she him. They're going to be together and something tells me, regardless of Quinten's situation, they'll make it work, just like we will."

Alex paused and felt his heart turn over in his chest. "Does that mean what I think it means?" He grinned.

"I'm coming to Tampa with you," Christina confirmed, and gasped when Alex took them into the water.

Alex cupped Christina's face and dived in for the first taste of her beautiful lips as his woman. Her long legs wrapped around his waist, her pelvis rubbed against his erection. Alex slipped his hands up her soaked, clinging dress, to get to her naked bottom.

He moaned and all thoughts of getting them

dry left his mind, as he lost himself in her arms and the pleasure between them.

I love watching Christina's nude body. The way she moves, the way her curves are well proportioned. Her breasts are round, high-tipped and perfect. The long legs: slim and golden fuse my fantasies.

Day 17

Quinten stood on legs that trembled and followed the guard through the maze of hallways and the steel gates. The mechanical opening and closing of the locks would forever remind him of his home for the past eight years. It wasn't something he'd forget easily. If ever.

Paperwork had been signed and in his hand he clutched the book Saige had once given him. Alex had found it and brought it to him once he'd been locked behind the gates of Harlington.

He loved his brother, and as much as it pained him to admit, it was Saige he hoped to see waiting for him. She'd given him back hope.

Warden Roscoe stood before him, looking exhausted, as though he hadn't been to bed yet. "I'm glad it's you that this is happening to. You've never belonged in here." The warden held his hand out.

Quinten hesitated and then took the offered hand. "Thank you."

"Here is your copy of the release. Keep it safe."

He tucked it into the book he carried.

The warden stepped to the door. "You ready?"

Was he ready? He'd been incarcerated for eight years. A lot could happen in eight years, and what about Saige? She'd have a life that didn't include him. What the hell was he going to do out there? His business had disintegrated when he'd been charged.

"Quinten, we need to do this."

Quinten nodded. "I'm ready."

Roscoe laughed. "I'm not sure about that."

Signaling to the guard, the door slid open with a final clang and the warden walked through. Quinten took a step, the absence of shackles caused him to falter—it had been so long. His head dipped to his chest and he closed his eyes. He inhaled and forced his feet to move forward. He felt, rather than saw, the moment he walked out of the jail and he came to a stop, his eyes still closed. He was terrified of who he would or wouldn't see when he looked up.

He no longer wore chains or the horrid blue pants and orange shirt that had been required. The guard had passed him a new pair of dark gray jeans and a pale blue T-shirt, along with new underwear and boots. They fit him fine, but he wondered where they came from because they weren't the clothes he'd been wearing when he was sentenced.

His thoughts scattered when he felt the soft touch against his fisted hand at his side. He looked down and then followed the arm up until he met the swimming eyes of the woman he loved.

She'd come for him.

He pulled her into his arms and held her close. So close that he was afraid of hurting her so he loosened his grip slightly.

"No," Saige protested and tried to get closer.

He buried his face in the curve of her neck and held on, his own tears running down his face and getting lost in his beard. He'd dreamt of this day for so long that, now it was here, and she was in his arms, he couldn't think of what to say to her.

Time had no meaning as they clung to each other, but eventually the coolness of the early morning started to register and so did the silence.

Cupping one side of Saige's face, he wiped away her remaining tears, placed a tender kiss to her lips, and smiled. He wrapped an arm around her shoulders and finally looked at the others.

The warden and guards had left them, but Detective Robinson and his brother stood to the side watching.

Slipping his hand down to Saige's, and intertwining their fingers, he moved over to Alex and pulled his brother against him for a one-armed hug.

Tears threatened again as he felt his brother's embrace. "I never thought this would happen." Alex kissed him on the side of his head. "It's such a damn relief to not have you inside anymore."

"Yeah, it is." Quinten let his brother step back, and turned to the other man. "Detective Robinson." He held his hand out. "Thank you, for everything." He glanced at Saige and back to the detective.

"You're welcome." Robinson cleared his

throat. "We better get moving before the press start showing up."

Quinten tightened his hold on Saige's hand because he wasn't going anywhere that didn't include Saige being with him.

She smiled and snuggled against his chest, kissing his hand that held hers.

"I'm driving back to Port Jude with Alex," the detective informed him, "and you're going with Saige for a few days."

Her arm pressed against his back at the detective's words. She looked up and smiled. "I'll tell you where when we're in the car."

He caught his breath and smiled with relief when she tugged him toward the two vehicles while he shivered in the early morning freshness.

"I have a sweater in the car for you." She smiled. "I meant to send it in with your clothes but I was so nervous, I'm afraid I forgot."

"Don't worry about it. I don't mind being cold. It's good to be walking in the fresh air without the prison walls surrounding me, and it's an added bonus to have you with me. To share my first minutes of freedom."

Saige nodded and came to a stop beside a

large, black SUV, Alex and Coulter behind them.

"Take care Quinten, and I'll see you when Saige decides to bring you back," Alex smirked, but Quinten could see the turmoil in his brother's eyes.

He bent low to Saige's ear. "Give me a minute."

She nodded and caressed his back. "I'll be here."

Quinten moved over to his brother and pulled him fully into his arms and held him tightly. "I love you," he admitted gruffly. "I'll never be able to thank you enough for always believing in me, for never giving up on me. I love you, bro." Quinten kissed him on his forehead and grinned.

"Go get your girl," Alex said.

The beach was quiet at this time of morning.

It had taken Saige two hours of driving to get them to the beach house that Coulter owned, but it was certainly worth it, and no one knew where they were.

Most of the trip had been done in awkward silence, but nothing had felt awkward about the way she'd touched him. She hadn't removed her hand from him since they'd left Harlington, and wherever she'd touched had set him on fire for more. She'd always been able to do that to him and he realized that some things never changed.

Saige was still the woman he'd fallen in love with so long ago, and just being with her now was a dream come true. He thought he'd never see her again. They both wore physical and mental scars from the past, and Quinten wasn't that blind that he didn't see that, but he believed together they could get past them and start to live again.

A rustling noise behind him drew his attention and when he turned, he caught Saige watching him as he sat on the steps that led down to the beach with a mug of coffee in his hands. His hair was windblown, which made him wonder why he'd bothered leaving it slightly longer on top—it constantly got in his eyes. But Saige's shiny auburn hair had been pulled back into a tie, looking neat and tidy.

At first, he held her gaze, but then she smiled and butterflies took flight in his stomach. Placing his mug down, he held his hand out to her. She hesitated before she slipped her hand into his and straddled his lap.

Quinten gasped, not only in surprise, but at

the feel of her being so close to him. So when she nuzzled into his neck, he did the most natural thing in the world and held her close.

He tried to fight the tears, he really did, but holding the woman he'd missed like crazy over the years had them streaming from beneath his closed eyelids. They made their way down his cheeks and into his beard as more followed. She was finally in his arms and he wasn't sure he'd ever be able to release her.

"I've missed you," she whispered, the sound of tears in her voice. "I know how that sounds, considering I couldn't remember you until recently. I've always felt there was someone there in the background, someone who needed me, except I had no way of finding him—you." Saige met his gaze, her own eyes as red as his. She offered him a gentle smile and pulled some tissue from her pocket. "They're clean. I figured I'd need them." She shrugged and dabbed at his face before seeing to herself.

Sighing, she settled back against him, and seconds turned into minutes as he closed his eyes and listened to the relaxing sound of the ocean— the first time in eight years that he'd heard it. It had been a daily occurrence in Port Jude—listening to the ocean—but until it had been taken away, he hadn't realized just how much he'd taken it for granted.

Opening his eyes, he kissed Saige on the top of her head and tugged the tie from her hair. She didn't stir. His fingers caressed through the strands of silk, and he was surprised by how much he loved seeing her with auburn hair. She was still the woman he'd fallen in love with and nothing would change that, he just felt a profound sense of relief that she still felt the same way about him—he'd spent eight years thinking the opposite.

He was finally home.

For the first time since she'd woken up in the hospital, Saige felt safe, and she knew that it was all down to the man who currently held her. The gentle caress through her hair lulled her to sleep, but she didn't want to sleep. She wanted to go and lie down with him in the large bed that she'd found in the master bedroom. She needed to be as close to him as two people possibly could be.

She had missed *something* and as soon as her

memories of Quinten had started to appear, she'd known it had been him that was missing from her life.

His arms around her as they listened to the ocean felt so familiar, and she ached for more—the more that she'd only ever experienced in Quinten's arms. She was nervous, because they hadn't been together since before he'd been arrested, which made her think that maybe he was just as nervous.

With a belly full of nerves, Saige kissed his cheek and nuzzled into his neck. She wiggled in his lap and smiled when she felt his reaction against her bottom. He gripped her hips and turned his face to meet hers as Saige reached up and gently sealed their lips together. The kiss stayed slow and sensuous as she wound her arms around his neck, the hard buds of her nipples pressed into his chest and arousal flooded her system. "Make love to me," Saige asked, her breath tickling along his lips.

Quinten's body quivered in reaction to her words, his fingers trembled against her face, his thumbs caressing along her cheekbones. Starring into her eyes, all the love he felt for her was there for her to see. "Have you—" He gulped and looked away, which clued Saige in as to what he asked.

She turned his face back to hers. "The only person to ever touch me in this way is you. You're the only one to have ever been inside of me. I don't know how else to say it."

"You said it just fine," he said. "I'm not sure I have the strength to move from here to the bedroom," he said on a soft laugh. "I'm nervous," he admitted.

"So am I, but I need to *be* with you."

Quinten watched her while an internal battle seemed to be going on inside of him. "I need that as well, don't ever doubt that. It's been so long, Saige. I'm afraid I'm going to hurt you."

"You won't hurt me." Saige climbed from his lap and held her hand out to him. "I trust you." She hauled him to his feet and smiled at the large bulge in his jeans.

He offered her a nervous smile as they slowly walked to the bedroom. Once inside, Saige let go of his hand. She quickly removed all her clothes and stood before him, fighting hard not to cover herself.

The look in his eyes as they roamed over her nude curves made her glad she'd taken the initiative. He kept straying back to her breasts, which made her smile—during their one night together, she'd discovered that he loved her breasts.

She stood directly in front of him and watched as he swallowed hard and closed his eyes. She took the opportunity to look at his groin. She'd kept her eyes above his belt, but now all bets were off. She wanted to see him, and not while he was fastened away.

Her hands flattened on his stomach, which quivered at her touch. It wasn't the only part of his flesh to tremble. Grabbing hold of the bottom of his shirt, Saige commanded, "Lift your arms up."

He did as instructed and as the shirt went flying to the floor, his eyes snapped open. "I'm not sure I'm going to get through this without embarrassing myself." He blushed. "It's been eight years, Saige."

"I know," she said softly.

Saige sat on the bed and slowly unfastened his jeans. Her hands trembled as she spread the opening apart.

He shoved the denim and briefs down his thighs, and heard Saige sigh with pleasure when his swollen penis twitched in her hand. The tip engorged with need while he throbbed before her eyes, leaking pearls of fluid.

"Saige," he growled, his fists clenched tightly at his sides. "I feel as though I'm about to come from just having your eyes on me."

"Not yet," Saige whispered, wanting just one taste.

Before he could move away, Saige bent and swirled her tongue around the flared head. His body tensed and his hands flexed.

Saige smiled and sucked him into her warm, wet mouth, relishing the salty taste of him. Her hand caressed his sac gently before it returned to his hard length.

Quinten shuddered, seconds before he pulled himself free. "I want to be wrapped around you, as close as I can get. I want to really love you, Saige."

She blinked back tears at his words and let him gently ease her down onto the bed while he kicked off his boots and jeans. When he lowered his body over hers, Saige couldn't help the gasp that escaped her lips at the feel of him against her while fully aware of his hardness brushing against her thigh.

He cupped her head with his hands and slowly

lowered his mouth, his tongue tracing the soft fullness of her lips before she captured his mouth with her own. His tongue sent shivers of desire racing through her, and raising his mouth from hers, he gazed into her eyes. "I love you," he whispered.

His lips traced a sensuous path of ecstasy from her neck to her breasts where he captured a nipple with tantalizing possessiveness. His hand seared a path down her abdomen and onto her thigh, lifting it to wrap around his hip. Instinctively, her body arched toward him.

"I'm ready for you, Quinten," Saige admitted, her fingers sliding through his hair to caress the strong tendons in the back of his neck. "I just want you." Her lips quivered as she confessed her need of him.

"You have me." He took her hand and guided it to himself. "Put me inside you." His voice broke and she felt him tremble above her.

His penis was rock hard and silky smooth as she guided the flared head to where she wanted him the most at that second, and then she welcomed him into her body as he slowly stretched her until he was fully seated. Her breathing was uneven and matched Quinten's as shivers of delight followed the slow rocking of his hips.

"*Saige*," Quinten hissed, his hand moving gently down her side to clutch her bottom against him, his fingers burning into her tingling skin.

"I know ... I'm so close ... please come with me," she begged as pleasure pure and explosive rushed through her.

Saige clutched at his back, and moaned, gasping for breath as her pleasure soared higher and higher until the peak of utter delight was reached, and then wave after wave of ecstasy throbbed through her with release.

Quinten hissed through his teeth, finding his own release in her body as he panted above her.

He panted, his chest heaving as he took them to their sides, and tucked her curves neatly against his own. Their bodies sated from the lovemaking.

"I love you too, Quinten," Saige mumbled against his chest as she snuggled against him, their legs intertwined.

He held her against him, gentle caresses of his fingers trailed back and forth along her back while their breathing eased as their earlier passion turned into heart felt love.

"Saige?" he questioned, when a finger traced the largest scar that she'd been left with. He bent his head and placed a soft kiss to the puckered skin on her shoulder. "I'm so sorry, baby."

"You had nothing to do with what happened to me. You have your own scars from that time as well." Saige cupped his face in her hands and kissed his scarred cheek, most of which was hidden under his beard. She then lifted his hand and kissed along the scar he'd gotten breaking into the shack. "I love you."

Her arms went around his neck as she laid her head against his shoulder, totally exhausted. He was still inside of her as he tugged the quilt over them and held her against him.

"Sleep, baby."

Quinten had slept briefly with Saige in his arms, and although he hadn't wanted to slip out of her silken sheath, he had, and left her sleeping.

He needed to clear the cobwebs inside his head, and to think, but so far he hadn't done much of anything, other than to stare out across the ocean.

He might have his life back, but what kind of future did he have now that his name was known. No one would hire him, even though his name had been cleared. He was a craftsman and he knew that it was something he'd never forget, although he was probably rusty at it by now. He could get that back.

To get his life back they'd have to move faraway from Florida. At least he had the money that the government had confiscated when he'd been convicted. Surely they'd give it back after everything. He wasn't rich by any means, but there'd be enough to live off for months while he searched for work. Saige would come with him. Wouldn't she? He smiled. She'd move wherever he wanted, just like he knew that he'd stay in Port Jude or Tampa if that was what she wanted.

"Hey."

He heard the smile in her voice seconds before she snuggled beside him. "I was just thinking about you." He wrapped an arm around her shoulders, needing that connection to her.

"What about me?" She grinned.

He laughed. "Not about you naked, at least, not

right now." He brushed her hair back from her face with his fingers. "I was thinking about *our* future, and how it might be better if we moved to a state where my name wouldn't be recognized. I was wondering if you'd want to do that." He covered her mouth with his, kissing her until she was breathless before she could answer. For some reason, now that he'd asked, he was terrified of what she would say. "If you don't want to move, then we'll stay."

"I think a move will do us both some good, and I think it will be best for you to start your business up again where people don't know your history. You've been cleared of all charges, but people can be weird." Saige wrapped her arms around his arm, and her head rested on his shoulder.

He was content to stay where they were, but knew that wasn't an option. As long as Saige was by his side, then his life would always be complete.

"Will you come somewhere with me?" Saige asked quietly.

Quinten frowned, and met her gaze. "Of course. Where?"

Saige looked nervously out at the water and his own apprehension reared its head. "Tell me."

He cupped Saige's chin and made her look at him. "I'm not going anywhere, so please talk to me, Saige."

"I remember everything apart from my time in the hospital. Two years of my life are still lost. I want to know why the smell of cleaning chemicals makes me physically sick. I want to go and visit the hospital and, hopefully, get to read the records they have from my stay there."

Quinten stayed silent as he felt his anger at Saige's treatment begin to rise. He hated that she went through everything without him. He should have been there with her, but he wasn't, through no fault of his own, but it still caused an ache in his heart.

"We'll go together." He lifted her into his lap and cuddled her to his chest. "Whatever happens from now on, we face it together." He rested his chin on the top of her head. "I love you, Saige. I never stopped, and it hurts deeply to know that I was kept away from you when you needed me the most."

"I guess in a way, I had it easy because I've only recently remembered you and what we had back then. I feel guilty for that. All those years you sat on death row, remembering me, and I was trying to live my life knowing that something was missing but not knowing what."

Saige wiped her eyes on the sleeve of her sweatshirt and met his gaze. "I love you, Quinten. I loved you before and I love you now." She smiled. "Will you make love to me."

Heat rose in his body as he whispered, "Yes."

They have managed to give the press the slip, but not me.

I will always find them.

The beach is lovely and quiet, which makes it easier for me to watch the couple on the steps of Coulter Robinson's beach house.

With the way Quinten starts touching Saige, I wonder if they have forgotten they're not in private.

Two minutes later, I answer my own question: yes they have.

Saige is now on her back with Quinten pressing between her legs, his jeans only just below his naked ass. He holds her wrists above her head while his mouth claims hers. Saige writhes under him, her legs locked around his hips, which hammer into her.

I never thought too much about watching other people having sex—I never understood the excitement. Except, now I'm watching Saige and Quinten, I'm aroused.

My breathing is heavy as I close my eyes and bring the image of Christina to mind.

I imagine her red lips are wrapped around my cock.

I ache.

I throb.

I pulsate.

I come in my jeans.

Day 18

Quinten spooned Saige all night, and instead of sleeping, he kept waking, thinking his imagination was playing tricks on him and she really wasn't in his arms. He felt a touch of guilt because every time he'd woken he'd made love to her over and over again, needing to be as close as he possibly could to the woman he loved—the woman he felt loved him just as much.

He smiled as Saige lay between his thighs, her head against his stomach, her fingers sliding through the hair on his chest.

"I'm not sure I'll ever be able to move again," she mumbled, her breath like a caress over his navel.

He couldn't keep the satisfied smile from his lips. "I don't mind keeping you in bed all the time, although I think I might need a rest."

She chuckled. "Mmm." She slipped her hand between them, over his hardening dick and massaged. Her gentle fingers tickled between his legs and just the feel of her touching his sac had his dick hard in an instant. "I'm not sure they're listening."

Quinten rolled Saige to her back and held her arms over her head. He nibbled at her neck, moving lower along her collarbone, and came to a stop as his mouth hovered over an erect cherry nipple.

Her cell vibrated across the bedroom floor. They must have knocked it off the bedside table at some point.

"Ignore it," she begged, and wrapped her legs around his waist to pull him closer.

He kissed the waiting nipple and moved off her to get the phone. "It could be important." He frowned down when he saw it was her father.

Saige seemed about as keen as he did when Quinten passed her the phone. "You better call him back. You've got a lot of missed calls from him," he suggested.

"I'll call him, but only if you come back to bed and hold me."

"Anything." He climbed on the bed behind her and cradled her between his thighs. His hands rubbed soothing circles on her stomach. "Call him and get it over with."

He felt Saige inhale and exhale before she lifted the cell and waited for her father to answer.

The minute he did, Richard's voice came over the phone loud and clear.

Saige held the phone away from her ear and gave it an odd sort of look. Quinten tugged her closer and held her tightly. "I'm here with you, baby," Quinten whispered. "Don't forget you can do anything."

She nodded and switched the phone to speaker. "Dad, I'm not saying where we are, but, yes, I'm with Quinten."

There was silence on Richard's end. "Do you know that Christina has left me for *Alex?* She could never keep her hands off that man. I should have gotten rid of the Petersons when I had the chance. They're all no good."

"Dad"—she rubbed at her brow, anger and embarrassment filling her face with heat—"you really can't blame Christina for wanting to be with the man she loves. You've had affairs for years with different women. At least Christina has only ever been unfaithful with the same man."

Richard spluttered, and Quinten struggled to hide his amusement. He'd known that Richard had affairs, but he'd forgotten about his brother and Christina, which kind of ticked him off.

"You would take her side."

Saige sighed. "I'm not taking sides and I've had enough of this conversation. Christina left because she was unhappy and, believe it or not, she's in love with Alex. I suggest you get over it and find someone else. I mean, it's not exactly going to be difficult for you."

"Saige!" Richard shouted as Saige hung up.

"Oh boy. He's never talked to me like that before."

Quinten kissed her bare shoulder. "You did good."

She turned her face to him. "Can we go to the hospital and get that over with? I want to be free to decide on where we're going to go and what our new life is going to be like.

He rested his forehead against hers. "Yes."

Her stomach was in knots as the hospital came into view and her hands fisted on her lap. Chills raced down her spine and she knew that whatever had happened inside that brick and mortar building hadn't been good.

"Hey," Quinten reached over and tried to pry her fingers open. The minute he pulled up outside the place, he turned to her and grabbed both of her hands.

Saige grabbed hold and turned fearful eyes to him. "I'm scared."

Quinten watched her before he climbed from the car and ran to the opposite side and opened her door. He tugged her out of the car and into his arms.

Saige buried her face in his chest and clung to him. "I'm afraid of what we're going to find out."

"Baby"—Quinten cupped her face—"whatever we find out, just remember you're not alone." He kissed her forehead. "We're together, Saige."

Saige searched his eyes, seeing pain and worry

in the hidden depths, but she didn't focus on that. She focused on the love she saw shining bright in his eyes. Reaching up, Saige gave him a lingering hug, and whispered, "I love you."

Intertwining their fingers together, she threw him a weak smile and turned to the hospital. The place didn't look welcoming. In fact, it looked like something out of a horror movie or *The X-Files*. If the sun hadn't been blazing down on them, she would have run the other way, regardless of what she wanted to know.

The three-story building was a dirty gray stone with small square windows that ran the length of each floor. There was no definitive shape to the structure and it looked like it had been dropped into place in the middle of nowhere.

As they approached the only door that they could see, Saige gripped Quinten's hand tight and let him lead her inside to the reception desk, which was a surprise.

The small area had pale yellow walls with white trim. Colorful flowers in a vase sat on the corner of the receptionist's desk, and the chairs for visitors looked welcoming and comfortable—such a contrast from the outside of the building.

"Can I help you?" a young woman asked, dressed casually in a white skirt with splashes of color, and a plain, pink sweater. She sat behind a glass partition.

Saige blinked, and cleared her throat. "We don't have an appointment, but I was wondering if Doctor Erikson was available to see us for a few minutes?"

"I'm sorry but Doctor Erikson is the director and I'm afraid you'll have to make an appointment if you wish to talk to him."

"Please," Saige begged. "I was a patient of Doctor Erikson's for two years. I left around six years ago." Saige looked at Quinten, who remained silent during the exchange, but she felt his presence and knew that he was with her.

"All I can do is let him know you are here, but I can't promise anything. What name should I give him?" she asked, her pen poised over the notebook on the clear desk.

"Saige Lockwood."

The pen slipped as she gave her name. Saige glanced at Quinten, who frowned at the young woman.

"I'll be back in a minute." The woman got up

and, after punching in a series of numbers by the door, disappeared through it.

"What—" Saige started.

"I think she recognized your name. But why?"

The door opened and a man who looked to be in his sixties entered. He stared at Saige for a few seconds before he indicated that they should follow him.

Her heart raced as the security door closed behind them. If Quinten hadn't been with her she doubted she'd have been so willing considering the chills that raced down her spine.

The hallways with plain walls and flooring loomed before them. Double doors between sections had to have a code punched into a security panel in order to move between the two.

She hadn't needed to ask who the doctor was. She'd known the minute she'd laid eyes on him. Doctor Erikson.

A memory teased her mind.

The sound of footsteps echoed against hard flooring. The beeping of monitoring equipment. Humming. Crying. Screams.

The hard bed beneath her covered in plastic

creaked every time she moved. Padded restraints in her peripheral vision terrified her. Blurred image of a man as he leaned over her. The covered overhead light caught her attention—she'd gotten used to using it to focus her mind.

A panic attack would mean more drugs. She hated the drugs. Couldn't think once they'd prodded her with thick needles. They hurt her so bad.

Saige reached up and rubbed her arm, her gaze on Dr Erikson. "You drugged me?"

"Yes. I knew it was only time before you remembered." He showed them into an office that looked to have seen better days. "Sorry about the mess. I couldn't find something." He cleared his throat and indicated with his arm that they should sit.

The silence stretched on until the doctor dipped his head and gazed at his entwined hands on the desk. "I'm going to be blunt so that I don't waste anyone's time. You're here because you want to know why you spent two years in this facility? You have some memory's but not all?"

Saige nodded and clung to Quinten's hand. The doctor noticed and stared at Quinten. "I'm glad

384 | TWENTY EIGHT DAYS

that you're finally together." He turned to Saige and winced. "When you were first brought here, you didn't speak and would spend hours staring into space. A week later, it was as though you'd woken up. That's the only way to describe it. You started asking for that young man." He nodded toward Quinten. "When he didn't come, you started to cry and beg for a cell phone. You didn't seem to remember what had previously happened—the abduction or selecting Mr. Peterson as your attacker. Your father didn't like how it distressed you not having Mr. Peterson with you."

"So, you're telling me that—"

"That you thought Mr. Peterson had abandoned you. That's what your father wanted you to think."

Saige heard Quinten curse under his breath as he wrapped his arm around her shoulders. He kissed the top of her head, and said to Erikson, "Go on."

The doctor stared at her sadly as though he was making a decision. Finally, he said, "I'm dying—" He held up his hand to stop them from saying anything. "After I found out and got over the anger … I realized that I needed to right the wrongs I have committed. I've spent the last few days writing a report for you. You'll probably receive it at your address in Tampa within the next day or two. I needed to tell you everything before I took it to my grave." He rubbed at his forehead and sat back in his chair, looking exhausted.

"What's in the report?" Quinten asked. "Please don't make her wait for your report to arrive. She's waited long enough."

"As I should imagine you have," the doctor added. "I wanted to avoid this because it isn't pleasant and it certainly wasn't legal."

A shiver ran through Saige at the doctor's words. Quinten tugged her closer.

The doctor sighed. "From the time you realized that Quinten would never be coming for you, until two weeks before you left this facility, we kept you drugged."

Saige had known that it had to be something like that but having it confirmed made her want to scream or hit something. The sad thing was that she didn't have any strength for anything right then. She'd been on an emotional rollercoaster for weeks and felt that she was going to crash anytime soon.

"Is that everything?" Quinten questioned, his head dipped to the side.

Doctor Erikson said, "Unfortunately it isn't, and I'm just going to say it. After you'd been here for a few weeks you were taken into surgery." He closed his eyes, and kept them closed. "I performed an abortion."

A pin dropped could have been heard in the silent room following Doctor Erikson's confession.

The clock continued to tick, but Saige couldn't form any words to describe the shock that she felt at hearing his admission. He'd taken Quinten's child from her body and all she felt was numb. Saige lifted her head to look at Quinten and realized that he was just as shocked.

Neither of them had expected that bombshell to be revealed and now they'd have to deal with it once they worked out how to do that.

"I've told you everything and it's also written in the report I've sent you. All I can say now is that I'm so sorry. I should have ignored the threat from your father, but I didn't."

"My father?" Saige whispered, hoping she'd misheard him.

The doctor hesitated and replied, "Your father threatened me and authorized the abortion and the drugs we used over the course of your stay here. You would have still been here to this day if I hadn't finally stood up to him and stopped administering the medication."

Quinten's concern for Saige had started to override the shock of their discovery at the hospital. She hadn't spoken since they'd left, apart from telling him to head for her father's house. He wasn't sure confronting her dad today was the best idea, considering how quiet and upset she was. He understood it though.

After everything she'd been through at the hands of Paul, and to have her own father responsible for taking their child, was unthinkable. His hands clenched around the steering wheel at the anger he felt, he just hoped they didn't get pulled over because his driver's license ran out years ago. He wasn't only angry at the loss of their child, he was angry that he hadn't been able to do anything to help her back then.

"Don't," Saige whispered, and placed her hand

on top of his. "What we learned today was a shock, but as long as we have each other, we can get through this, right?"

He swallowed and nodded, emotion too close to the surface for words.

Saige moved closer and rested her head on his arm. He slipped his hand to her thigh and intertwined their fingers when her hand slipped under his.

"I'm sorry."

He frowned, and pulled the car over to the side of the road.

He turned to face her and cupped her face, placing a tender kiss to her quivering lips. "I'm the one who should be apologizing. It was my fault everything happened. Your father didn't like me. I was married and I wasn't good enough for you."

"I love you, Quinten. He should have accepted that." She sighed, heavily. "I'm not even sure I want to confront him now, or even talk to him."

He kissed each eyelid and lingered over her brow. "As much as I hate to say this, I think we should go and see him now. It will get it all over and done with and we can move on. You need to hear it from your father's mouth. I also want him to apologize to you."

Saige offered a sad smile. "I don't know what I'd even want him to say or do, and I'm not sure an apology is going to cut it. What happened is too disgusting and I hate him for doing that to me—to us. We're both victims, Quinten."

He closed his eyes and, not for the first time, he wished that he could go back eight years to when his life was somewhat on the right track.

Sick to her stomach, Saige held tight to Quinten's hand as they walked toward her father. How did her father justify what he'd done to her? Until her memory had returned she'd always presumed she'd been daddy's girl. In a way she had been, but she'd been manipulated.

It was Quinten's strength that held her together, even though she knew he'd suffered at her father's hand. He'd been right though, and she did need to hear her father's reasoning. Deep inside she knew it had everything to do with her father's refusal to accept Quinten as the man she loved. She hated that she'd let her father direct her life for so long without realizing he had.

Her father sat alone by the water with a bottle of beer in his hand. Only the slight turn of his head indicated he knew they were there.

"He called me," her father started. "I didn't think you'd come after what he told you."

Quinten ushered her closer and pulled her down onto his lap as he sat on one of the three vacant chairs. His arms around her waist kept her anchored.

"Why?" she asked.

Her father was silent for a long time and just when Saige thought he wouldn't say anything, he started talking. "Peterson had been arrested for murder and your abduction. I couldn't let you have his child. I kept you drugged because I didn't want you to remember him and possibly remember that it had been someone else who took you. I wanted you away from him, and everything that happened gave me the opportunity for that to happen."

Quinten wiped the tears from her eyes with trembling hands. She knew that he blamed himself for what happened to her, but she didn't. She didn't blame him for any of it.

"Did you know the real killer was Paul?" she asked, the thought just crossing her mind.

"Because if you thought I'd remember someone else taking me, that tells me you knew it wasn't Quinten. You let the real killer walk free?" she accused, angry. "You gave him the opportunity to kill again."

He ignored her comment and turned to look at her, his eyes red-rimmed. "I didn't know it was Paul." His voice shook. "I didn't know who it was. I knew that I could protect you and keep you safe, so I let the investigation run its course. During the course of the trial, I realized that Quinten was probably innocent. I honestly thought that the jury would come to that decision. I was surprised when he was sentenced to death, because of how little evidence they actually had." He dropped his chin to his chest.

"Was your inclination to punish me really because of Saige or because of my brother sleeping with your wife?" Quinten asked, barely controlled anger behind his words.

"I won't discuss Christina with you," he hissed.

They had their answer.

Saige had had enough and stood. "I'm leaving Florida with Quinten." Her father flinched at her words. "We want a life together and I want to help him rebuild his carpentry business." She couldn't help the tears that ran unchecked down her face as she looked at her father—the man who was supposed to protect her from evil. "That's what love is all about, and I love him, Dad, I love you, too, and that's why my heart is breaking."

She fought back the sob and her dad stared at her, his eyes filled with anguish but she didn't care. He couldn't understand how much his actions had hurt her. "I love you, but I don't love who you've become. You have destroyed so much and you nearly destroyed my happiness and my love. Quinten is both of those and you would have let him go to the execution chamber to keep him away from me. I'm leaving Florida, but I can't have a life with you in it and after today, I never want to see you again."

Saige tightened her grip around Quinten's hand and turned to head toward the car.

"Saige?"

She ignored her father's call.

"Please ... Saige ... Quinten!"

She closed her eyes and turned to face him. Her father had stood, looking unsteady beside the chair.

"I ... I know it's probably too late, but I'm sorry. I'm sorry for everything." He looked at Saige. "I love you, honey." He held Quinten's gaze. "Saige is precious, please look after her and keep her safe."

Quinten glanced at her and pulled her into his arms, holding her close.

So Saige and Quinten knew what Richard Lockwood had done to her. The man deserved everything Saige had said to him and more. They had both let Richard off lightly, which shocked me.

Her father had pushed for the conviction of Quinten, which was what I had wanted, but he'd also let the real killer—me—go free. How can a father justify that: supporting his daughter's abductor? To all intents and purposes that was what Richard Lockwood had done.

But he'd gone a step further by committing his daughter to the 'nuthouse' and subsequently authorizing the abortion of her child.

If they didn't make the man pay for that then I will. Because after my brief chat with Dr Erikson, I now have a copy of the confession he'd written to Saige.

Day 19

Quinten lay snug behind Saige with an arm draped over her waist, and the other she used as a pillow. He watched her sleep, her features finally relaxed from the stress of the day.

He'd wanted to say more to her father for what Richard had done to his daughter, but he could see how broken Saige was with the day's discovery.

What he hated to admit was that he understood where her father came from. His daughter had been abducted, abused, and the man her father thought responsible was the man his daughter was in love with. She had been pregnant with his child. Quinten understood, but couldn't accept the way that her father had gone about dealing with it, or the drugs that he'd authorized. Saige should have been given a choice. Deep in his heart though, he knew that Saige would have never believed that he was guilty, and she'd have kept and cherished their child.

When he was with Saige, he used to dream of having a little girl who looked just like her mama, with hair so blonde and soft, and eyes so blue. He would have cherished her just as much as he did her mother. As the first tears started to run from his eyes, he wondered if their baby had been a boy. His son would have been a miniature of him, and would have loved baseball, fishing and so much more.

Quinten buried his face into the back of Saige's neck and, while she couldn't witness his despair, Quinten gave way to the tears he'd held back all day. He had held himself together because he saw that Saige had needed that, but it had been difficult when his heart had been breaking all over again for the life they'd created with love, and then had taken away from them.

He froze when Saige started to turn, and when

she met his gaze, she tugged him down to her chest and held him while he broke down. Great racking sobs shook his body as he held onto her as tight. Saige ran her fingers through his hair while she silently cried with him, the unevenness of her breathing giving her away.

The one constant in his life was Saige, but the rest of his life was in turmoil. He hadn't had a chance to catch his breath since he'd been freed from Harlington, and he felt like he was drowning with no direction.

Saige had mentioned his carpentry, and really, that was all he knew, but after being away from it for so long, he wasn't sure that he even wanted to go back to it. He wanted a new life away from everything he had ever known—a new life with Saige by his side.

His girl had been through so much that he was surprised she hadn't walked away from him when the doctor had delivered the news to his relief, she hadn't. He felt guilty for even thinking that she would, but everyone he'd ever known had walked away from him, except Saige and his brother.

Everything always came back to the girl in his arms, who cried herself back to sleep.

He was glad, and as he slipped from the bed, he cast one more glance over his shoulder before he closed the bedroom door.

Saige smiled as she watched Quinten turn another page in the book he read. They'd had a quiet day of not much talking, but there'd been a lot of touching—a soft caress to her arm or a hand to his back. She needed his touch as much as he obviously needed hers.

After the news from yesterday, Saige had been at a loss about what to do or how to move forward, but for Quinten being by her side, she wouldn't have gotten through the night—they'd helped each other, and now she needed to be closer.

Rolling from the sofa she laid on, Saige walked on her knees toward Quinten, smiling when his eyes landed on her. He closed his book and let it drop to the floor before he reached for her.

Saige climbed on top of him and, when her head rested against his chest, she sighed in pleasure. "This is where I'm supposed to be."

"I agree with you," Quinten mumbled, moving around to a more comfortable position. "I never thought I'd get the chance to hold you again." He kissed the top of her head, his arms holding her close.

"It's my fault that you spent eight years behind bars."

"Hell no!" Quinten tugged her up so he could look into her eyes. His hands gently cupped her face, his thumbs caressed along her cheekbones. "You had nothing to do with me being sent away. Nothing, Saige." He brought her forehead to rest against his. "I have never blamed you, and I never will. I blame the justice system." He wrapped her tightly up in his arms again. "You're as much a victim as I am."

Saige let her tears soak into his shirt, and reminded him, "I killed our baby," she sobbed.

Quinten paused. "They had you drugged, and they kept you that way. What they did to you was illegal and once we get the report the doctor said he sent to you, we'll pass it over to Coulter and let him deal with it."

"Okay." Saige tried to dry her face up with the sleeves of her sweatshirt, but didn't quite succeed. "I need a tissue." Climbing from his lap, Saige went into the bathroom and used toilet paper before she washed her face with cold water in the basin.

"You okay now?" Quinten asked, coming up behind her and trapping her between the vanity and his warm body. He kissed her neck, and rested his chin on her shoulder so that they both stared into the mirror.

Saige reached up with one hand and caressed his face, noticing the faint lines from where Jocelyn had used her nails. Quinten turned and kissed the palm of her hand.

"I love you, and I hope you don't mind me telling you all the time," Saige whispered.

"I've waited years to hear you say those words to me again, so I'll never get tired of hearing them." His hands slipped around her waist, his hardness obvious against her bottom. "I love you more than I have words to describe," he admitted, his voice thick with longing.

"I really want your baby, Quinten." Saige bit her lip, wondering why she blurted those words out, but once Quinten got over the shock of hearing them, his lips twitched and he smiled all the way to his eyes.

"We haven't exactly practiced safe sex, so I'm guessing that's going to happen sooner rather than later, but are you really ready for that after what we've discovered?" he asked, a worried frown on his brow.

"I'm angry that my father agreed to an abortion without even telling me I was pregnant. To me, that is worse than him keeping me drugged for two years. Although, I'm upset that the life we created with love was taken, I don't have one memory." Saige said, heartbroken. "I'm not making any sense."

"I understand what you're trying to say. You're saying that you didn't know, so how could you mourn for something you had no clue about. In this case, our child."

"I don't want to think about it anymore and I want to try and put that in the past as much as I can, because the thought of someone invading my body in that way makes me want blood. That report will be given to Coulter, regardless of my father being responsible."

Quinten tugged her sweatshirt free of her shoulder and pressed his warm lips against her skin. "A can of worms has been opened and Coulter's out for blood. Trust him."

"I do ... Will you take my mind off everything,"

Saige asked, and pressed against the arousal he couldn't hide even if he tried.

"You sure?" he asked.

"More than sure." She smiled, and tugged her sweatshirt off and pushed her leggings to the floor. She cupped her breasts and watched him gulp when his eyes landed on the large mounds through the mirror.

"Wait." Quinten looked around and grabbed a towel to cover the edge of the vanity before he pushed her against it. "Spread your legs."

She did and then felt the gentle caress of Quinten's palms over her bottom and the tickle of his fingers between her thighs. His breath was warm against her skin as he nuzzled into her neck.

"You have too many clothes on," she hissed between her teeth when he removed her hands from her breasts and replaced them with his own, rolling and pinching the hard nipples between his finger and thumb.

"Not for long." In two seconds, he managed to remove his sweats and shirt, and pushed his penis between her thighs. The heat of his body warming her through.

Saige pushed back and, reaching between her

thighs, rubbed the head of his shaft with her thumb.

His hands trembled against her skin as he lifted one of her thighs up, and brought her knee onto the vanity. "Hold steady."

She couldn't do anything else, and then she felt him nudge into her. Once he was seated inside of her, he brought her leg down. She clenched around him. "So good," he grunted.

His hand held onto her breasts as he started a slow glide in and out. She wouldn't be able to hold on for long because of the way he made her feel—like she was his and his alone.

"I love you, baby," he whispered against her neck. "Never forget how much I love you."

"Never," she agreed.

Day 20

Coulter observed Paul Lewis through the one-way glass as the man sat silently next to his lawyer. Every now and again, Paul would lean over and whisper something to the lawyer, and it seemed to Coulter that he was almost … *excited*. He really couldn't figure the man out.

Lost in thought, Coulter vaguely registered the arrival of the DA and Special Agent Nero Soren. The FBI Agent had arrived just before Paul Lewis had been arrested. The Fed was intense and missed nothing.

The DA, Gregory Bishop, cleared his throat. "He has no idea what he's going to face in prison, does he?"

Coulter sighed. "No, and that worries me." He glanced at Greg and Soren, and then back to Paul. "He said he wants taking care of. Who confesses to murder for that?"

Greg stared at Paul and laughed. "I guess he does."

"He has gone into detail about each murder except the first one. In my experience, serial killers never forget the first life they take. They remember it, and try to better it. Why doesn't Paul Lewis remember?" Soren said. "It makes no sense."

The Agent became thoughtful. "His confession seems too neat and tidy, regardless of all the evidence backing up his confession. The other DNA bothers me. I don't believe it belongs to another victim like he, *suggested*."

"Then go and ask him." Greg shrugged.

Coulter glanced at Soren and then met Greg's eyes.

Greg continued. "He's talking, regardless as to what his lawyer has advised. It's as though he has no secrets, so ask and see what he says—how he reacts."

Coulter turned his gaze back to the two-way glass and wondered what was really going on in the head of Paul Lewis.

"I'll stay and watch," Greg commented, and probably used it as his way of telling him he didn't have all day.

Coulter nodded and walked from the room followed by Soren. They took a minute in the hallway and Coulter ran a hand down his face, exhausted. The case had kept him awake at night because something niggled at his conscience but what was the big question.

He glanced at the door and before he could have second thoughts, he pushed his way inside.

Paul Lewis sat straight in the chair when he saw him and Soren, but the man's lawyer frowned and whispered something to Paul, who ignored whatever was said.

"Detective Robinson. Special Agent Soren," Paul said. "I was told that I wouldn't see you both again until the trial so this is a nice surprise." He moved around on his chair as though he was *excited*.

That word again.

"I wanted to go over some questions with

you." Coulter took the chair across from them, and his frown deepened when he glanced at Paul who eagerly awaited the questions.

Soren relaxed against the wall behind Coulter so he could observe.

Coulter sat back in the chair and held Paul's gaze. "Tell me why the college girls were killed one way, and Fern and Tracy another, and what I can't understand is why you have no recollection of your first kill—that doesn't normally happen with a serial killer." He'd leave Jocelyn and Saige out of it for now.

Without a pause to think, Paul answered, "I was rushed and drunk with the first girl. That memory isn't really there. Fern though, was in the wrong place at the wrong time. I didn't intend to kill anyone else, but she caught me sneaking around outside of her building. She threatened to scream and would have given me away. So I silenced her. It felt good to silence her." Paul grinned and then looked sad just as quickly.

He continued. "I really didn't want to hurt Tracy, but she followed me one night and saw me digging up the jewelry box, which I buried after I put the trinket from Fern inside. After I left she went and dug it up to see what it was." He looked remorseful for once. "I knew someone had been around, messing with my things, and then Tracy acted weird around me, and I just knew. I went to her house the night when Alex was there and heard her tell him that she knew who had taken Saige." Paul glanced at his lawyer, who looked exasperated with him.

"Paul, what else?" Coulter prodded.

"I had to keep her quiet, so I took her out into the woods and killed her. She fought me. Made me angry. I didn't want to hurt Tracy, but I couldn't stop. I'm sorry."

Coulter rubbed his brow and couldn't find any hesitation in Paul's answers—nothing that raised a red flag saying he lied.

"What about Jocelyn? You said that you loved her."

"Detective Robinson," the lawyer said, annoyance in his voice, "my client has been asked these questions over and over again. I know that's the norm but he's already been charged. You have the evidence and you have his signed confession."

Coulter ground his teeth together to keep his mouth shut until he could talk without his own annoyance showing.

"We will continue to ask your client questions until we are satisfied with the answers." Coulter proceeded to look at Paul. "Jocelyn?"

Paul stayed silent and stared at his hands on the table. "I thought she loved me. She didn't." His voice hardened. "She was going to betray me. Once Quinten had been sentenced to death, she had second thoughts and was going to tell you that Quinten was innocent and that it was me. I didn't believe her at first, but as she started to walk away from me, I realized she would tell you. I was angry and upset so I struck out and attacked her. She begged me not to hurt her, but I did. She was like all the others, *a whore.*"

Over the many years that he'd been a detective, Coulter had seen and heard things that would give others nightmares, and in all that time he'd never met anyone like Paul Lewis.

"Why did you blow up my truck?" Coulter asked, catching Paul Lewis by surprise.

Paul's reaction told Coulter that he knew nothing about it.

"I ... um. Truck?" Paul mumbled. "I don't know anything about a truck."

"That I do believe." Coulter was tired of Paul and the case. He needed some fresh air—Amber—to clear his head.

He stood and shoved his chair under the table. "Why, Paul? Why kill those women within hours after they'd been with Alex?" That was one thing that had been on his mind.

Paul looked up and held his gaze. "Because Alex is the evil brother, not Quinten. I wanted to lead you to him but you never once thought that he killed anyone. I must have done something wrong to set him up, huh? I won't make that mistake again."

Coulter and Soren left the room.

Soren glanced at him. "I think he's going to be convicted." He nodded and left Coulter in the hallway.

Coulter sagged against the wall outside of the room. Paul Lewis was totally, utterly crazy.

Day 21

Quinten clutched Saige's hand in his as they rode the elevator up to her apartment in Tampa. He'd been nervous to leave the beach house and the wide-open space of the beach and ocean for an apartment building in the much larger city—he hated it.

If it hadn't been for the report from Dr. Erikson, then he doubted they'd have come back so soon. But here they were and he tried to keep his apprehension to himself, although with the quick glances Saige kept giving him, he didn't think he'd succeeded.

She squeezed his hand, and smiled as the

doors of the elevator opened and they stepped out. "We're right here," Saige said, and opened the door.

He was surprised at the wide-open layout of the apartment when they stepped inside. Floor to ceiling glass walls along two sides of the apartment opened it up even more, and he could see Tampa stretching out on the horizon to the ocean. Everything was in white and pastel, but it was the brown, leather chair that held his gaze. It was so out of contrast to the rest of the apartment that he smiled to himself.

"The chair"—she smiled, and wrapped her arm around his waist—"something told me I had to bring it with me. Now that I have my memories back, I'm glad I did."

"I am as well. We really got to know each other on that chair." Quinten smiled, and bent his head to kiss Saige on the top of hers. Not only had they spent time talking, but he'd sat in that chair with Saige in his lap every night for a month in frustration—every smile, every touch, had affected him deeply.

Movement from the corner of his eye, drew his attention.

Saige lifted her gaze, but kept her arm around his waist. "Tamsyn, I wasn't sure if you were home."

He frowned because the other woman didn't look too friendly, as Saige moved out of his arms—her fingers intertwining with his.

"What's wrong?" Saige asked.

Tamsyn disappeared and a minute later returned with two large suitcases. "I'm sorry to do this without notice, Saige, but I'm moving in with my boyfriend." She shrugged.

Tamsyn tugged the cases to the door and turned back to Quinten. "I'm glad you're both back together. I'm sorry." She left.

"You okay?" Quinten glanced at Saige's stunned expression.

"I can't believe she left so abruptly." Saige bit her bottom lip, and he reached out and rescued it from her teeth with his finger.

"We weren't close," she explained, "nor best friends—roommates ... I'm really okay with her leaving." Saige sighed. Then she said, "At least we have the place to ourselves." She smiled and shrugged. "C'mon, I'll give you a tour."

He watched Saige but she smiled. "I promise

you that I'm fine with her going. We hardly spent time together—usually we'd chat over morning coffee, but that was it. Not often either."

He nodded and followed Saige while he tried to ignore the panic that had started in his gut. He'd never been claustrophobic before but he had a feeling that that was what was wrong with him. The large windows in the main part of the apartment had views of other apartment buildings, and the other side, the ocean. He spotted the lounge chairs on the balcony, and he knew where he'd be coaxing Saige to sleep tonight.

Saige worried with Quinten having sat out on the balcony since they'd reached her apartment hours ago. He'd made all the right noises as she showed him around, but now she felt that something was off with him.

They needed to talk.

Grabbing two beers from the fridge, Saige made her way toward him and smiled when he tugged her down onto his lap instead of the separate lounger. His arms tightened around her as he nuzzled into her neck. "I love holding you like this, smelling you," he chuckled.

"Smelling me, huh?" Saige made herself comfortable so that she could see his face and offered him an amused smile. "What's wrong?" She caressed along his brow and down the side of his face, tracing along the faint scars down his cheek.

"Honestly, I'm finding all this difficult."

"Oh." Saige dipped her eyes and wondered what he referred to as being difficult.

"Not you, Saige." He cupped her chin. "I need space—" He quickly cut off his words and tightened his hand on her hip. "I'm not explaining myself very well."

He closed his eyes and tucked her head under his chin. "I've spent years in a small space where I had to wear chains if I left the cell. Now that I'm free, I need open spaces, and I'm struggling being in the city with so many people. I'm struggling being inside this apartment." He kissed her forehead. "You've only made this place half a home though."

She was surprised he remembered what they used to talk about—her dream place. "I used to want a lot of color and *space* with our books sharing shelf space, and the old, brown leather chair close by so that we could both curl up and snuggle together while reading or just relaxing."

"That's right, and the only thing you got right is the chair," he observed and she realized it wasn't a criticism but a genuine observation. "When we start to build a home together we're going to have that color. I'm going to build us the most amazing bookcase for your books—I've no idea where mine are—and it's going to be our place. It's going to be ours, babe. I can see it now."

Her tears would soon start to soak into Quinten's shirt but there was no way he wouldn't know so she lifted her face and let him see how much his words affected her. "I want that more than anything."

He smiled and wiped her eyes with his thumbs, or rather he tried to. She laughed and knocked his hands away. "I've got this."

He watched her closely and asked, "So, have you given any thought as to where you want to live?"

She smiled and straddled his lap, her hands held loosely on his shoulders. "What about Montana? It's full of large spaces and less people. We can choose somewhere that isn't over populated."

"Are you choosing Montana because of what I just said about needing peace and quiet or have you given it some thought?" Quinten tipped his head and watched Saige closely.

"I was thinking a complete change to Florida. Somewhere that has nice summers, but cold winters. I think we're both ready for the change and we'll be able to choose whether or not we want to be around people or not. Have a town close by with a convenience store. Driving distance to a larger city maybe for a once a month large shopping trip, and we need schools close by."

Quinten threw his head back and laughed. "You do have it all planned. Anything else?" he asked, his eyes darkening the further his hands slipped up her thighs.

She grinned. "I know you really won't like this but you'll just have to live with it for now." She watched him frown and continued. "This apartment is mine, Quinten. I bought it with money that had been left in a trust for me when my mother died. I'm going to sell it and get us a home in Montana that we both love. I know you're a proud man, but until we get ourselves sorted, you're going to have to forget about where the money is coming from and just enjoy being with me." She bit her lip, hoping he would just agree.

"I can do that for you, but as soon as the money I'm owed comes through and I'm working, we're going fifty-fifty, and that isn't open for discussion." He grinned. "However, what I might let you open for discussion is how much I want you, how much you drive me insane, how much I'll always need you by my side, and what we'll never discuss is who loves who the most because I'm pretty certain we'll never agree on that one."

Saige silently agreed and swooped down to capture the lips that always captivated her.

I am naked walking around my apartment enjoying the feel of freedom from the restriction of my clothing. My vengeance hasn't finished and is only really getting started, but what I've learned over the years is to be patient.

I glance through the windows.

And there they are—half-naked on the balcony for anyone to see. I'm so glad I can stare without being seen thanks to the privacy glass.

My heart pounds in my chest as I watch Quinten and Saige. She rises up and then slowly takes her lover inside her body. The gentle roll of her hips tells me exactly what they are doing. Quinten gently suckles at her breast.

My penis pokes out from my body—large and solid.

Then I feel a warm mouth wrap around my aching flesh. Hands on my thighs. Glancing down, I groan at the naked girl on her knees before me, her red lips look amazing on my cock.

As my lust rises, I move my gaze back to Saige and Quinten, except I'm not seeing them anymore.

I'm seeing Christina's naked body as she rides me.

I'm seeing her large breasts bounce.

I feel the wetness between her legs as I pound into her.

I feel the warmth of her release all over me.

I feel the tightness in my groin.

I slip deep and when the girl on her knees swallows around the head of my cock, I immediately release.

"Oh, Christina!" I moan in my head, but actually moan out loud, "Oh, Tamsyn!"

Day 22

After a call to Coulter to see if they could go back to his beach house for a couple of weeks, Quinten helped Saige pack her things up. He didn't have much—a week's supply of clothing, as well as sneakers and work boots that Saige had bought him as soon as she knew he'd be released. Alex would have the rest of his gear ready to go with them when they moved to Montana.

The minute Saige had suggested where they should move to, he'd liked the idea without even having to think about it. He'd probably be able to get more carpentry work out there as well because they tended to keep within a country theme.

Although his specialty was woodcarvings, he used to build kitchens, and made to order furniture. He was pretty sure it was a skill that one didn't forget.

The worry about their future was there, but he felt more positive about it and about being able to provide for Saige, and any children that might follow.

He'd love to see Saige pregnant with his child and he refused to think about what they'd already lost through no fault of their own. His girl was strong, stronger than anyone he knew, but he couldn't help wonder if she was really alright.

Her father could go to hell for all he cared, but at the end of the day, Quinten would follow Saige's lead because, until she'd met him, her father had raised her well.

"Hey, what's wrong?" Saige asked, snapping his attention back to her delectable bottom as she leaned over the bed, watching him over her shoulder. "And don't go getting any ideas." She chuckled. "Coulter will be here soon to help us down to the car and away from this place."

"I'm sure I can keep my hands to myself for an hour or so ... I'm happy, Saige." He dropped his ass to the end of the bed and met her gaze when she paused in what she was doing. "I'm finally free to be with you after so long." He held his hand out to her, which she took and sat beside him. "But, I'm also worried about you and what your father has done to the relationship between you both."

Saige said. "As long as I have you by my side then I'm happy too, Quinten. When I had no memory of you, there must have been something there because I brought our chair with me to Tampa. As soon as I started to remember, I longed to be with you, and then when I remembered everything about our time together, I knew nothing would keep me from you once you were free ... I'm heartbroken about my father and really don't know what's going to happen, especially after I give Coulter the report."

Quinten wrapped an arm around her shoulders and kept her close. "What they did to you was illegal, and I'm guessing Coulter will make sure they don't get away with it. He's your father, Saige, are you sure that you're okay with that?"

"You think I should just ignore what he's done." She tried to pull away but he wouldn't let her.

"No, I'm not saying that. I want your father to

pay. I'm angry with him and I'll never want him near you or any children we may have in the future. He somehow manipulated the evidence against me, which lost eight years of my life with you. He did the unspeakable to you, so no, I don't want you to ignore what he's done." He inhaled and slowly exhaled to calm his temper at the thought of her father. "I just want to make sure you're okay with taking this further, but I'm going to be right by your side no matter what happens. Do you hear me?" He slipped a hand to the nape of her neck and cupped the back of her head.

Saige swallowed a few times, but he was relieved that, for once there were no tears. "I'm angry and upset that he isn't the man I thought he was. There's still part of me that feels I should protect him, but I can't."

He sighed in relief because he knew that he would have had to say something to the detective if Saige had decided against it. Quinten wouldn't have been able to walk away without making sure Saige was protected.

"I'm glad that's cleared. Let's buzz Coulter in," Quinten said, and after a quick kiss to her lips, he did just that.

❖

Coulter smiled when Quinten opened the door to him and Amber, showing them inside. Minutes later he watched as Saige led Amber out onto the balcony to admire the view of the ocean.

"You're looking a lot better than the last time I saw you." Coulter observed.

Quinten had looked gaunt when they'd met him at the prison for his release, and even though it had only been five days since then, Colter noticed that the other man had been well taken care of and even had a bit of a tan.

"That's what happens when you have the love of a good woman who believes in you." Quinten smiled and offered him a seat. "Thanks for coming to help us get away from here. It's like a zoo out there. With Paul's confession and my innocence being announced, the press are everywhere, trying to get an exclusive."

"Yeah, the front of the station is a nightmare as well." Coulter sat forward and stared at the envelope on the coffee table between them.

He knew what was inside because Saige had already told him, which made him angry. He never would have expected that of Richard Lockwood. The man had never come across as anything but the loving father. His attitude toward his wife, Christina, had given Coulter thought, but hell.

"It hasn't been opened?" He glanced at Quinten.

"No." Quinten ran his hand over his face and glanced toward Saige. "She didn't want to read in detail what had been done to her."

"And you?"

"I just got out of prison. I think if I read that, I'd end up back there, and I'd be guilty this time." Quinten leaned forward and rested his elbows on his thighs, his head dropping into his hands.

He let Quinten get himself under control, and picked the letter up. Keeping it sealed, he put it in his pocket and placed a receipt for the letter on the coffee table.

Nothing would prevent the current investigation from being derailed. Everyone involved would be named and he'd leave it up to the DA to wade through the charges, and to decide who needed to be held responsible.

"Hey." Saige placed her hand to the back of Quinten's neck, a look of concern crossed her face.

"Everything okay?"

Quinten smiled and, sitting back, tugged Saige down to his lap. Amber sat beside Coulter on the sofa and slipped her hand into his. Coulter turned, offered her a smile, and squeezed her hand to reassure her things were fine.

"Coulter has the report," Quinten said, but Coulter figured it had been unnecessary because Saige had glanced at the table as she walked over with Amber.

"Can you tell us what's likely to happen now?" Saige asked as worry marred her brow.

"Paul Lewis is different from other killers I've arrested. I'm still not a hundred percent convinced that he's guilty of everything he's been charged with, except this time around, there is a lot more evidence that the man we have is guilty as charged." Coulter shrugged. "He actually said that he wanted to lead us to Alex because he was the evil brother. Do you know what that means?"

Quinten frowned and sighed. "Alex could be an asshole when he wanted to be, and he'd always have a dig at Paul whenever he came across him, until I put stop to it. I'm the younger brother, but I'm sure that I was the more mature one." Quinten sat back and closed his eyes. "Alex changed and I realize now that it must have been when he started having an affair with Christina. He grew up."

Coulter nodded and accepted Quinten's explanation. For a man as unhinged as Paul Lewis, that would be a good enough reason to want to get back at Alex.

He was glad that Amber was with him. She gave him peace. And after everything that had happened, he felt like he'd become friends with Saige and Quinten, and he wanted to help them.

Amber stood and tugged him up with her. "I think it's time to help you both make the big get away." She smiled.

"I meant what I said, you both can use the beach house for as long as you want to," Coulter said.

Saige moved over to them, reached up, and hugged him. "Thank you. You have no idea how much that means to us." She stepped back and hugged Amber.

"Let me get some shoes on, then we're ready to go."

He watched her leave the room and turned to

Quinten, whose eyes also followed Saige.

"She's stronger than me. She'll be fine," Quinten observed.

They'd all be fine, eventually.

Day 28

The day he was supposed to die.

Quinten rubbed at his chest not really knowing how he was supposed to feel—thankful, relieved, happy, they all really meant the same thing except he couldn't help the gloom that had settled over him when he woke during the early hours of the morning. He managed to slip from the bed without waking Saige, and was now on his third cup of coffee. To him, being able to help himself to coffee or food at the drop of a hat was an extravagance, and one that he'd never take for granted again.

For the past six days since they'd arrived back

at Coulter's beach house, Quinten had gotten into a routine that involved coffee and sitting on the steps leading from the house to the beach to watch the sun rise or set.

He loved the time alone to think, but, if he was honest, he loved the time here with Saige all the more. He needed to get a handle on his need to be able to see her at all times during the day, or to check on her when he entered the house to grab another cup. She didn't mind, but he needed to stop.

Fabric rustled as Saige climbed into his lap, a sheet wrapped around her. He smiled and groaned when she wiggled around. "I woke and you were gone," she complained. "Hold me close."

"I couldn't sleep." His arms slipped around her waist. "Please stop wiggling around on my lap." He pressed a kiss to her neck and groaned when she turned and straddled him.

"What are you thinking about?" Saige asked, her hands rested against his chest, his on her hips.

Smiling, he reached up and caressed her face with a finger. "I was thinking that I was supposed to die today," he admitted softly. He gave a sardonic smile, and quickly hurried on when he saw Saige's bottom lip quiver. "I'm thinking that I'm a very lucky man to be given another chance at this thing called life, with you beside me."

Saige nodded and he could see the struggle for her not to cry, so he cupped her face with one large hand and her neck with the other. He brought her closer until their lips were a breath apart. "I want to make a new memory for this day, Saige, I've waited a long time to hold you again, so I don't want to waste another minute. I don't have anything to offer you—"

"You have everything to offer me, Quinten," Saige interrupted. "You love me. You make me happy, and I love you with every beat of my heart." She leaned forward the inch that separated them and placed a soft kiss to his lips. "Now finish what you were saying."

Quinten cleared his throat because there was one hell of a lump of emotion stuck in there. "Will you marry me, Saige?" His heart thumped widely in his chest while he watched all the emotions his question had created in Saige flutter across her face.

Saige slipped her fingers through his trim beard to cup his face. "Yes," she whispered and pressed her lips to his. "Yes." She giggled and started placing kisses all over his face. "Yes." The sheet was tossed aside and his breath caught in his throat.

She was nude beneath.

"You've been sitting in my lap naked?" A stupid question considering he could see the answer for himself.

He caressed over her shoulders, down her arms and back up. His hands itched to touch more flesh as he slowly moved and cupped both her breasts and rubbed her nipples with his thumbs.

His body reacted to the sight of Saige straddling him without any clothes on, and his swollen flesh under her bottom hurt from being restrained.

"You're so beautiful." He kissed along her collarbone and the valley between her breasts before he suddenly moved and captured her lips.

Her hips undulated over his jean-covered dick and, if she weren't careful, he'd come before he even got out of them.

"I need you," Saige moaned, and scooted off his lap, reaching for his zipper. "Lift." And that was all it took to take his jeans to his thighs, which trembled the minute Saige wrapped a hand around his solid length.

Saige sighed, and dropped her head into his lap.

"Mmm," he mumbled, as pleasure shot through him like a volcano when her warm mouth lapped at the head of his dick.

His fingers tangled into the strands of her hair and just when he thought he was about to blow his load, he pulled her off him. "No more. I want to come inside you while you're coming on me."

Her eyes darkened seconds before she straddled his lap. She stroked his shaft, driving him crazy. "Put me inside you," he begged between gritted teeth.

Saige smiled and held him poised at the place he wanted to be more than anything right then. And as she slowly sank down on him, Quinten's eyes rolled with pleasure.

Fully seated on him, Saige ground down and rocked. His hands went to the arch of her back as he pressed his face between her breasts. He nuzzled, first one breast, then the other before he captured a nipple and sucked.

His eyes rolled when she tightened around

him in the position she was in, her hips grinding faster. When his lips captured hers, his hands went to her bottom and held her open and moved her on him.

The hard nipples rubbed against his chest as she bounced but, when she wrapped her arms around his neck, he lost momentum, his dick buried so deeply inside of her that he couldn't breathe.

And then he felt the first flutters of intense pleasure around his shaft. Seconds later, she convulsed in his arms—he shuddered and joined her in release.

Minutes later, Quinten held Saige tightly in his arms while he was still buried inside her silken body, little aftershocks still rocked through their systems.

Saige sat back on his lap and ran her fingers through his beard. "I love this." She smirked. "I love how it feels against my skin."

His eyes lit with mirth. "So you wouldn't want me to get rid of it, huh?"

"No way. The beard stays." She laughed. "I love looking at you, but yeah, I love how it feels." She pressed a kiss to his lips and became serious when she met his gaze. "Can we marry soon? We've been apart a long time and I don't want to waste one more second."

"Yes ... Are you sure, Saige?" His heart was in his throat while he watched her eyes fill with tears.

"I've never been more sure of anything before." She kissed him. "I love you," she whispered.

He held her tightly and only released her slightly when he realized his hold was too strong and that she needed to breathe. "I love you, too."

She smiled. "I think we need to head inside and get more practice at making babies."

"What?" he mumbled.

"We're getting married *soon*, and even though it's going to take time to accept what happened to me against my will, it isn't going to stop me from having your children. I want lots of babies, Quinten."

He had no words, so instead, he kissed her on the tip of her nose before he carried her inside and made slow, sweet love to her.

❖

I am back in Boston with a new plan already settled in my thoughts. The lovely Tamsyn is with me and has no idea about who I really am or what I am capable of—she will eventually.

Quinten should have died today, but he didn't because Saige suddenly had to know the truth.

Well, they say the truth will set you free and I guess in Quinten's case, it really did. He won this round and I plan on leaving him and Saige alone, unless of course, they decide to interfere with my new plan.

Day 365

Saige sat in Quinten's arms and drank her mug of decaf coffee in silence as she watched Alex and Christina sitting opposite them. Dinner that night marked the last night of Alex and Christina's visit at their new home in Montana. The couple had a late night flight to catch back to New York, where they'd both settled.

Christina had certainly seemed a lot happier with Alex, and he'd always seemed to need her close.

Although she loved having them, she couldn't wait to have the house back to just Quinten and her. She missed the closeness she would usually share with Quinten throughout their home. Not to mention that she had some good news to tell her husband of ten months.

Unconsciously, her hand slid to her belly, a soft smile on her lips that she hid when she yawned into Quinten's chest.

Christina laughed. "I think it's time we left and let you get to bed."

"I'm sorry." She smiled. "I can't seem to stay awake these days."

"Hmm," Christina mumbled, and Saige caught the other woman hiding a smile as she stood.

Saige placed her mug on the coffee table with the others and found herself on her feet when Quinten stood and steadied her. He kept her close with an arm around her back and his hand on the curve of her hip.

"Are you okay?" he whispered, as he nuzzled into her neck.

"I'm fine."

Twelve months ago, the warrant for his execution had been signed and he'd had twenty-eight days left on earth. That had shaken Quinten to his very core because he'd been innocent. He thanked God every day for the second chance at life he'd been given with Saige.

Just thinking about Saige, his eyes found her as they always did. He smiled as his wife hugged his brother and Christina goodbye, which caused Quinten's heart to swell with love for the amazing woman. Her strength and resilience, after everything they'd both been through, had known no bounds. Her love and compassion held him together on the days when his past really got to him.

Saige stood back so he could hug Christina, and then it was his brother's turn. Men or not, he pulled Alex into his embrace and held him tightly. "Thank you," he whispered. "Thank you for everything."

Alex held tight and the brothers embraced for a long time before Alex stepped back. Quinten couldn't place the emotion on Alex's face as he backed up to the driver's side.

Quinten frowned and wrapped his arm around Saige when she snuggled into his side.

"What's wrong?" she asked, and kissed his chest.

"I'm not sure."

Before Alex disappeared into the car, he stopped and looked at them. "I'm sorry, Quinten." He turned and looked out at the mountains that surrounded the house before turning back to Quinten and holding his gaze. "You never should have been blamed for the college girls." His face was serious, then he smiled like the old Alex before he climbed in the car and drove off.

Day 366

Dear Mr. Peterson,

Things aren't going too well for me here, at least, nothing like I thought they would. The food is okay but the mattress is so lumpy that I think I'd rather sleep on a bed of leaves on the forest floor. Perhaps, it wouldn't be as scary as this place. They have really bad people inside these walls and they keep threatening to do bad things to me.

I wish someone could help me.

I only killed one girl.

You see, I know who killed those girls, because I had an obsession with him. He had the life that I wanted, but knew that I could never have. Who would look at me the way the girls looked at him? So one night I followed him thinking that he was meeting up with a woman, except he went to that shack. I saw what he did to that first girl. I didn't see everything, only the ending, which is why I've never been able to tell the police about that first one.

I was prepared for the second one though, and I watched and waited. When he left to go home for the night, I snuck into the shack and that's how I got the souvenir. I had a good collection, too bad they didn't let me keep it.

He loved frightening them. They were terrified of him, and of me. I learned a lot from him and used my new skills to kill that lying bitch, Jocelyn. She deserved everything that she got.

But the real killer isn't behind bars, is he?

They had the wrong brother all along. I know the college girls killer is you, Alex Peterson. But don't worry, I won't tell. I'm good at keeping secrets.

Paul Lewis

Alex folded the letter and tossed it into the fire, watching as it became engulfed in flames. He waited until it turned to ash before heading toward the bedroom to join Christina. She was finally completely his, and nothing or no one would take her from him.

Day 367

Coulter smiled as he watched his six-month pregnant wife, Amber, waddle through the homicide department toward him. She'd never looked as beautiful and his heart had never felt so full. Amber had broken down all of his defenses with just one kiss, and she'd owned him since that day.

Patting his lap when she made it to his desk, he laughed when she raised a brow.

"In the office, Detective?"

"Ignore them. I need to hold you."

Her eyes softened, her arm wrapped around

his neck, and her bottom landed snug against his groin. Perhaps that hadn't been the wisest decision he'd ever made.

Amber chuckled and whispered, "We need a lunch break at home."

He pinched her bottom. "Behave in the office."

She rolled her eyes but he could see laughter in them.

Coulter rested his large hand on her swollen belly, and let out a sigh of contentment as their baby kicked against his palm.

"Something's bothering you," Amber guessed, and ran a hand through his hair. "You can talk to me. You do know that, right?"

"I know and I always do. Paul Lewis is heavily on my mind. I retire from the force in two months and although I don't regret that, I wish I were convinced that Paul was guilty of killing those girls."

"Have you told anyone your thoughts about him?"

He knew she meant his captain or partner.

"I've talked it through with the Captain and Agent Nero Soren, from the FBI. The Captain thinks we have the right man. Soren isn't completely sold on Paul Lewis being the college girl killer. He's taking another look at the files."

He sighed heavily against his beautiful wife. "The jury obviously thought we had the right man because they convicted him. This time the case wasn't based on the DNA match alone." Coulter sighed. "Serial killers *always* remember their first kill. I haven't heard of one who hasn't, until now."

"I wish I could help you. I feel so helpless."

He kissed her sweet lips and rested his forehead against hers. "You help me by just being at my side. You help me because I have you waiting for me at home, growing our child within your body. You help me more than you'll ever know, Amber." He captured her lips once more before he buried his face in the curve of her shoulder.

He knew he couldn't keep the last part from her, so he quietly admitted, "I received a letter today. I suspect it's from Paul Lewis."

Amber raised a questioning brow. "You did?"

"I haven't opened it. I will. Later."

His wife offered him a wry smile and kissed his cheek.

❖

Unable to settle, Coulter sat in his study with a whiskey in one hand and the unopened letter from Paul Lewis in the other. His wife had poured him the drink and sent him into the room, pointedly looking toward the letter on his desk.

He was tired of the job. Tired of the case. It was why he would retire from the force soon with full pension. He couldn't wait to be home with Amber and their child. He never thought he'd be a father for the first time at forty-nine.

The next couple of months couldn't come soon enough.

Sighing heavily, he placed the empty glass on his desk and used the letter opener to slice into the envelope. Straightening the paper on his desk, he read the short letter.

Dear Detective Robinson,

I wondered if you ever investigated Alexander Peterson?

Yours,

Paul Lewis

❖

It's been twelve months since I was in Florida, and even though we haven't communicated, Paul Lewis remembered what he was supposed to do.

The letters have arrived.

Now all I have to do is wait and observe, just like I've been doing all this time.

The thought of playing with Christina excites me beyond anything. I never thought I would become obsessed with the blond whore.

I've decided that I will let her live and she can watch as everyone else tries to catch the tail between their legs.

In the end I will win.

THE END

The Next Victim
2018

Synopsis

For nine years Faye Ingram had lived with the harrowing guilt of what became of her sister. After all it had been her fault that Kelsey had been driving home from college that dark night...*hadn't it?*

Their parents blamed her.
Kelsey's boyfriend blamed her.
Kelsey's friends blamed her.

The killer hadn't only taken her sister from her family and friends; he'd taken Faye's life...and now it was time to claim it back.

FBI Special Agent Nero Soren understood Faye's need for answers, except the more questions she asked, the more he feared for her safety. His instincts told him that the killer they hunted was hunting a prey of his own, but was the prey *Faye Ingram* or *Christina Peterson*?

Agent Nero Soren along with his partner, Agent Logan Reddick, raced to find the killer before he claimed *the next victim.*

Available Autumn 2018

Cover Design by Abigail Higson

Dear Reader

If you liked *Twenty Eight Days,* I would appreciate it, if you would help others enjoy this book too by recommending it to your friends, family, and book clubs by writing an honest, positive review on Amazon, Barnes and Noble, Kobo, iBook Store, Goodreads, etc.

Acknowledgements

Editors: Nadine Winningham & Sirena van Schaik
Editor/Proofreader/Cover Designer: Abigail Higson

BETA Readers: Emma Clifton, Kathrin Magyar, Lynne Garlick, Sonya Covert & Stacie Mayer-Hamburger

A big thank you to Nadine for her encouragement, advice, and plotting sessions during the writing of this book. I'm sure I drove you nuts!

To my family who had to search through washing baskets for clean clothes, had 'something quick' for dinner, lived in an upside down house, while I concentrated on this book, I love you all.

Kathrin, thank you for organizing me (which isn't easy), being my overseas travel partner, and for the plotting and ideas for the next book, The Next Victim.

Lynne & Cara, thank you both for your friendship. Lynne, you read every word I write, even the brief chapters for books that won't get written for years to be completed—thank you!

A special mention to Alan Farrelly, you know what for! Thank you!

Other books by Rona Jameson

Come Back to Me
Summer at Rose Cottage
Twenty Eight Days

Books written by Lexi Buchanan

Bad Boy Rockers
Book 1: Sizzle
Book 2: Spicy
Book 3: Sultry
Book 4: Savor
Book 5: Sinful
Book 6: Silent Night (Novella)

McKenzie Brothers
Book 1: Seduce
Book 1.5: The Wedding (Novella)
Book 2: Rapture
Book 3: Delight
Book 4: Entice
Book 5: Cherished
Book 5.5: A McKenzie Christmas (Novella)

De La Fuente Family (McKenzie Spinoff)
Book 1: Love in Montana
Book 2: Love in Purgatory
Book 3: Love in Bloom
Book 4: Love in Country
Book 5: Love in Flame
Book 6: Love in Game
Book 7: Love in Education

McKenzie Cousins (McKenzie Spinoff)
Book 1: Baby Makes Three
Book 2: A Business Decision
Book 3: Secret Kisses
Book4: Kissing Cousins

Jackson Hole
Book 1: From This Moment
Book 1.5: When we Meet (Novella, in the back of From This Moment)
Book 2: New Beginning (coming soon)

Romantic Suspense
Lawful
Stryker

Standalone Novella's
One Dance
Educate Me
Pure

Holiday Season
Kissing Under the Mistletoe
A Soldier's Christmas

About the Author

Rona Jameson is an emerging author of romantic suspense. Her more explicit contemporary romance books are written under pseudonym, Lexi Buchanan.

For more information:
ronajameson.com
ronajamesonauthor@gmail.com